When It's Over

When It's Over

Roy Glenn

www.urbanbooks.net

Urban Books, LLC
300 Farmingdale Road, N.Y.-Route 109
Farmingdale, NY 11735

ISBN 13: 978-1-64556-653-3
EBOOK ISBN: 978-1-64556-654-0

First Trade Paperback Printing September 2024
Printed in the United States of America

10 9 8 7 6 5 4 3 2 1

This is a work of fiction. Any references or similarities to actual events, real people, living or dead, or to real locales are intended to give the novel a sense of reality. Any similarity in other names, characters, places, and incidents is entirely coincidental.

Distributed by Kensington Publishing Corp.
Submit orders to:
Customer Service
400 Hahn Road
Westminster, MD 21157-4627
Phone: 1-800-733-3000
Fax: 1-800-659-2436

When It's Over

Roy Glenn

Chapter 1

Monika Wynn ran up the stairs of a building under construction until she reached the eleventh floor. Once she reached that level, she exited the stairwell and proceeded to her spot in the front of the building, where she set up her Remington Model 700 rifle and aimed it at the office of Bamidele Renault, a captain in the Burundian rebel militia. He was in his office waiting for word from Lieutenant Abeba Omenuko about a three-vehicle convoy of arms preparing to get underway en route to members of the Popular Front for the Liberation of Burundi.

"Alpha to Omega, in position and standing by."

"Acknowledged," Carla responded.

Renault would be Monika's target for the day. All he had to do was stand up.

In another part of Bujumbura, the economic capital of Burundi, three Nissan NV350 panel vans containing QBZ-95B-1 5.8-mm carbine assault rifles, a weapon designed and manufactured by Norinco in the People's Republic of China, prepared to move out with a two-man detail assigned to each vehicle.

"Epsilon to Omega," April said. "Subject vehicles have left the compound and are proceeding on the established route. I am in pursuit."

"Acknowledged, Epsilon. Omega to Gamma. Status report."

"Gamma is in position and standing by," Travis informed. He was positioned at a red light, five miles ahead of the convoy's current location.

"Acknowledged, Gamma. Subject vehicles will reach your position in approximately two minutes."

"Acknowledged, Omega," he said and looked through his binoculars. "Subject vehicles in sight." Travis took the device from his pocket, and as the lead vehicle approached the red light, he engaged the device. The light changed to red and all three cars slowed to a stop.

"Epsilon to Gamma. I am in position."

"Acknowledged, Epsilon," he said and pressed the button to detonate the two cars parked on either side of the third vehicle.

As the fire burned, the first two vehicles drove away from the scene quickly. Travis pulled up on a motorcycle and shot the driver of the third vehicle before he could react. When the second man tried to exit the car, April fired and hit him with two shots to the chest.

"Go!" she shouted to Travis. "I'm right behind you!"

"Gamma to Omega, two enemy combatants down. Joining pursuit of target vehicles."

He drove off, leaving April to secure the weapons and take care of the bodies. Once she had accomplished her task, she got in the third vehicle.

"Epsilon to Omega. Subject vehicle secure."

"Acknowledged. Convoy is ten miles ahead of you on the established route."

"Acknowledged. In pursuit," April said, driving the truck with the weapons.

"Omega to Delta. Go ahead with your traffic," Xavier responded.

"Subject vehicles approaching your location. ETA three minutes."

"Acknowledged, Omega. In position and standing by."

"In range in three, two, one."

Once the lead vehicle passed his position, Xavier spread spikes across the road just before the second vehicle arrived at his position. When the car drove over the spikes, the tires burst just as Travis rolled up on the motorcycle. He fired at the passenger when he tried to exit the vehicle and hit him with two shots to the chest. The driver got out firing and got off a few shots before Xavier shot him.

"Second enemy target disabled." He got on a motorcycle as April pulled up.

"Acknowledged, Delta."

As Travis and Xavier sped off, April secured the second vehicle and called for the Burundi Army so they could take possession of the weapons.

"Omega to Beta."

"Go ahead."

"Third enemy target approaching your location."

"Acknowledged, Omega. Beta is in position and standing by." Nick raised the Compact EMP Launcher. "Enemy target in sight."

"In firing range in three, two, one, fire."

On command, Nick fired the projectile, which hit the hood of one of the Nissan NV350 panel vans as it passed, and it slowed to a stop.

"Third enemy target disabled," Nick said as Travis and Xavier rolled up on their motorcycles. Both driver and passenger exited the vehicle with their hands raised and surrendered.

When the convoy didn't arrive at its destination, a call was made to Lieutenant Abeba Omenuko.

"Damn it all to hell," he shouted and banged his fist on the desk.

He was now responsible for telling Captain Renault, who didn't take hearing bad news well. In fact, he was well known for shooting the bearer of bad news. Omenuko grabbed the bottle of rum from his desk drawer and took the bottle to his lips. After a couple of big swallows, he put the cap back on the bottle and returned it to the drawer before he left his office. He knocked lightly on Captain Renault's door.

"Come!"

Omenuko took a deep breath and turned the doorknob. "Excuse me, Captain," he said nervously.

"What is it?"

"The Burundi Army seized the convoy with the weapons."

"Fuck!" Captain Renault shouted. He hit his desk with both hands and stood up.

"Got you," Monika said and fired.

She hit Captain Renault in the head and packed up her Remington.

"Alpha to Omega, enemy combatant neutralized. Returning to base."

"Acknowledged, Alpha. See you when you get here."

Chapter 2

Two BBKs (Bad Boy Killer gang) were driving on a long stretch of road when a Chevy Silverado driven by Baby Chris pulled in alongside them. He cut in front of the trailing vehicle and then blocked its path. Marvin stood up in the bed of the Silverado and opened fire on the BBKs with heavy weapons, killing both occupants as they tried to exit the vehicle.

In another part of the city, in a black cargo van, Angel and Bowie, armed with AK-47s, slammed into the driver's side of the vehicle driven by three BBK members. When the car crashed, Angel exited the cargo van and opened fire. Bowie jumped out quickly and slid a disk under the vehicle. Then he rushed to the van, got back in, and once Angel was aboard, he sped off . . . just before the car exploded.

Axe and Press waited impatiently for their prey for the evening to come out of The Bellview Ballroom. As soon as the three men exited, they opened fire with AK-47s. One of the BBKs rushed to get behind a car for cover and opened fire on Axe and Press. Realizing they were outgunned, the BBKs' plan turned to retreat, and they began shooting their way back to the ballroom. Axe fired and hit one in the back as he ran. Press took aim and shot another before he reached the door, and he went down. The last man was able to get off a few shots before Axe shot him in the head just before he made it inside.

In the aftermath of Ryder killing Truck, Truck's old gang, the BBKs, some would say foolishly, declared war. Although Kojo, who Truck sold for, only responded with a strongly worded statement that future violence would not be tolerated, it was delivered by one of his men before Marvin shot him. Montel Rigby, the head of the BBKs, thought he had no choice but to go to war with Barbara Ray, who ran The Playhouse.

The Playhouse, or just "The House," was a gambling spot called Sweet Nectar until Barbara took over. She renovated the place, expanded the dance floor, and turned it into a dance club, which attracted a younger crowd and substantially increased her gambling revenue. However, she decided to focus on expanding her legitimate businesses. Therefore, Black assigned Barbara's captain, Jackie Washington, to take over at The Playhouse and run the war from there.

"Feel free to use whatever resources you need," Black told Jackie the first night she took over at The Playhouse. "But I'm sure your crew can handle them without involving the rest of The Family."

"Agreed," Jackie had said that night.

To this point, she hadn't gone all out against the BBKs, choosing, instead, to simply respond to their incursions with superior force and mass casualties.

"I thought that they would have lost their heart to fight by this time, but no. Montel Rigby is stubborn."

"Maybe if you targeted him . . ."

"I have, but the muthafucka is way off the grid and doesn't like to show his face."

"Somebody knows where he's hiding."

"Amanda Lindsay would be my choice. She's his girlfriend, but she's as hard to find as he is."

"Make it happen," Black said and stood up.

"Where you off to now?"

"Sherman."

"Tell him he owes me a grand."

"For what?"

"He'll know," Jackie said.

"There's one more thing."

"What's that?"

"I need you to put somebody at Barbara's new spot."

"The legit one?"

"Yes."

"Why? Barbara can protect herself."

"Michelle is working there after school."

"Done," Jackie said, coming from behind her desk to escort Black to the door.

"I'll tell him. I'll see you tomorrow," he said and left the office. "Good night, Fiona."

"Have a good night, Mr. Black," she said as William stood up. "You too, William."

He blew her a kiss and followed Black out of the office. Once they were in the car and had driven off, William asked, "Where to, Boss?"

"Roll by Sherman's."

"You got it," he said and drove in that direction.

When they arrived at Sherman's house, it was late, so Black called Sherman because he didn't want to wake up his wife, Ester.

"What's up, Mike?" he answered.

"Open the back door, old man."

"Coming."

Sherman went to open the door and then led Black back to his media room.

"Where's Bobby tonight?" Sherman asked.

"Date night with Pam," Black said.

Sherman laughed.

"Now that all their kids are gone, Pam wants to go out."

"You and Shy got a date night too?"

"No. Cassandra thinks she needs to be home with her boys and ride shotgun over Michelle when she's there. Which is less and less these days."

"She likes the streets, just like her daddy."

"What are you watching?" Black asked on his way to the bar to fix a drink. He poured a drink for himself and then held up the bottle. Sherman held up his glass.

"*The Barefoot Contessa.*"

"Bogart," Black said nodding because he was a Humprey Bogart fan and sat down with his drink.

"And Ava Gardner."

"I hear you got RJ hooked on these old movies."

"That and Ester's cooking." Sherman shook his head.

"What?"

"I know, being Bobby's son, everybody sees him as the heir apparent to take over for Rain one day, but right now, I don't see it."

"Why is that?"

"Too much on his plate. With Venus and the new baby boy and having to deal with the angry girlfriend . . ." he said about Mia Rubio, who had just returned from her European tour opening for Cristal. "Between those two and the promotion business he's got going, he's not focused. I mean, he gets done what I need him to handle, but still."

Black thought briefly about Michelle. "Just because he's Bobby's son don't make him the heir apparent. He needs to earn that spot just like Rain earned it."

"She eats and sleeps nothing but this Family."

"True."

Black paused to think about her judgment in not telling him about involving The Family in Gavin Caldwell's business, not once but twice.

"I don't think there's anything to worry about. I don't see Ms. Robinson giving up the job any time soon."

"Who said I was worried? I'm just expressing an opinion."

"So, tell me something I don't know."

"Kojo's whole house is in disarray."

"I knew it would be. What's up with that?"

"After Ryder killed Truck, he discovered they had a snitch in his house." Sherman laughed. "Turned out to be one of the boy's top people. After that, Kojo, or more correctly, Sienna Petrocelli, had Arron Copeland killed because he was the one that brought her in."

"That only leaves Truck's brother, what's his name?"

"Drew Mack."

"Anybody taking advantage?"

"That would be Kendrick Nance."

"What can you tell me about him?"

"Not much. Other than he used to work for the Kings."

"When you find out more, I wanna hear about it."

"You know you got it." Sherman stood up. "You want another drink?"

"No." Black drained his glass. "I promised Cassandra I wouldn't be in the streets all night, and I got another stop to make." He stood up. "You say hello to Ester for me."

"I will," Sherman said and saw Black to the back door. When William saw him coming, he started the car.

"Where to now, Boss?" he asked when Black got in. "Ready to call it a night?"

"No." Black paused. "Take me to Veneshia's."

Back in the day, when Black took over the gambling operation from Andre, he beat a gorilla pimp named Silky to death one night after witnessing him beating one of his women. Silky's women gathered and watched quietly.

"Kick his ass," one of his women said softly.

"Yeah," another said.

"Kill that muthafucka, Black!" Veneshia shouted, and that started a chant. "Kill him! Kill him!"

After killing their pimp, by right and tradition, those women belonged to Black. He cleaned them up and found them somewhere to ply their trade safely, with Veneshia serving as his bottom girl. This position gave her status and power over the other women working for her daddy, and, much to his regret, Veneshia still called him by that name. When they arrived at Veneshia's, Joe, who had been running security for her for years, greeted Black and William.

"Evening, Mike."

"What's up, Joe?" Black said as he and William attempted to follow house rules and surrender their weapons.

"No need for that, Mike. I think I can trust you not to start no shit." he laughed, "At least you ain't gonna start shit you can't finish," Joe said and allowed them to pass. "I know Veneshia will be happy to see you."

"I know."

Over the years, she had become one of his best sources of information on the streets. Black knew that every once in a while, he had to stop by there, pay her some attention, and show her the respect to which she was entitled.

"Daddy's here!" one of the women shouted enthusiastically when Black and William came into the room.

The rest of the women at the house quickly got to their feet and formed what amounted to an inspection line. It was one of Veneshia's rules. Black shook his head and sat down since he had no interest in looking over the women.

"They're all yours," he said to William as one of the women hurried to get him a drink before she got in line just as Veneshia entered the room. This was a good thing because the inspection line was more about Veneshia and her expectations in her daddy's presence than it was about Black. And each woman knew there were consequences for making her look bad in front of her daddy.

"Daddy!" she exclaimed. "This is such a pleasant surprise."

"Evening, Veneshia. You look very nice tonight," he said of the Marchesa Notte, off-the-shoulder lace midi-dress she wore. The dress was black, as was most of her wardrobe, a holdover from her days as his bottom girl when he wore black just about every day.

Veneshia smiled brightly. "Thank you, Daddy. I'm glad you like it," she said, walking the line behind William. "Too much makeup," she said to one, and she quickly went to fix it. "That outfit is totally inappropriate for you. Go change." She stood in front of her girl with her hands on her hips.

"Yes, Veneshia," the woman said and rushed off.

"What are the rest of you standing around for?"

"Nothing," they said collectively, leaving the room with William so Veneshia could talk to Black alone. As she came toward him, Black stood up and gave her a hug and a kiss on her lips.

"How are you, Veneshia?"

"I could find something to complain about, but nothing is happening in my world that I can't handle."

"What can you tell me about Kendrick Nance?"

"He used to work for the Kings. Now, he's trying to fill the void the Caldwells left and push Johnny Boy's pawn out."

Black chuckled. "What about Kojo?"

"They're falling apart after Ryder killed Rodney Mack, and they killed Shanice Hardaway. She was a police informant, you know." Venishia took Black's glass. "Kendrick Nance is trying to be the next big thing."

"He into anything other than drugs?"

"He's got some women he runs out of The Burke Hotel."
She fixed him another drink and one for herself and
handed it to him before reclaiming her seat.

"Thank you." Black shot the drink. "They causing any
problems for you?"

"Not so far. The bum bitches he has working for him
are little more than streetwalkers. They are no competi-
tion for my women."

"You let me know if you do, and I'll put Rain on it."

"No need to involve Black Widow. If they cause me a
problem, I'll handle it like I have been doing for years,
Daddy. I certainly don't need Rain."

"I know you don't. And I meant no disrespect."

"None taken, but if I see where they're a problem I can't
handle, I *will* let you know."

Black stood up. "All I can ask."

"Leaving so soon?"

"Yes." He handed her his glass. "I promised Cassandra
I wouldn't be in the streets all night."

"You say hello to Mrs. Black for me," Veneshia said,
standing up and walking to the door in the main room
with him.

"Good night, Veneshia."

"Good night, Daddy." Veneshia got on her toes to kiss
him on the cheek. William separated himself from the
woman he was talking to and followed Black to the door.

"Where to?"

"Home."

Chapter 3

Once Black got home, he saw the light coming from the media room. When he opened the door, he found Shy watching a movie on television. He came in and kissed his wife, and sat down.

"I wasn't expecting you to be home so soon."

"You did say not to stay out all night. I assumed that you had something in mind."

"I do," she said and turned off the television.

"Thought you were watching that?" Black said as Shy stood up.

"Not really. Just something to do while I waited up for you," she said, leading her husband by the hand out of the media room and upstairs to their bedroom.

Shy came toward him and helped him get undressed. Once he was naked, she stepped into his embrace and felt the warmth of his being enfold her. She removed her nightgown and crawled onto and stretched out across the bed. She sighed and arched her back when he palmed one of her nipples, squeezing it gently as his other hand caressed her waist and her hip. When he squeezed her curved ass and lifted her legs, Shy wrapped them around his waist and stared into his deep brown eyes. He kissed her at the same moment he entered her. It took her breath away.

"Oh, Michael."

He held her cheeks, and he moved in and out of her while she worked her hips in rhythm with him. Shy was caught up in how magnificent it felt to have him inside her. She panted her pleasure as his lips brushed around her neck, her chest. As their bodies slammed into each other, Black's hand traveled his beautiful wife's warm, naked body, enjoying the smooth, soft skin of her luscious curves. After all these years, he still couldn't get enough of her.

Their eyes locked as Black slid in and out of Shy, hitting her spot. She rotated her hips, moving slowly, then fast, and then slowing again. Shy slowed her pace enough to kiss him, and he pulled her on top of him. As he plunged his thickness inside of her, she grabbed her breast and pushed her nipple into his mouth. Black licked and sucked her nipple and could feel the tension simmering within her. She kept gliding her hips, looking down at him. The look in Shy's eyes set him on fire.

Shy rode him harder, moving up and down faster, slamming her hips into him. Black grabbed her ass, and his dick swelled inside her. She rode him harder and faster, slamming her body down harder. When her walls clenched around him, he pumped harder and faster. As her tits bounced up and down, Black kissed Shy to silence her screams of passion. She rolled off him and snuggled up next to him, and soon, she fell asleep in his arms.

In the morning, at six thirty, Shy's alarm went off. She silenced the alarm and sat in bed before kissing Black and heading for the shower. Although she had interviewed several people, she still hadn't hired anybody to replace Reeva Duckworth, who had been murdered by Tabitha Morrison months ago, so Shy was still running her own business.

She was out of the house by seven fifteen and arrived at her office at seven thirty. She wouldn't return home until after seven in the evening most days. Therefore, what was once their morning ritual now fell entirely on Black. He was left to wake up his children and prepare them for school. Now, it was Black who went to see about Mansa and took him into the room with Joann. Then he went and knocked once on Michelle's door.

"Get up."

"I'm up," she shouted back.

Michelle was 18 and was going to college that fall. She and her girlfriends, Tierra and Sharkiesha, all applied to and had gotten accepted at Columbia. Now, Mr. and Mrs. Black were just waiting for the words *apartment off campus* to come rolling out of her mouth.

She came out of her room dressed and ready to leave. Her father entered Eazy's room and stood over him until he got out of bed and headed for the bathroom. Downstairs in the kitchen, M, who was always up no later than six, cooked breakfast and prepared lunch for the children. Once they were gone, Black got back in bed.

He had a meeting later that day with Deana Butler, the head of the real estate division, Jaila Bell, the head of the finance division, and Ian Jenkins, the head of the construction division. They were meeting to discuss the construction of commercial office space, but that wasn't until that afternoon. Later that afternoon, he would meet Shy and the wedding planner, Lakedra Delray. Wanda was getting married that weekend, and Black had promised to throw her the biggest, pull-out-all-the-stops, over-the-top, extreme wedding ever.

"What you know about planning a wedding?" Shy asked when he told her about it.

"I know how to hire a wedding planner," he replied, which meant that Shy would be working with the wedding planner, and he would write the check to pay for it all.

That was the reason for that afternoon's meeting. As he sat there listening to his three department heads talk and sometimes yell at each other, Black's mind drifted to his disappointment in Rain, who, without telling him, had backed his play and involved Jackie and Carter in the murder of Caldwell Enterprise associates Greg Mac and Drum. At the time, he was focusing on his legitimate businesses, and Rain was carrying the title of boss of The Family.

Wanda suggested that he should exile her to an island in the Bahamas the way he had done her when men sent by Nado Benitez almost killed her. Black vetoed that idea because her actions in the matter hadn't involved them in a drug war as Bobby did when he backed Leon in his war with Rico. But it did force him to seriously question her judgment, just not enough to take away her power and position. He was impressed by how she handled herself during their recent run-in with the Albanian mob.

"What do you think, Mike?" Deana asked.

"Huh?"

"What do you think?"

"About what?"

"About the financing for the project?"

"I'm sorry. My mind was someplace else. What are we doing with financing?"

"Jaila wants to apply mixed-use principles to the project."

"Okay, explain mixed-use and explain why we're considering it."

"It is a kind of urban development that blends multiple uses, such as residential, commercial, cultural, institutional, or entertainment, into one space, where those functions are, to some degree, physically and functionally integrated," Jaila said.

"What are the advantages and disadvantages of mixed-use development?" he asked. As Jaila elaborated on the advantages and disadvantages, Black once again got caught up in his own thoughts.

"So, what do you think?" Deana asked again.

"I think we should vote on it," he said. "I know you're for it. What do you think, Jaila?"

"It could work for us," she said.

"Ian?"

"It could be a construction nightmare—or the best thing we could do. It just depends on several factors."

"All right, let's do it," he said, and then they broke back into their usual talking/arguing.

An hour later, the meeting broke up and Black headed to Shy's office to meet with the wedding planner. That didn't take long. Lakedra Delray did a quick review of everything that was supposed to happen, the way it was supposed to happen, and waited for him to hand her the check that he had in his pocket. With his work for the day complete, Black stood up.

"I'm about to get outta here."

Shy chuckled. "If I didn't have so much to do, I'd be walking out with you."

He sat down on the edge of her desk. "Well, Mrs. Black, if you'd hire one of the many people you've interviewed . . ." he said and allowed his voice to trail off.

"I know, but I haven't found the right person," Shy said, and Black said her following line for her.

"Reeva is hard to replace," he said and stood up.

"Well, she is. I'll walk you out," she said and stood up. They walked to the lobby together.

"What time do you think you'll be home?"

"I don't know," Shy said and got on her toes to kiss him.

"See you when you get there. Good night, Vandy. Please let Erykah know I'm gone."

"I'll call her and tell her. Good night, Mr. Black," Vandy said, and Shy watched her husband walk to the car where William was waiting.

"Where to, Boss?"

"Take me home."

He started the car. "You got it."

Chapter 4

The big day finally arrived. Wanda and James Austin were getting married. Everything was set. The wedding and the reception were to be held at the Midtown Loft & Terrace, one of the most prestigious and desirable event venues in New York City. The wedding would be on the beautifully landscaped terrace with a view of the fantastic Manhattan skyline. Then after the ceremony, the wedding guests would move to the stylish reception in the elegant Midtown Loft.

The terrace, with its retractable, enclosed rooftop, featured new hardwood oak flooring, high ceilings, dimmable lighting, an in-house illuminated bar, a dance floor, and a VIP room. Although a member of The Family was getting married, it was not a Family wedding. The venue accommodated one hundred seated guests, and The Loft, where the reception was to be held, accommodated 160 seated guests. Therefore, the guest list was limited to invited guests only. Because Wanda, at this point, was more a businesswoman than a gangster, in addition to her immediate family, many of Wanda's guests were clients and business associates.

As far as The Family was concerned, the invited guests included Black, Shy, and their children, Bobby and Pam, of course. Their daughters, Brenda and Bonita, flew in from California. Since her boyfriend, Cole, was in jail awaiting trial on an armed robbery charge, Barbara, who was dressed elegantly in a Mônot one-sleeve cutout gown,

was there with Tahanee. She selected a Chiara Boni La
Petite Robe stretch jersey fishtail gown. Marvin and
Judah came alone and wore black Ralph Lauren men's
formal tuxedos. They ran into Barbara just as she arrived
at the terrace to be seated.

"You here by yourself?" Barbara asked Marvin.

"Yeah, there wasn't enough seating for me to bring
somebody," he lied, and Barbara knew it. She was with
Wanda when planning the guest list and knew she'd
included a plus one for Marvin.

"I see." Barbara winked at Tahanee and looped her arm
in Judah's. "Then you wouldn't mind escorting me to my
seat?"

"I would be honored to," he said, and Judah escorted
her.

Dressed in an azurite ML Monique Lhuillier strapless
gown, Mia Rubio was there with RJ. They sat next to his
sister and Marvin. Venus sat next to Bobby, and Pam was
there with his son. She looked terrific in the Balenciaga
long glove-sleeve stretch gown she selected.

Nick had brought his entire team home after com-
pleting their mission in Bujumbura, Burundi. He was
in attendance with April. She looked elegant in the Kay
Unger Antoinette cap sleeve column gown. Although
she was uncomfortable in it, Monika looked stunning
in her Safiyaa crepe draped-side gown, as well as Carla,
who was wearing a Talbot Runhof metallic cape-back
trumpet gown, accompanied by her husband, Xavier.
Travis and Jackie were also there. She hadn't seen him
in months and was overjoyed to have him home. She
looked very sexy in the violet Sachin & Babi Deliah flared
one-shoulder gown.

Rain was there, as was Carter, and she made a point
of sitting in a different row from him. Since she decided
to abort his baby, she'd wanted little to do with him. It
bothered Carter, but he was handling it in his own way.

Looking gorgeous in her Valentino pleated silk cape gown, the surprise wedding guest was Jada West. During her time setting up and operating the bank in Nassau, Wanda got a chance to get to know Jada, and the pair formed a friendship that built on mutual respect.

Her maid of honor was her longtime assistant, Keisha Orr. She wore a steel-blue dress Greco ruffle cutout floor-length gown that Khaite designed. Although they weren't bridesmaids, Shy and Pam wore the same dress.

Since neither James nor Wanda was all that religious, they had chosen to have a traditional wedding ceremony. Reverend Jones would preside over the exchange of vows, and he would have the honor of announcing them for the first time as a married couple. Once the guests were seated, it was time for the processional. After her mother was seated, other members of James and Wanda's immediate families were escorted down the aisle and sat on either side of the altar. Her father had passed several years earlier, so Wanda asked Black and Bobby to walk her down the aisle.

"You ready?" Black stood up and spoke when he heard the wedding music. Both he and Bobby were wearing black Ralph Lauren men's formal tuxedos. However, they wore steel-blue vests matching Keisha, Shy, and Pam's dresses.

"As I'll ever be," Wanda said, and Bobby held out his hand to help her up.

Wanda looked incredibly beautiful in the custom Ysa Makino off-the-shoulder wedding dress with a detachable overskirt and all-over embroidery and beaded detail.

"Well, let's do it," Bobby said, and the assembled guests looked on as they walked down the aisle.

"Thank you. Please be seated. Today, we gather to lift Wanda and James up to celebrate ever-lasting love. In the presence of their beloved family and friends, they will pronounce their love through this ceremony and begin a lifelong journey together.

"On this day, we offer gratitude for the blessings that have been bestowed upon Wanda and James. In this fast-spinning, always-changing world, they have finally found peace and comfort in each other. This ceremony is a tribute to their unique love story and a promise of a beautiful future. Nothing is more romantic and sacred than standing before all those dear to your hearts to declare your love to each other.

"Let us begin. Please repeat after me to offer your commitment. 'I, Wanda, take thee, James, to be my lawfully wedded husband. To have and to hold from this day forward. For better, for worse, for richer, for poorer, in sickness, and in health. To love and to cherish, until parted by death.'

"'I, James, take thee, Wanda, to be my lawfully wedded wife. To have and to hold from this day forward. For better, for worse, for richer, for poorer, in sickness, and in health. To love and to cherish, until parted by death.'

"Wanda and James," Reverend Jones continued, "as you exchange your rings today, you are also reinforcing your faithful commitment to trust, love, and romance. Each ring serves as a constant reminder that you are loved. Your beloved is giving you the most precious gift on earth through love."

The couple exchanged rings.

"By the power vested in me, before your families and friends, I now pronounce you man and wife. Please seal your marriage with your first wedded kiss."

Chapter 5

"Good evening, Mr. Garrison."

"Fantasy," Carter turned quickly, "how are you?"

"I'm doing fine. What about you? How are you this evening?"

"I'm great. You look amazing," he said of the red Zuhair Murad Bettina beaded chiffon cape gown the beauty had selected for the occasion.

"Thank you very much for saying so, Mr. Garrison. You're looking very handsome yourself." Carter was wearing a Brooks Brothers Regent fit one-button tuxedo. "You wear a tuxedo well. You should wear one more often."

"Can I get you a drink?"

"As much as I'd love to, I cannot. I have to go to the office to assume monitor duty. The rest of the team is flying back to Juba tonight. They just came for the wedding."

Carter finished his drink. "I understand. Can I drive you there?"

"That would be wonderful. It will give us a chance to catch up." She looped her arm in his and looked around for Jada. "I wanted to speak to Ms. West before I left, but I don't see her."

Carter looked around. "I don't see her either."

"That's okay. It's nothing pressing. I'll speak with her tomorrow before she goes back to Nassau."

The pair walked off together. "I take that as meaning you'll be here for a while?" Carter asked as they headed for the exit.

"That is what I want to speak with her about."

"So, your secret mission for Wanda is over?"

"It is."

"I wasn't aware that you still worked for Jada."

"That's because I technically don't. I am officially assigned to Monika and her team. My checking with Ms. West is more of a courtesy."

Fantasy hoped that Jada would insist that since she had finished working undercover for Wanda, she return to Nassau to complete her training. Although she enjoyed the challenge of working with Monika and the team, Fantasy thought that she was better suited to work with Jada and reclaim the position she once held before, as Jada put it, she "shamelessly threw herself at Carter." At that time, she had visions of replacing Simone, who had betrayed Jada's trust, and she met her demise as a result.

Carter chuckled. "I guess that's why you're going to the office and not with Jada," he said as they left the ballroom.

Rain angrily watched Carter leave the reception with Fantasy. At that point, she had no claims on him, but she still thought it was disrespectful that he would leave with her after all they had been through together. She reminded herself that their not being together was her idea.

"But still . . ." Rain shot her drink.

"But still what?" Alwan asked, even though he had a good idea. After witnessing the interaction between Carter and Fantasy, he figured that was what she was talking about.

"Nothing. Let's get outta here. I need to come up outta this dress and get comfortable." Rain was looking hot in her purple Markarian magnolia off-the-shoulder corset gown. She laughed. "No place for my guns," she said and got up from the table.

After speaking with the newlyweds and wishing them well, Rain went to say good night to Black and Shy before she left. Once she had gone home to change, she went to her new hangout. With Carter still occasionally occupying the office at JR's, she had taken to hanging out at Purple or Deep Purple, the restaurant lounges she owned with Mileena Hayes and Yarissa Dash. Carter avoided those spots because of his prior relationship with Mileena, so it was the perfect spot. Rain was out one night when she went to a concert hall featuring rock bands to collect money from someone who had been ducking her.

The concert hall was practically empty that night, but Rain saw the potential for the place. She talked to RJ about possibly bringing some acts he was working with there. Once he saw the place, with its huge stage and the large open area that sat between the stage and stadium seating, he agreed and arranged to host Lola Luv there. It was an overwhelming success.

Two weeks later, they featured Monte Cole. After he packed the house, Rain had seen enough. She bought the spot, renamed it Purple Rock, and featured P Harlem for the grand opening. The current headliner was Mia Rubio, but there were plans to showcase talent from *The Breakout*. In this popular television reality series, up-and-coming artists compete for a chance at a recording contract from Big Night Records, which was hosted by Black's sister, Scarlet.

While she operated out of JR's, anytime she was in the club, Rain spent the entire night in her office alone, drinking Patrón and watching porn. At Purple Rock, she reserved a booth near the stage for herself, where she spent her nights now. Watching all that porn had her on edge, and since she wasn't fucking anybody and, at that point, had no plans to, it was just frustrating.

"What's up, Rain?" RJ said as he took a seat at the table. Mia headlined the show, so he was at Purple Rock every night.

"Nothing. What's up with you, RJ?"

"I'm good," he said, but he wasn't.

With Mia headlining the show, his being at Purple Rock every night didn't sit well with Venus. Although he really liked Mia and was practically living with her, he and Venus, whom he still loved, recently had a baby boy they named Robert Ray the Third. She was still living with Pam and Bobby, and RJ would spend the entire day at his parents' house so he could be with his son. That didn't sit well with Mia, and both women gave him hell about it.

"How's she doing tonight?" he asked as her song ended, and the crowd gave her a standing ovation.

"That answer your question?" Rain asked. "They love her."

"How long you gonna let her play here?"

"Another week, maybe two," he said, but what he really wanted at times was to get her back on the road. While she was touring Europe with Cristal, things were much quieter and less stressful. "Scarlet has been trying to get her back in the studio to work on new material."

"Who you gonna bring in next?"

"I was thinking about doing a *Breakout* show with some of the more popular acts from the last few seasons."

"What about Roselyn Pierce?" Rain asked about last season's winner. "When we gonna see her up in here?"

"Honestly, I don't think you will. Her agent has been acting funny. It's mostly my fault." Mia had been working with Scarlet when they met, and he had pushed to get Mia's debut album out before Roselyn could get in the studio. "She thinks that Roz should have been the one to tour Europe with Cristal." He laughed. "That and the fact that Gladys signed Mia before she got her on the show has a lot to do with it."

"What about the other muthafucka from last season?"

"Jerry Brinson? We didn't sign him."

"And what does that mean?"

"It means I have no idea where he is or what he's doing."

"You want me to send Alwan to talk to her agent and make her a little more 'cooperative'?"

"Money's been on that, but it hasn't mattered so far." He paused. "I take it that you really want Roz?"

"I do. I ain't really feeling the *Breakout* losers' showcase."

RJ laughed. "They're not losers; they just didn't win."

"Okay. See what you can do to get Roselyn Pierce up here for me. If you can't get her, we'll try the losers' showcase for a week and see how it goes."

"Roselyn Pierce may cost you more," RJ began. "I can bring the *Breakout* showcase for less than you're paying for Mia."

Rain laughed. "Now, I really don't want the losers. What about The Regulators?"

"You mean P, Monte, Lola, *and* Scarlet?"

"*And* Cristal."

"That's doable. Cristal may be hard to pull off, but it's doable."

"Why?" Rain said as Mia closed out her set and took a bow to a standing ovation.

"Something in her contract about playing small venues."

"She played The Four Kings," Rain commented.

While Cristal was in drug and alcohol rehab, she worked with Scarlet on new music, which she performed at The Four Kings when she got out. That night, Cristal officially became a member of The Regulators.

"That was because Scarlet asked her to."

"You tell her that I would consider it a personal favor if she would appear here."

RJ chuckled as Mia came off stage and headed for the table where they were sitting. "An offer she can't refuse."

"An offer she *shouldn't* refuse."

"You want her to appear solo or with The Regulators?"

"Shit, both if I could get her."

"I'll put it to Gladys and her agent."

Rain laughed. "You tell Gladys the same thing you tell Cristal, that I would consider it a personal favor," she said, knowing that Gladys was scared to death of her.

"Shit, you know Gladys is scared of you, right?"

"I know."

"Hey, babe." Mia sat down and kissed RJ. "What y'all talking about?"

"Getting Cristal to appear here," Rain said.

"It's like that, huh? Tired of hearing me every night," Mia said jokingly, but she was a little hurt by it. She was enjoying appearing there nightly. "You'd rather have Her Majesty," she said because after spending months touring Europe with her, Mia didn't like Cristal and was tired of her shit.

"It's not like that," Rain said. "It's not that I'm tired of hearing you, and the crowd loves you."

"I never intended for you to become the house performer. And I wanna get you back in the studio to work with Scarlet on your second album," RJ said.

"I see," Mia said with a fake smile as Rain's phone rang.

"This Rain," she said and got up from the table.

When Rain walked away, Mia dropped the fake smile and turned to RJ. "You just want me back in the studio all day and night with slave driver Scarlet and then back on the road, don't you?"

"It's not like that."

But it kinda was. His life was simpler when Mia was on the road. Now that she was back, RJ had to deal with both his sometimes difficult and demanding baby mama and Mia, the angry girlfriend.

Mia folded her arms across her chest, and her pouty lower lip dropped. "Yes, it is, and you know it. Don't think I don't know what was going on with the two of you while I was putting up with Cristal's shit. That way, you can spend more time with your precious Venus."

"Where is this coming from? You know I be over there to be with my son."

"You don't have to be there to see your son. You can take him sometimes. That way, I could spend some time with him."

"I do. The three of us have a good time when I get him on weekends," RJ said as Rain returned to the table.

"What do you know about Kendrick Nance?" she asked and saw the look on Mia's face. It was the same frustrated and angry look she knew all too well from her days dealing with Carter.

"I know some of his people like to gamble at Mama's," RJ replied. Mama's Country Kitchen was one of the gambling and number spots that Rhianna ran along with the gambling at Samson's Bodega. "Why, what's up?"

"Nothing. His name has been coming up a lot since Black asked me about him."

"I'll check him out and get back to you."

"Cool. I'm out."

Rain wasn't ready to go, but she had been around them before and knew that Mia had no problem arguing in front of her. Not wanting to get involved in their shit, it was time to exit.

"You two have a good night." Alwan came up behind her. "Let's get outta here," she said, and he followed Rain to the exit at Purple Rock.

Chapter 6

It was billed as The Brawl in Montreal, A Night of Champions. A fight between middleweight champion Genesis Rodriguez and undefeated Canadian champion Jacques Gauthier for the IBC title. After a string of high-profile wins, former middleweight champ Frank Sparrow had gotten Marvin's fighter, Alex "The Bronx Bomber" Benton, on the undercard to fight Blaise Tremblay, the current NBO Canadian welterweight title-holder. The fight was to be held at the Maurice Richard Arena at Olympic Park in Montreal, Quebec, Canada.

It was a big night for Marvin. He knew that a good outing for Alex would get him into the welterweight title conversation, so he was excited. He was there at ringside with Joslin Braxton. He had been seeing Savannah Russell, who worked for Frank.

However, after talking with his uncles, Mike and Bobby, about fishing off the company dock and shitting where they all gotta eat, he began to back away from her. He started seeing LaSean Douglas, but she had gotten too clingy, so he gave her space. Joslin was different. They would get together when one or the other wanted to fuck, and then they'd go their separate ways until the next time, which made her the perfect mate for the time being. She was surprised to get an invitation to the fight, but she wasn't about to turn him down.

Black and Bobby had made the trip with their wives, Shy and Pam. Rain Robinson was in the house, but she didn't want to be bothered with Carter, so she missed the last fight. This time, she wasn't letting him dictate what she did. She expected him to show up at ringside with Fantasy on his arm, but she was surprised that he came alone. Since Jackie was Marvin's captain, she had a vested interest in The Bronx Bomber's success, so she was there with Fiona.

Where Venus had no interest in the sweet science, Mia Rubio was a big-time boxing fan, so she was there with RJ. Although she wasn't really into boxing, Barbara was there with Tahanee to support Marvin. Baby Chris and Payton Cummings were there, as was Judah. Once again, he was accompanied by one of the dancers from his spot. He didn't bother to introduce her, and nobody asked. Jada West was the surprised attendee to the fight, dressed elegantly in a Raisavanessa beaded palm knit dress. She was there with her associate Clayton Edmonds, who was Congressman Martin Marshall's chief of staff.

"In the red corner, wearing silver and black trunks, with a professional record of thirteen big wins, eleven of which came through knockouts and no defeats, Alex 'The Bronx Bomber' Benton."

Seeing that Alex was not only the underdog but also the visiting fighter, he got a polite round of applause.

"Fighting out of the blue, his professional record consists of twenty-five wins and three losses, with nineteen knockouts, please welcome the reigning NBO Canadian welterweight champion, Blaise Tremblay."

The assembled crowd sprang to their feet and gave their champion a thunderous round of screaming applause.

"I gave you your instructions in the dressing room. Remember to protect yourself at all times and, above all, obey my commands at all times. When I say 'break,' I want a clean break. In the event of a knockdown, you will be directed to go to a neutral corner. Are there any questions? I expect a good, clean fight. Touch 'em up, and good luck," the referee said, and the fighters returned to their corners to await the bell to begin round one.

Black leaned across Shy. "You wanna bet on what round it ends?"

"Make it easy on yourself."

"The usual?"

"You're on," Bobby said, "I say it goes five."

"I say he stops him in the seventh," Black said and sat back.

"What's 'the usual'?" Shy wanted to know.

"A dollar," Black said as the bell rang to start round one.

Alex practically ran across the ring and began hitting Tremblay with hard lefts and rights. It forced the Canadian champion to cover up, and he eventually reached out to smother his opponent and wait for the referee to separate them.

"Box."

Once the referee stepped out of the way, Alex was back in Tremblay's chest, throwing punches in bunches. He held on.

"Punch your way out," the referee commanded, but Alex kept throwing hard rights to Tremblay's ribs. The referee separated the two combatants.

"Box!"

The referee stepped back again, and Alex went back to working the body. Black leaned close to Marvin. "He's gonna punch himself out."

"No, he's not, Uncle Mike. Tremblay is a notoriously slow starter, so we trained for this," Marvin said confidently as his fighter kept up the pressure and forced Tremblay to the ropes.

"Get off the ropes!" his corner man screamed, and his fighter covered up and tried to get Benton off him with a pawing jab that seemed to have no effect. He eventually held on again.

"Punch your way out," the referee commanded, but once again, Alex kept throwing hard rights to Tremblay's ribs. The referee separated the two fighters.

"Box!"

Before Tremblay could get off the ropes, Alex jabbed his way in and threw an overhand right to the jaw that staggered Tremblay as the bell rang to end round one. Appreciating a good fight, the crowd sprang to its feet as The Bronx Bomber returned to his corner. Marvin leaned close to Black.

"He's gonna box and work the jab this round, Uncle Mike," he said, and Black nodded.

"I don't think Tremblay's gonna make it to the fifth round, much less the seventh," Bobby said.

"You may be right," Black said as the bell rang to begin round two.

As promised, Alex met Tremblay in the center of the ring, moving laterally to his right and throwing the left jab that snapped Tremblay's head back. Known as a boxer/puncher who liked to work inside and could take a punch, Tremblay followed Alex around the ring, looking for an opportunity to engage his opponent. Alex stopped the lateral movement, set himself, and threw a three-punch combination that ended with a big overhand right that connected and dazed Tremblay. He held on, once again, and waited for the referee to separate the combatants.

"Box!"

Knowing that Tremblay was dazed by the overhand right, Alex threw a pawing jab, and when Tremblay tried to step in, he threw the overhand right. It connected to the jaw, but it didn't daze him this time. He put his shoulder in Alex's chest and began throwing hard shots to the body. This time, it was Alex who held on.

"Punch your way out," the referee commanded. Tremblay kept going to the body until the referee separated the two fighters.

"Box!"

Alex quickly moved the fight back to the center of the ring and resumed his lateral movement, throwing the crisp left jab and a straight right hand that Tremblay seemed to have no answer for. He kept pawing with the jab and a lunging right that caught Alex on the chin. He pushed Alex against the ropes and stepped inside. Tremblay went straight to the body with lefts and rights. Alex covered up and then threw a wicked uppercut. He followed that punch with an overhand right that caused Tremblay to step back as the round ended. Both fighters returned to their corners.

"He's gonna finish him this round, Uncle Mike. Watch and see," Marvin leaned close to Black and said.

"I guess we'll see," Black said, watching The Bronx Bomber, who remained on his feet between rounds. When the bell rang to begin the third round, Alex rushed across the ring again, hitting Tremblay with hard lefts and rights to the body. The two fighters exchanged blows in the center of the ring, and Tremblay hit Alex with a head shot.

He got back on his bicycle and resumed a lateral movement, working the jab and the straight right. When Tremblay lunged in, Alex caught him with an overhand right that put him on his back. The once-partisan crowd sprang to their feet as Alex retreated to a neutral corner. The referee picked up the count.

"Four, five, six, seven."

Tremblay got to one knee.

"Eight."

Tremblay got to his feet to beat the count. The referee checked his gloves and looked closely at the fighter.

"Box!"

Alex rushed out of the neutral corner and got back on Tremblay, backing him to the ropes with a five-punch combination ending with the overhand right that Tremblay hadn't had an answer for since the fight began. He stumbled as he tried to escape the ropes, and Alex forced Tremblay back against the ropes. He used the now punishing left jab to measure him for the straight right hand.

Tremblay tried to hold on, but Alex moved to his left and kept throwing the jab and the straight right. As Tremblay took those punches and didn't throw any in return, the referee stepped in and took a long look at him. He was about to stop the fight when Tremblay held on.

"Punch your way out."

Alex separated himself from Tremblay, took a step back, and threw a wicked uppercut followed by an overhand right that stopped Tremblay, and his body collapsed to the canvas. The referee picked up the count as Alex went to a neutral corner.

"Four, five, six, seven, eight." Tremblay got to one knee, but the count continued. "Nine, ten," the referee said as

Tremblay finally got to his feet. The referee grabbed him and waved his arms.

Alex came out of the neutral corner and took a lap around the ring before he did a summersault. He jumped up on the ring ropes with his hands raised in victory. The ring announcer entered the ring as the referee raised Alex's hand.

"The winner by knockout and still undefeated, Alex The Bronx Bomber Benton."

Chapter 7

"Prestige Capital and Associates, how may I direct your call?" Vandy asked.

"Good morning, Vandy. Erykah Morgan, please."

"Who should I say is calling?"

"Patrick Freeman."

"Do you mind if I place you on a brief hold?"

"Not at all, Vandy," Patrick said, and before too long, Erykah came on the line.

"Erykah Morgan."

"Good morning, Erykah, it's Patrick. How are you this morning?"

"I'm well."

"Is Mike in?"

"Not yet. But I do expect him today. I just have no idea when."

"Have him call me. It's nothing crucial."

"I'll give him the message," Erykah said.

She ended the call and looked at the time. It was almost eleven thirty, and she knew that he had a meeting scheduled with Jaila, Deana, and Ian at one that afternoon, so she debated with herself over whether she should call him. She knew he attended the fight that past weekend in Montreal and didn't know when he would return. She decided to call Elise, Shy's assistant, to see if she had made it to work that morning.

"Camb Overseas Importers, how may I direct your call?"

"Elise, it's Erykah."

"Hey, girl, what's up?"

"Is Mrs. Black in this morning?"

"No. They returned late from Montreal, so she called and said she wouldn't be in today. Why, what's up?"

"Mike's not here either. I knew they went to the fight, so I'm not surprised they're not here. Thanks, Elise," she said and called Black's cell phone. It went straight to voicemail, so she called the house.

"Hello," a very groggy Shy answered.

It was Shy's first time in Montreal, and since it was one of her husband's favorite places, he wanted to show her the city. Therefore, the Cessna didn't touch down in New York until five that morning.

"Good morning, Mrs. Black. It's Erykah. I am so sorry to wake you up, but I am trying to reach Mike, and his phone is going straight to voicemail."

"Michael." She elbowed him.

"What?"

She held out the phone. "It's Erykah."

"Hello."

"I am so sorry to wake you up, but your phone is going straight to voicemail."

"What's up?"

"You have a meeting scheduled with Jaila, Deana, and Ian at one this afternoon. Do you want me to reschedule?"

"Yes. First thing tomorrow morning," Black said and was about to end the call.

"One more thing before you go."

"What's that?"

"Patrick wants you to call him. He said it's nothing crucial."

"Thanks, Erykah, I'll give him a call."

"That's all I got, Mike."

"Okay. I'll see you tomorrow," Black said and reached across Shy to hang up the phone. He rolled over, she moved close to him, and they both went back to sleep.

When Black woke up a few hours later, he reached out for Shy, but she wasn't there.

"Cassandra!" He called her but got no answer. He got out of bed and got his phone. Once he was back in bed, Black turned the phone on and called Patrick.

"Mike, I'm glad you called."

"What's up?"

"When you get some time, I need you to come down here and sign the papers for that land deal."

"Can't you have a courier bring them to the house for me to sign?"

"I could, but there are some things that I need to talk to you about." Patrick paused. "Like I told Erykah, it's nothing crucial. We just need to talk."

"Can I get with you tomorrow morning?"

"Sounds good. What time should I expect you?"

"Pencil me in for eleven o'clock."

"See you then." Patrick hung up the phone, and Black got out of bed and headed for the shower. Once he was showered and dressed, he went downstairs to the kitchen and was surprised to find Shy in there with her mother and mother-in-law, and M was showing Shy how to cook Broccoli-Stuffed Chicken. He stood by and watched quietly.

"Once you've mixed the broccoli and cheese, you place half in the center of each chicken breast, like this," M said and demonstrated. "Then you fold the long sides over the filling and fold the ends up."

"Like this?" Shy asked.

"Perfect," M said as she got some toothpicks. She handed a few to Shy. "Then you use toothpicks to hold it together."

"Like this?"

"Yes, that's it. Now, put them in the baking pan seam-side down. Cover the pan with foil, and we're gonna bake them for thirty minutes," M said, taking the pan and putting it in the oven.

"That was pretty easy," Shy said.

"Then you'll be doing more cooking?" Black asked, and it startled everybody.

"Michael," she said, wiping her hands. "How long have you been standing there?"

"Not long." He walked up behind her and put his arms around her waist. "Long enough to see you doing something I never thought I'd see." He kissed her on the cheek. "I'm proud of you."

"Thank you, Michael. I couldn't let our daughter learn to cook, and I don't."

"She's tired of Michelle and her smart mouth," Joanne said.

"That too, Mommy," Shy admitted.

"So, I guess I don't have to ask what's for dinner."

"No, you don't," she said. "We're having broccoli-stuffed chicken with veggies and barley pilaf or herbed potatoes."

Later that evening, once the children got home from school, the family ate and enjoyed the first meal that Shy ever cooked. After dinner, Bobby arrived at the house, and Black left with him.

The following morning at ten forty-five, after meeting with Jaila, Deana, and Ian, Black got off the elevator at Wanda Moore and Associates for his appointment with Patrick Freeman. He was caught off guard when the elevator doors opened. Susan Beason stood there, dressed in a black and gold Balmain embellished sleeveless mini-dress and Balmain alma leather strappy sandals that showed off her amazing legs and made them pop.

"Hello, Mike. This is a pleasant surprise."

"Hello, Susan."

She was the soon-to-be ex-wife of Daniel Beason. He and his late partner, Elias Colton, had gotten involved with members of the Troka Clan, an Albanian criminal organization, and barely came away with his life. But it cost him his marriage. Now, the soon-to-be single Susan had turned her attention to Black despite Shy's warning to stay away from her husband.

"I don't like how you look at my husband," Shy said when she confronted Susan at a Women of the Association of Black Business luncheon.

"Your husband is a handsome man," she said unapologetically that day, and it pissed Shy off.

At the time, Shy was convinced that Daniel Beason was involved, if not responsible, for the death of Reeva Duckworth and had come to the association luncheon that day to question Susan about where Beason was hiding so she didn't pull out her gun or scratch her eyes out when she said it.

"How are you, Susan?" Mike asked.

"I'm doing very well, thank you for asking." Susan stepped closer to him and looked up into his intense eyes. "I had an appointment with my tax lawyer, Jelani Joseph, and you were the last person I expected to see."

"I'm here to see my lawyer too."

"There was so much that Danny was into that needed to be dealt with that, between Jelani, the criminal lawyer, and the divorce lawyer, I'm here all the time."

"I can't even imagine."

"When you finish with your lawyer, you should let me take you to lunch, and I can tell you all about what I've been going through since I last saw you."

"As tempting an offer as that is, sadly, I have to say no. When I get done here, I have another appointment," Black lied. The only thing that he had planned for the rest of the day was to get with Bobby. "Can I get a rain check?" he asked and regretted it as soon as the words left his lips. He knew what Susan's intentions were, as did Shy, and he vowed to stay away from her.

"I'm gonna hold you to that, Mike," Susan said and pressed the button for the elevator. The door opened. She got on the elevator. "Tell Cassandra that I said hello," Susan said with a big smile as the doors closed.

Black chuckled. "I plan to do that as soon as I see her," he said aloud as he headed toward Patrick's office.

He knew from experience that Susan would go out of her way to mention it to Shy the next time she saw her. He didn't understand the game Susan was playing with Shy, but he knew it was a dangerous one for her.

When Black got home that afternoon, he was surprised to find Shy there. She was getting into the whole cooking thing and had been looking up recipes of things she'd like to try to cook during her downtime at work. She'd found a recipe for Lemon Garlic Shrimp Pasta, and since she wasn't busy at work, Shy came home to cook. She was in the kitchen with M, Joanne, and Michelle, so he couldn't blurt it out the second he saw her.

"Hi, Daddy," Michelle said when he entered the kitchen.

"Hello, ladies. How's everybody doing tonight?" he asked and kissed Shy.

"We're fine, Michael," Shy said as she tossed shrimp in the same pan with garlic, crushed red pepper, oregano, and spinach.

"This is becoming a habit with you, ain't it?" he asked.

Shy shook her head. "I wouldn't go that far. The kitchen still belongs to M. I just saw a recipe I wanted to try," she said, carefully spooning cooked pasta into the pot.

"Exactly my point. You, looking up recipes."

"I know, that's what I said," Michelle paused. "Looking up recipes is Grandma's and my thing."

"You're not jealous, are you?" Black asked.

"No, not at all. I'm just surprised, that's all."

"I hope not. I was kinda hoping that this would be something we could all do together," Shy said, stirring in butter, Parmesan, and parsley.

"Mix that until the butter melts, and then add the lemon juice," Michelle said, reading from the paper that her mother had printed.

For her part, M sat quietly, smiling, because this was what she wanted to happen when she suggested it to Shy. At the time, she had noticed that Shy and Michelle were butting heads over the slightest little thing and hoped that cooking would be something to bring them together. Of course, that was going on when Shy took the keys to Michelle's car and grounded her for having no concept of what a curfew meant. Since then, Michelle had learned to respect Shy's wishes, all was forgiven, and now Michelle drives her father's Alfa Romeo.

After dinner, which was delicious, the family retreated to their spaces. Mr. and Mrs. Black were in the media room, but instead of turning on some music or the television, Black went for it. But he eased into it slowly by asking about her day.

"What about you, Michael? How was your day?"

"I had a meeting at the office with Patrick."

"How is he doing?"

"He's doing fine. He said to tell you hello." He shifted in his chair. "Someone else said to tell you hello."

"Who?"

"Susan Beason," he said, and Shy's eyes narrowed.

"Where did you see her?"

"She was at the law office."

"Because you recommended her to them," Shy said, and he could hear the disgust in her voice. "What did the bitch say to you? Because I know it was more than to tell me hello."

"She invited me to have lunch with her."

"What did you say?"

"I told her I couldn't because I had an appointment." He felt it best, at that second, to leave out the part about him asking her for a rain check.

"That bitch is gonna make me hurt her," Shy said and punched Black in the shoulder. It wasn't hard, but it got his attention.

"What was that for?"

"Because this is *your* fault, Michael."

"Me? I didn't do anything."

"That's the point. You're not doing anything to discourage her."

"What do you mean?"

"You should have told her that you couldn't have lunch with her because you are desperately in love with your wife. Tell her that you are not the least bit interested in her or anything else she has to offer. Did you do *that*?"

"No, but—" he began, but Shy quickly cut him off.

"Ain't no buts about it, Michael. If you are not doing anything to discourage her, all you're doing is encouraging her, and she gets bolder and bolder because she thinks you're into her."

"I am not doing anything to encourage her," Black said, and Shy held up her hand.

"Either you stop her, or I will," Shy said, pointing in his face. Then, she got up and left the media room, slamming the door behind her.

Black relaxed. "That went well."

Chapter 8

The Caldwell Task Force, which Lieutenant Rachael Dawkins headed, was formed by Deputy Inspector Cavanaugh and the Assistant United States Attorney, Dennis Allen. The task force was formed for the express purpose of taking down the Caldwell Enterprise. They wanted to put Curcio Family member, the late Johnny Boy DiLeonardo's, handpicked man, Kordell Jones, aka Kojo, into the drug market. Johnny Boy, who'd been a problem for Black and The Family since the early days, was serving time for a parole violation and passed on his knowledge of how to run a drug trafficking organization to Kojo when Big Tony wanted to have a greater presence in the market.

Between the work of the task force and Rain trying to cover her tracks, Butch Caldwell decided to move his family's business to Arizona. With its mission accomplished, the task force was disbanded, and her team was integrated into the organized crime task forces' investigation of Rocco Vinatieri. Therefore, Dawkins didn't tell them that she recruited Veronica Isley, who had graduated in the top five at the police academy, and placed her as a deep cover operative inside Kojo's organization.

She assumed the identity of Shanice Hardaway. Kojo was unaware the real Shanice Hardaway was in witness protection after providing information on her uncle Jimmy Hardaway's drug and racketeering businesses.

Shanice was introduced to Arron Copeland, one of Kojo's lieutenants, when she had outgrown one of his dealers and began moving enough weight to get Kojo's attention. He made her one of his lieutenants.

She began feeding tips to Detective Sergeant Marita Bautista and her strike team, and they were doing real damage to Kojo's organization, posting one big seizure after another and locking up his people. That ended the day that Officer Billups tapped on Deputy Inspector Cavanaugh's door, walked in, and asked about Officer Veronica Isley.

He sent her image to Joey, who sent it to Kojo's consigliere, Sienna Petrocelli, and she sent her head of security, Brendon Walker, to kill her. She caught one in the chest and the other in her stomach. The impact of the shots took her off her feet. Isley was able to crawl to her phone and call 911.

"Officer down this location."

Miraculously, Officer Isley survived her wounds and was given a medal for Meritorious Police Duty, awarded for highly creditable acts of police service over a period of time. On the other hand, Lieutenant Rachael Dawkins was not given a medal for her service. She had run an unauthorized undercover operation that, despite netting several arrests and massive drug seizures, resulted in getting an officer shot in the line of duty. They took her lieutenant bars, bypassed sergeant, busted her back down to detective, and suspended her without pay for a month.

"Further proof that no good deed goes unpunished," Kirk said when she came to his apartment after her hearing. "Forget the arrests and the seizures."

"Tell me about it." she plopped down on his couch. "I'm just glad that Veronica survived the shooting and completely recovered."

"Oh, yeah, she's fine. But what about you? To me, you deserve better than to bust you down like that."

"I can't prove it, and it probably wouldn't matter if I could, but I believe that Cavanaugh gave her up."

Kirk laughed. "Of course, he did. Cavanaugh used to occupy the space in Big Tony Collette's back pocket. So I'm sure he belongs to Angelo now that he's the boss of that house. The word on the street is that Kojo works for Angelo."

"What am I gonna do now?"

"I could put a good word in with the captain, get you back into Major Case."

"If you could do that, it would be great," Dawkins said.

"Yeah, I could do that for you." He sat down next to her. "I miss having you as a partner."

That was a month ago. Dawkins had served out her suspension, and now, she was pulling up at a crime scene to meet Kirk. When she entered the gambling house where the murders had been committed, the assembled police and crime scene technicians gave her a light round of applause.

"Welcome back, Detective," one or two said. Others just gave her a high five or fist bumped as she passed on her way to Kirk and the bodies.

"Good to be back," she said. *I think.*

"About time," he said when she walked into the room. Dawkins paused to look at the door frame and noted that the door had been kicked in.

"The captain's 'welcome back and behave yourself' lecture took longer than I expected."

Kirk laughed. "Did you promise to be a good little cop and not run any more unauthorized ops?"

"On the straight and narrow from here on out," she said, but she had it in her mind to go after Deputy Inspector Cavanaugh and the Assistant United States Attorney,

Dennis Allen, for what they had done to her. She just had no idea what going after them would look like and whether she should involve Kirk in her plan.

"What you got?" she asked, looking around the room at the four dead bodies. One was lying on the floor, and the other three were seated at the poker table.

"Near as I could tell, the shooter kicked in the door and shot the houseman before he could get his gun out," Kirk began.

"Eliminate the threat first," Dawkins said.

"Then he shot the three of them before he robbed the joint." He held up an evidence bag. "They found .45-caliber shells."

"Any witnesses?"

"Not to the shooting, but uniforms are canvassing the area."

"Any ID on our victims?"

"Nope. None of them had a wallet or any ID on them. I'm thinking the killer took them."

"Thorough," Dawkins said as a uniformed officer entered the room.

"Excuse me, Detectives."

"What you got?" Kirk asked.

"One of the businesses across the street has surveillance cameras."

"Let's go check it out," Dawkins said, and they left the crime scene to watch it. "Has the coroner established a time of death?"

"Between two thirty and three thirty this morning," Kirk said as they arrived at the store.

Once the video was queued to the estimated time of death, the detectives sat and watched until Dawkins said, "There he is."

"Pause it!" Kirk exclaimed when the shooter looked directly into the camera.

They took the surveillance video back to the precinct to be processed, and facial recognition was run.
The detective had been following up on the death of
Arnold Bruguier, who was found dead in a bathtub filled
with water in his hotel room. He was fully clothed, and
Lorazepam, a drug used to treat people with anxiety that
has a risk of abuse and addiction, which, if misused, could
lead to overdose and death, was found in his system. The
circumstances of his death suggested suicide or murder;
both were considered possible explanations. Kirk had
been investigating the case in both directions when they
got the call identifying this robbery suspect.

"Thanks, Pete," Kirk said and ended the call. "Our
suspect's name is Chet French, aka Big Frenchie."

"What's his deal?"

"Armed robbery and did some time for aggravated
assault," Kirk said, reading through the information that
Pete had sent him. "Got out six months ago." He paused.
"That's interesting."

"What's that?"

"Known associates. He shared a cell with Kendrick
Nance," Kirk said as they headed for his car.

"Who's that?"

Kirk stopped and faced Dawkins. "He's the product of
your hard work," he said, opening the car door for her to
enter.

"What's that supposed to mean?" she asked when he
got inside the car.

"He used to work for the Kings before he got locked
up for possession with the intent to distribute, but more
importantly, he's trying to fill the void left by you running
off the Caldwells and all but dismantling Kordell Jones's
operation."

"You think there's a connection between them?"

"No telling." He read further. "I got a last known address for French."

"Let's go get him," Dawkins said, and the detectives headed for French's apartment.

Kirk beat on the door. "Chet French! Police, open up!" he shouted and got no answer.

"What do you wanna do?" Dawkins asked, and Kirk looked around the hallway.

"I'm gonna have a look inside," he said and proceeded to pick the lock.

"Excuse me, but I believe this comes under the heading of breaking and entering, you know, since we don't have a warrant."

"Really?" he questioned and opened the door.

They donned gloves and went inside to have a look around.

"Check this out," Dawkins said.

"What you got?" Kirk asked and went to her.

"Looks like he was surveilling Mama's Country Kitchen," she said and handed Kirk the images she'd found.

"Next target, maybe?"

"It's worth a drive-by, don't you think?" Dawkins asked.

"I think so," Kirk replied, and the detectives left the apartment.

Chapter 9

Mama's Country Kitchen was a gambling spot that Rhianna McGrew ran for Sherman Williams, and it was also a popular soul food restaurant. Big Frenchie found a space across the street and parked his car. He was hungry, so he thought about getting a plate of corn bread, baked macaroni and cheese, collard greens, and southern fried catfish to go before he robbed the place.

"How fucked up would that be?" he laughed and checked his gun before he got out of the car. Big Frenchie retrieved a gym bag from the trunk, closed it, slung it over his shoulder, and then walked toward the restaurant.

When he stepped inside, he stopped and took a deep breath. The food smelled so good that he thought again about getting a plate instead of robbing the place. He thought seriously about ordering, taking the food to the car, and then returning and robbing the place. However, instead, he shook his head and headed for the rear of the restaurant, pulling his mask up as he walked. Once he reached the door, he set himself and then kicked it in.

"What the fuck?" Percy, the houseman, shouted, and Big Frenchie raised his silencer-clad weapon and shot him in the chest before he could reach his gun. Then he turned and fired at the four men that were playing poker, killing them instantly.

Big Frenchie grabbed the gym bag from his shoulder and filled it with the money on the table as quickly as he could. Once he had the cash, he walked up to Percy's body, kicked him out of the way, and got the bank before slinging the bag over his shoulder and heading for the door.

At the same moment, Rihanna hung up the phone and exited her office. She had just locked the door when Big Frenchie ran out of the gambling room.

"What the fuck?" Rihanna shouted, and Big Frenchie raised his silencer-clad weapon and fired a couple of shots at her as he ran.

She got the Ruger Max .380 from her thigh holster and fired back, but he was out the door. She ran outside after him and kept firing until he got to his car. Rihanna had to take cover behind a car when he returned fire and then got into his vehicle. Big Frenchie started the car, dropped it in drive, and sped off with Rihanna firing until her gun was empty.

Rihanna went back inside Mama's. "You all right?" Evette, the restaurant manager, asked.

"I'm fine," she said as she rushed past her going to the gambling room.

Rihanna opened the door and was horrified by Percy's body stretched out on the floor and the four gamblers at the table. Two were facedown in their own blood. The impact of the shots had knocked the other two out of their seats, and their bodies lay on the floor.

"My God," Evette said as Rihanna closed the door to the gambling room and went into her office. She shut the door and took out her phone.

"What's going on, gorgeous?" Sherman asked when he answered the phone.

"We got robbed, Boss," she said quickly and sat down at her desk.

"How much?"

"I don't know yet, but we got civilians down."

"Damn it all to hell," he said and banged his fist on the armrest. "You call RJ?"

"Not yet. You were my first call."

"I'll take care of it," Sherman said and hung up to call RJ.

Rihanna got up from her desk and came out of the office. She had just opened the door to the gambling room and stepped inside when Kirk and Dawkins walked up behind her.

"Looks like we're a little late for the party," Kirk said, catching Rihanna off guard. She spun around on her heels.

"Kirk," she said as he and Dawkins donned gloves and approached the bodies.

Dawkins checked one of the bodies. "He's dead, but the body is still warm." She looked at Rihanna. "This just happened." When Rihanna said nothing, she took out her phone and called the precinct. "I'm going to assume you didn't call the police."

Rihanna rolled her eyes. "Just about to, Detective."

"Yeah, right," Kirk said and looked at the bodies. "You know who did this?"

Rihanna thought for a second before answering. "I didn't get a good look at him, but I did shoot at him when he ran," she admitted since there was evidence of the firefight.

"Where's the gun you used?" Dawkins asked.

Rihanna held up her hands. "I'm reaching for my gun," she said and then got it from her thigh holster and handed Dawkins the .380, who put it in an evidence bag.

Kirk knelt and picked up one of Big Frenchie's expended shells. "They are .45-caliber shells."

"You think it's our boy?"

"I'm sure of it." He stood up. "But we'll see. This is a Mike Black spot," Kirk said and walked out of the gambling room.

"And?"

"That means that cameras cover every inch of this place. We'll get a look at him." He thought for a second. "Just to be on the safe side, go ahead and call for a warrant now."

Twenty minutes later, RJ arrives at Mama's with Judah. He was at Doc's when he had gotten the call about the robbery from Sherman. When he arrived, RJ was surprised to see all the police, emergency vehicles, and the coroner's van outside of the usually quiet spot.

"What the fuck?" RJ questioned.

Judah chuckled. "Somebody must have called the cops," he said as they parked on the perimeter of the crime scene.

"No shit," RJ said and got out of the car.

"I doubt it was Rhianna," Judah said as they walked. "Must have been one of the customers."

"Probably," RJ said as they approached the restaurant and wondered if he would attempt to bypass the crime scene tape or if he even wanted to. "Shit."

"What?" Judah questioned as RJ stopped in his tracks.

"Kirk."

"Fuck is he doing here?" Judah asked as Kirk saw them, smiled, and came their way.

"Robert Ray, Junior," Kirk said loud enough that it got the attention of the technicians processing the scene, and they looked in RJ's direction.

"He's all yours," Judah said, dropped his head, and returned to the car.

"Where's Judah going? I wanted to say hello. I haven't seen him since Doc was murdered."

"Maybe he doesn't want to talk to you," Dawkins said, smiling. "You *are* a cop, and I hear some people don't like to talk to the cops."

"Wonder why?" Kirk paused. "Naw, that couldn't be the case. What do you think, RJ?"

"He's doing fine, Kirk."

"So what's going on?" Kirk asked.

"You tell me. I just got here," RJ said. That was when he saw Rhianna, and they made eye contact. She shrugged her shoulders and mouthed the words, "*I'm sorry.*"

"You got robbed. Your houseman and four civilians are dead."

"I'm sure you'll have the guilty party in custody soon, Kirk."

Kirk nodded. "I'm just surprised, that's all."

Figuring that he would talk to Rhianna later, RJ started to walk away from the detectives, but they walked alongside him.

"What surprises you, Kirk?"

"That there's somebody out there stupid enough to rob one of your uncle's spots."

"I don't know what you're talking about," RJ said. When Judah saw him coming, he got in the car.

"Of course, you don't. I know your uncle Mike is a legitimate businessman, right?"

RJ stopped abruptly and faced Kirk. "Is there something in particular that you want?"

Kirk got in his face. "Don't get cocky on me." He leaned closer. "There's no statute of limitations on murder," Kirk said softly, reminding RJ that he knew that he had murdered Sterling, Venus's old boyfriend, and would use it if he felt RJ was getting out of line.

RJ put up his hands in surrender. "Nothing but respect for you, Kirk."

"I thought so." Kirk stepped back. "Now that we have that established, do you have anything that you want to tell me?"

"No, sir." RJ nodded at Rhianna and then turned back to Kirk. "Is it all right if I go, Detective?"

Kirk looked at Rhianna and then back to RJ. "You can go." He glanced at his watch. "They should be done processing the scene in about an hour. Why don't you come back then, and you can talk to Rhianna?" Kirk said, walking away with Dawkins.

"What was that about?"

"I know that he killed his baby mama's ex. Threw him off the roof of a parking garage."

"Oh," was all that Dawkins said as they returned to the crime scene.

Chapter 10

They weren't calling it a date night, and they certainly weren't calling it a double date, but that night, Press and Nia Kelly, Axe and Desiree Gaynor were going to have dinner at Cuisine. For Axe and Desiree, this was a big event. It would be their first time going somewhere other than a hotel and doing something other than fucking. You see, Desiree was the soon-to-be ex-wife of Davis Gaynor. Axe sent Press to collect once his gambling losses surpassed $50,000. It had nothing to do with the fact that while he was losing at poker and lost a lot, Axe had his wife bent over in the storage room. When Davis found out about the affair, he refused to pay.

"Go ahead and kill her lying, cheating ass!"

At Axe's request, Press took Desiree to the Hyatt Place in Yonkers that night, and his relationship with her had grown until it reached this milestone. But if the truth were to be told, Axe really wasn't feeling the whole out-in-public thing. It was mainly because Desiree had been hanging out at the club with Nia, and she would tell her about all the places that *"her man"* took her.

"Axe never takes me anywhere but to bed, ain't that right, Axe?"

So there they were.

But they weren't the only ones having dinner at Cuisine. That evening, Mike Black was there with his children. They had just come from seeing a movie, Mason Grant's new action thriller, *On The Run,* and stopped in to eat before they headed out to New Rochelle.

Their server, Adrianne, had filled the table with lobster cocktails, smoked salmon appetizers, the soup of the day, mixed green salad bacon, and Roquefort blue cheese. Black had the bone-in filet mignon and veal Milanese. It was sautéed jumbo shrimp scampi for Michelle and chicken Parmesan for Eazy.

Axe leaned close to Press. "I mean, we gotta go over there and show respect," he said as they watched other members of the Family, Clinton Demonte and Cleveland Andrews, one by one, approach the table.

"You sure it's cool? He's out with his children. I don't know if it's cool to interrupt family time."

"You've never met his daughter, Michelle, have you?"

"No."

"You need to," Axe laughed. "We might be working for her one day."

"I don't know, Axe."

"You ain't scared to meet the boss, are you?"

"No."

Axe stood up. "Then come on. Excuse us, ladies," he said, and Press got up as Jarell Quincy, who ran numbers for The Family, approached the table.

"How are you, Mike?" Jarell said, shaking hands with Black and nodding in respect to Michelle and Eazy.

"I'm doing good, Jarell. What about you?"

"If you could get a message to Carter that I need a minute of his time, I'd appreciate it."

"Anything I can do for you?"

"No, Mike," Jarell said. "Nothing to trouble yourself with. I just need a moment of Carter's time," he said, being mindful of the chain of command.

"No problem, but if you don't hear from Carter, I wanna know about it."

"Understood. Enjoy your meal," Jarell said and walked away.

"There he is," Black said as Axe approached the table. Michelle smiled and waved.

"What's up, Mr. Black?" Axe asked, and Black stood up to shake his hand.

"How are you, Axe?"

"I'm good." He turned to introduce Press. "This is—"

"Omari Preston," Black said with his hand out. "I've been hearing many good things about you and the work you've been doing."

Press shook Black's hand enthusiastically. "It's an honor to meet you, sir."

"The honor is mine." Black sat down.

"We're not gonna take up any more of your time, Mr. Black," Axe said. "I just wanted to show respect."

"Your respect and your service are most appreciated," Black said.

"How are you, Axe?" Michelle asked.

"I'm fine, Ms. Black," Axe said and bowed respectfully. And with that, he and Press returned to their table and their lady friends.

"He knows who I am," Press said on the way.

"Trust me, Mike Black knows everything," Axe said as they reclaimed their seats.

But that evening, they weren't the only ones who enjoyed the hospitality of the supper club. Kordell Jones, a.k.a. Kojo, was in the house as well. In his quest to meet Mike Black, he had made a habit of coming to Cuisine at least once a week for dinner in the hope that Black would be there. Kojo had been going there for months, and finally, Black was there.

"What are you doing?" Brendon Walker, Kojo's head of security, asked when he started for the table.

"I'm going to talk to him," Kojo said and kept walking.

"This is a bad idea," Brendon said as he followed Kojo.

Black saw him coming, as did William. He got to the table just in time to stop Kojo. Black signaled to let him come.

"I've been waiting a long time for this. Mind if I sit?"

"I do mind," Black said, but Kojo boldly sat down anyway.

Brendon, who knew this was not good, stood behind Kojo and noticed Axe and Press standing behind him. He looked around and saw that Jarell Quincy, Clinton Demonte, and Cleveland Andrews were coming quickly toward the table.

He leaned in and whispered to Kojo. "We should go."

"What do you want?" an annoyed Black asked.

"I thought it was long past time you and I met."

"Why?"

"What do you mean?"

"Why do I need to meet you?" Black sat back. "As far as I'm concerned, you're nobody. You're just somebody we gotta deal with out of respect for Angelo. Get him outta here."

Axe and Press grabbed Kojo and snatched him out of the chair. When Brendon started to move toward them, Clinton Demonte discreetly put a gun in his back. "I wouldn't," he said and took Brendon's gun. Black called William over.

"Take him to the parlor and wait for me," Michelle heard her father say.

She watched as what would one day be her men escorted Kojo and Brendon out of Cuisine. Michelle had heard him say, *Take him to the parlor* before, but she never knew what it meant. She just knew that it wasn't good.

"What was that about?"

"Just somebody who thought he was entitled to something he wasn't. Nothing for you to be concerned with."

Michelle looked at her brother. He had gone back to eating his food. She shook her head because he could be so naïve despite her urging him to listen and pay attention to everything.

Black watched them until they had left the Cuisine, and after they finished eating, they left the restaurant, and Michelle drove them home. When they arrived, Black retreated to the sanctuary of the media room while Eazy excitedly told his mother all about the Mason Grant movie before he went upstairs to his room.

When he did, Shy joined Black in the media room. Michelle hung around the living room, waiting and watching as Mr. and Mrs. Black eventually came out of the media room and went upstairs. But she knew her father and knew it wouldn't be long before he returned downstairs.

He was passing through the living room to the front door when he saw Michelle sitting there.

"What are you doing in here?"

"Waiting for you."

"What's up?"

"Mind if I ask you a question before you go, Daddy?" she asked, and Black stopped.

"What's that?"

"What's 'the parlor'?"

Black looked at Michelle for a second or two and thought about saying, *Nothing for you to be concerned with*. Instead, he came and sat down next to her. "Why do you want to know?"

"Because I've heard you say that before, and I want to know what it means. Is the parlor an actual place? What happens there?"

Black pointed at her. "You didn't answer my question. You just asked more questions. But I still want to know why you want to know if the parlor is a place and what happens there."

Michelle paused and had to think of a better answer than *because I wanted to know*. She decided to tell him the truth. "Because I need to know everything that goes on in this family."

"Now, we're getting somewhere. Why do you need to know everything that goes on in this family?" he pressed her.

"Because one day, it might fall to me to be the boss of this family," Michelle quickly said as if she were glad to say the words out loud finally.

"The parlor is an actual funeral parlor," Black said nonchalantly. In so many ways, he was proud of his girl, but at the same time, she was, and always would be, his little girl, and she was in such a rush to be a gangster. With every fiber of his being, he wanted to protect her, but he knew she was right. One day, Michelle Black would be the boss of this family. It was his job to shape the empire, both legal and illegal, that she would one day be in control of.

"So, you saying 'take them to the parlor' is, what, just a way of saying to kill them?"

"No." Black took a deep breath and exhaled. "At the funeral parlor, there is a crematorium we've used to dispose of bodies for years."

"What?"

"You heard what I said, Michelle. We take people there so they disappear without a trace. No blood, no bodies, no murder weapon, no evidence."

Michelle sat quietly for a second or two as she chewed on the mouthful that her father had just fed her.

"I understand," she finally said, and it made sense to her. "Is that what's gonna happen to the man from earlier today?"

"His name is Kordell Jones, and yes, that's what's gonna happen to him."

"Can I go with you?"

"No." Black stood up.

Michelle stood up. "Please."

"No. And don't tell your mother I told you about the parlor." He sat back down, and Michelle did too. "Sometimes, I think I let you know and see too much." He put his arm around her. "But then I think that if you were a boy, your mother wouldn't have as much of a problem with it."

"And I would have grown up in my rightful place at your side." She folded her arms across her chest. "Instead of listening at the door."

"No, you would have been in the room with me," he said, thinking about Eazy's lack of interest in the family business. "You learn what Barbara has to teach you, and when the time is right, you can assume your rightful place. Until then, listen and pay attention to everything. One day, it will all serve you well."

"Yes, Daddy."

Chapter 11

"Okay, William, let's go."

"Where to?"

"The parlor."

"No doubt," William said, and they headed out of the house.

Things were quiet at the parlor, or at least they were now. When they arrived, Jarell Quincy, Clinton Demonte, and Cleveland Andrews took it upon themselves to savagely beat Kojo and Brendon before they left them with Axe and Press. They took no part in the beating because, as Axe pointed out on more than one occasion, "Mr. Black said to take them to the parlor, and that's it. He didn't say nothing about beating the fuck outta them."

Those words fell on deaf ears as Quincy, Demonte, and Andrews did their worst, and when it was over, and they had beaten Kojo and Brendon damn near to death, they stopped, and suddenly, Andrews was the voice of reason.

"This isn't what the boss wanted."

That was when Edwina arrived at the parlor. "What the fuck are you assholes doing?" she asked when she saw what they had done. She didn't wait for an answer. "Y'all get the fuck outta here!"

When Axe and Press started to leave with them, Edwina stopped them. "Mike wants you two to stay."

When Black arrived at the parlor with Willian, Axe, and Press were waiting patiently for them. Black took a look at Kojo and Brendon and shook his head.

"What happened to them?"

Press started to answer, but Axe stopped him. Black chuckled. "Let me guess. Quincy, Demonte, and Andrews got a little carried away, leaving you two to deal with the mess."

"Edwina made them leave," Axe said as Black approached Brendon. He was on his knees with his hands tied behind his back. His face was a twisted and bloody mess.

"Where's Edwina?"

"She went to the store. She said she'd be back," Axe reported.

"Either of you know what goes on here?"

"No, sir," Axe said. "But I've heard stories."

"What have you heard?" Black asked as Edwina came into the room.

"Evening, Mr. Black."

"What's up, Edwina?"

"Nothing much. Since the three amigos brought them in, I wasn't sure what you wanted to do with them," Edwina said because not everybody knew what happened there.

"They're in for the full treatment," Black said, and William laughed.

"I'll go get everything ready," Edwina said, going to get the cremation chamber ready to give Kojo and Brendon the "full treatment."

"So, what have you heard?" Black asked when Edwina left to prepare the cremation chamber.

"That niggas get cremated here."

"Right." Black nodded. "You know why the two of you are still here?" he asked and got no answer. "You two are still here because you work for Fiona," Black said, referring to the murder corporation that Jackie had formed to accept murder contracts. "Chances are that in that line of work, you'll need to use Edwina's services."

"The full treatment," William joked.

"Right," Black laughed along with him.

Black took out his gun and put it to Brendon's head. Kojo closed his eyes as Black shot him. His body jerked like it was he who had taken the bullet. Then Black walked up to Kojo and put the gun to his forehead.

"Open your eyes and look at me," Black said calmly. Kojo opened his eyes. "You're going to die tonight. But I'm guessing that you figured that out already." Black sat down next to him. "But I want you to know that it's nothing personal. I don't know you or anything about you. You're gonna die, one, because you interrupted me when I was out with my children, and I take family time very seriously."

"Told you," Press whispered to Axe.

"But the real reason I'm gonna kill you is because of Johnny Boy," Black said and shot Kojo twice in the head.

"Right on time," Edwina said when she returned. "I'm ready for them."

Now that both men were dead, Edwina prepared the bodies and removed their jewelry, and then she checked for medical devices and prosthetics. After that, Kojo's body was placed in a rigid cardboard container that was completely combustible. Then the body was moved to the cremation chamber and placed in a retort, which was heated to between 1,400 and 1,800 degrees Fahrenheit. At that temperature, the body burns, and the bones turn to ash. The cremation process takes between two to three hours.

"Where to, Boss?"

"Take me out to Yonkers," Black said and relaxed in his seat. "I need to talk to Joey."

"On our way," William said, heading out to Yonkers and the private club where Angelo Collette used to run his crew. Now that he was boss of the Curcio Family, the spot had been taken over by Angelo's right-hand man, Joey Toscano.

William rolled down the window. "Mike Black to see Mr. Toscano," he said to the two men who met the car when he parked.

"Wait here," one said and walked away to check.

Black shook his head. "Not like the old days," he said, remembering when this was Angelo's spot. "A lot of new faces."

It wasn't long before the man came back to the car. "Mr. Toscano will see you now."

William got out and opened the car door for Black to exit, and they went inside. Once inside, they surrendered their weapons. William sat at the bar, and Black was escorted to Joey's office.

"Mikey!" he said when the door opened, and Black walked in.

"How are you, Joey?" Black asked and shook his hand.

"I'm great. Can I get you something to drink?"

"Whatever you're drinking is fine," Black said and sat down.

"Nonsense!" Joey said and went to the bar. He picked up a bottle of Rémy Martin Louis XIII. "I got you."

"I expected no less."

"What, you think because Angee ain't here no more that I don't have what you drink?"

"I meant no disrespect," Black said as Joey handed him a glass.

"What can I do for you, Mikey?"

"I need to make you aware of something." Black took a sip. "That's good."

"What's that?"

"Kojo is dead."

Joey nodded. "It was only a matter of time. Honestly, I'm surprised he lasted this long before somebody ended him."

"It was only out of respect for you and Angee that Rain didn't kill him."

"I know, Mikey, and to tell you the truth, there won't be a lot of people who will miss him, the arrogant fuck." Joey raised a glass. "It'll save Sienna the trouble of pushing him out."

"Just thought you should hear it from me personally," Black said, finishing his drink.

"I appreciate it." Black stood up. "Before you go, Mikey, let me ask you a question."

"What's that?"

"What about Sienna?"

"What about her?"

"You got any problem with her?"

"Nope. And to be honest with you, I'm the least of her problems."

"What do you mean?"

"You know as well as I do that her house is in disarray, and the wolves are circling."

"Kendrick Nance." Joey stood up and shook his head. "Between him and fuckin' Bautista's fuckin' strike team putting points on the board . . ."

"I thought you dealt with everybody the snitch gave up."

Joey followed Black out of the office. "Shanice, or whatever the fuck her name was, knew their whole operation inside and out, so Bautista is still coming at her hard."

"That's fucked up. Bautista's a dog with a bone."

"Tell me about it, Mikey."

"Cavanaugh can't rein her in?"

"He's treading lightly. After he crashed the Caldwell Task Force, too many eyes were on him to shut her down."

When Black entered the bar area, William stood up and started for the door. Black shook Joey's hand.

"Tell Angee I'll get with him when things quiet down," Black said, following William out of the club.

Chapter 12

With towering volcanoes and stone temples, Bali, Indonesia, provided Wanda and James an unforgettable backdrop for their honeymoon. Black and Bobby may have paid for it, but Shy and Pam arranged for them to stay at the Bulgari Resort Bali in an ocean-view villa with a plunge pool and magnificent, unobstructed views of the Indian Ocean. The newlyweds spent a week relaxing on the private beach, dining at Il Ristorante, the hotel's signature restaurant overlooking a reflection pool amidst the cliffs of Uluwatu. At the spa, the couple indulged themselves in deep Balinese massages with exotic oils and herbs and the placement of warm volcanic stones on the chakras, the body's seven energy centers, facial treatments, and body wraps, all done at the ocean's edge. They had a wonderful time and returned to the city aboard Black's Cessna Citation. Now that they were back in the city, Wanda and James invited the Blacks and the Rays to join them for dinner at The RH Rooftop Restaurant.

James raised his glass to make a toast after a delicious meal of lobster rolls, shaved ribeye on charred garlic bread, broiled salmon, and roasted chicken. "Wanda and I want to thank you for everything you've done."

"The wedding, the reception, and the honeymoon were all amazing, and we had such a great time," Wanda added.

"It was our pleasure," Shy said.

Pam raised her glass. "I hope the two of you will be very happy together."

"Well, since we're making toasts," Bobby raised his glass, "I want to wish the two of you all the best and a lifetime of happiness."

"Thank you, Bobby," Wanda said, and James nodded in agreement.

"And if you don't keep her happy," he paused and smiled, "let's just say that it won't go well for you, James," Bobby said jokingly, but he was serious.

James chuckled and put his arm around Wanda. "You don't have to worry about that, Bobby. Making Mrs. Austin happy is my purpose in life." He kissed her on the cheek.

"I already made a long-ass speech at the reception, so I'll just say you're welcome and wish you all the best," Black said.

"Thank you, Mike," James and Wanda both replied.

When it was time to leave, Black tried to pay the check, but James insisted.

"This is our party," he said, dropping the American Express Centurion Black Card on the bill.

Once he paid the check, they all rose and headed toward the exit, with Wanda and James holding hands. They were followed by Black and Bobby, with Shy and Pam trailing behind them. When they exited the Ninth Avenue building, a black van came to a screeching halt, and the side door suddenly opened.

Before Black and Bobby could react, one man armed with an automatic weapon opened fire. As Shy and Pam ducked back into the building for cover, Black and Bobby hit the ground and waited for their opportunity to return the gunman's fire. When the shooting stopped, Black and Bobby sprang to their feet, drew their weapons, and fired at the van as it sped away.

"Oh no," Shy said when she came out of the building and saw that Wanda and James had been shot. She rushed to the bodies.

"No," Black said when he saw them. "Call 911, Pam!"

When the ambulance and the paramedics arrived, James and Wanda were taken to Mount Sinai West Hospital. James was pronounced dead on arrival, and Wanda was rushed to surgery with multiple gunshot wounds to the chest and stomach.

"This Rain."

"Wanda's been shot, and James is dead."

"Fuck," Rain reacted. "You know who did it?"

"Not yet. I need you to meet me at Mount Sinai West."

"On my way," she paused. "Black?"

"Yeah."

"I'm sorry."

"I know, just get here."

Rain ended the call. "Wanda's been shot. Take me to Mount Sinai West Hospital," she told Alwan, and he drove her there.

"What's going on, Mike?" Patrick asked when he answered the phone.

"Wanda's been shot, and James is dead."

"Oh my God. Is she going to be all right?"

"She's in surgery. We're at Mount Sinai West. I need you to send somebody here to deal with the police."

"I'm on my way, Mike."

"Thank you, Patrick."

"No problem. I'll be there as soon as possible," Patrick promised, and he hung up the phone and got ready to head out.

Chapter 13

Now that they had reviewed the security video from Mama's and were able to verify that it was Chet French who had robbed the place, and they watched him kill the houseman, Percy Albertson, Detectives Kirk and Dawkins were on their way to his apartment to arrest him. Kirk parked in front, and after donning bulletproof vests, they entered the building with their weapons drawn. They had reached the sixth floor and were walking down the hall when they saw a man coming out of French's apartment. Both detectives raised their weapons.

"Police!" Dawkins shouted.

"Don't move!"

The man raised his weapon and opened fire at the detectives. With their backs pressed against the wall, Kirk and Dawkins stood completely still until the shooting stopped. Then the man ran down the hall to the back staircase.

"Was that French?" Dawkins asked as they followed him down the hall.

"No!"

"Who the fuck is he then?" Dawkins asked.

Once they reached the stairwell, they saw the man running up the stairs to the seventh floor, so they followed him. The man ran through the hall, stopped, turned, and fired. Kirk and Dawkins retreated to the stairwell as he fired, and then he kicked in the door of an apartment and rushed in. When the detectives reached the apartment, they saw the man go out the window to the fire escape.

"I got him," Dawkins shouted and went out the window behind him. Kirk turned and ran out of the apartment and down the stairs.

Out on the fire escape, the man stopped and fired at Dawkins. She returned his fire and continued chasing him. When he reached the bottom, the man jumped down and turned to run toward the street. But that was when Kirk punched him in the face, and the blow put him on his back.

Kirk stood over him. "Where the fuck do you think you're going?"

Dawkins jumped down from the fire escape and stood over the man with her gun drawn. "He's going to jail, that's where he's going. You're under arrest for attempted murder."

Once they had him cuffed, they took the suspect to the precinct. The man's name was Baker Wright. He was the brother of one of the men that French shot in a robbery. He had come there to kill him for what he had done.

Kirk and Dawkins were at their desks in the squad room when their lieutenant came out of his office and went to where they sat.

"I need to see the two of you in my office," he said and returned to his office.

Dawkins looked at Kirk. "Right behind you," she said, and they got up and followed the lieutenant.

"What's up, Lieutenant?"

"Wanda Moore has been shot, and her new husband is dead."

"Oh shit," Dawkins said, and Kirk said nothing but found himself getting a little emotional. Not only had he known Wanda for years, but they also had sex several times. Dawkins glanced at him.

"Is she all right?" he finally asked.

"As far as I know, she is still in surgery from multiple gunshot wounds to the chest."

"Where did it happen?" Dawkins wanted to know.

"They were coming out of The RH Rooftop Restaurant."

"Does Black know?" Kirk asked.

"He and Bobby were there when it happened. She was taken to Mount Sinai West. The case has been assigned to Ninth Precinct Detectives Miller and Riley. But I want the two of you on this."

"They aren't gonna appreciate us big footing their case," Dawkins pointed out.

"You think I give a fuck what they appreciate? I already cleared it with their lieutenant. I need you to find out who did it before Black turns the streets red."

Kirk stood up and started toward the door. "He at the hospital?" Dawkins asked as she rose.

"Where else would he be?" Kirk told his partner, and once they left the lieutenant's office, they went to Mount Sinai West.

When the detectives arrived at the hospital and found Black, he was there with Shy, Bobby, Pam, and Rain. She had just arrived and offered her condolences.

Shortly after that, Kirk and Dawkins entered the waiting room. Patrick stopped them as he had with Detectives Miller and Riley and every other cop that tried to talk to Black.

The detectives showed Patrick their badges. "We'd like to speak with Mike Black."

"What can I do for you, Detective Kirkland?" Patrick asked.

"I just told you. I want to talk to Black."

"Mr. Black—" Patrick began.

"Black!" Kirk shouted to get Black's attention. When he looked and saw Kirk and Dawkins, Black signaled for Patrick to let them come.

"Kirk."

"How is she?"

"She's still in surgery," Black stated, and Shy rolled her eyes at the detectives. She'd never had any use for cops, and despite their relationship, Kirk was no different.

"You know who did it?"

"No."

"Would you tell me if you did?"

"I really don't know who did this, Detective. But you know I will."

"And when you do?" Kirk asked.

"Is this your case, Detective?" Black asked instead of answering his question.

"We're on it."

"Then who were those other two assholes who came up here?"

"Miller and Riley," Shy spit out angrily.

"Officially, it's *their* case," Kirk chuckled. "So, at some point, you may want to talk to them, but like I said, we're on it. Can you tell me anything that would help us find who did this?"

"No, Kirk, I can't," Black lied because he had some ideas about who was responsible for Wanda getting shot and murdering James. Even though he'd just had Kojo killed, Black didn't think that Sienna Petrocelli or anybody in what was left of her organization had anything to do with it. On the other hand, the BBKs were a different story.

"Even though I know that you won't, I urge you to let the police handle this," Kirk said, and Black stood up. He held out his hand.

"Thank you for coming." He turned to Dawkins. "Always a pleasure to see you." He looked at Rain. "Walk with me, Ms. Robinson. You too, Bob."

"Think about what I said," Kirk expressed as he and Dawkins followed the three out of the waiting room.

"I will," Black replied, walking down the hall with Bobby and Rain as Kirk and Dawkins looked on.

"You think he will?" Dawkins asked.

"Hell no. As soon as he finds out who's responsible, those three are gonna unleash bloody hell on them."

"We need to find them first." Dawkins watched Black walk away.

Knowing his connection to Angelo and, by extension, Deputy Inspector Cavanaugh and Assistant United States Attorney Dennis Allen, the former lieutenant thought about asking for Black's help in paying them back for what they had done to her, but this was not the time or the place. As she left the hospital with Kirk, Dawkins thought she would take her issue to Jada.

"Who do you think did this, Black?" Rain asked as the three walked down the hall.

"I have no idea. I was about to ask you the same question."

"I don't know. I been playing nice lately."

"What about you, Bob?" Black asked.

He'd noticed that Bobby had been uncharacteristically quiet. The only thing on his mind was finding who did this and killing them. He imagined that Bobby felt the same way.

"No clue. I know it's nothing I'm doing. I haven't even fucked anybody's wife or girlfriend lately," he chuckled. "Maybe it's Daniel Beason."

"Daniel Beason? Why would he do that after we took the Albanians off his neck?" Black questioned.

"It might be about Susan."

"Oh, hell no!"

"Who's Susan?" Rain asked.

"Beason's wife."

"You fuckin' Beason's wife?" she asked, shocked that he would cheat on Shy.

"No, I'm not fuckin' her."

"No. She just set it out for you," Bobby laughed.

"Anyway," Black looked at Rain, "start asking questions. I wanna know who's behind this."

"I'm on it," she said as they returned to the waiting room just as the doctor arrived to talk to them. She stopped at the door to wait for them.

"How is she?" Black asked as Shy and Pam joined them at the door.

"The surgery was successful. We were able to remove all three bullets," the doctor said.

"Thank God," Pam said.

"But she hit her head hard when she was shot, resulting in traumatic brain injury accompanied by swelling and an increase in intracranial pressure. Therefore, I thought it best to place her in a medically induced coma." She paused. "The goal of a medically induced coma is to reach a level of sedation that will give the brain vital time to rest and heal."

"Can we see her?" Bobby asked.

"She's in the intensive care unit. Are you her family?"

"They're her brothers," Shy said.

"You can see her one at a time," the doctor stated.

"You go ahead, Bob," Black said, and he followed the doctor to ICU. Then he turned to Rain. "Find out who did this."

She nodded. "What are you gonna do?"

"After I see Wanda, I'm going to The Playhouse to talk to Jackie; see if she heard anything."

"I'll let you know if I find out anything."

"Before you go, tell me what's up with the robbery at Mama's."

"Some nigga they call Big Frenchie is the one who did it. Word is that he's down with Kendrick Nance. Sherman and RJ are on it." Rain paused. "And one more thing."

"What's that?"

"Kirk and Dawkins showed up right after it happened."

"Great."

"I'll get with Sherman, see what's up, and get back to you."

"Do that."

"I'm out," Rain said and left the waiting room.

Once Bobby came out, Black entered the intensive care unit to see Wanda. He stood by her bedside and held her hand.

"I swear on Vickie's soul, I'm gonna find who did this." Black squeezed her hand. "You get stronger and open your eyes. Everything's gonna be all right, I promise you that." Black leaned forward and kissed her forehead before leaving the ICU. Then he went back into the waiting room and approached Shy.

"I'm going to The Playhouse to talk to Jackie; see if she heard anything."

"I understand." Shy hugged Black and kissed him on the cheek. "Be careful and come home to me."

"I will." He looked at Bobby. "Let's go."

"I'm gonna hang around here."

"I understand."

Although he always wanted Bobby to ride with him, Black understood where his head was and why he felt he should stay. The three of them had been close since they were children.

"I'll let you know what's going on," Black said, heading for the door. William was sitting there. "Let's go."

He stood up and followed him out. "Where we going?"

"The Playhouse."

When Black arrived at The Playhouse, he went straight toward the office.

"She in?" Black asked Rook as he got to the door.

"She's always in," he said, knocked on the door, and opened it for Black.

"I'm sorry about Wanda," Jackie said the second Black came through the door. "You know who did it?"

"Not yet. You heard anything?"

"I got people out asking questions, but I haven't heard anything. What happened?"

"We were coming out of a restaurant with Wanda and James when a van rolled up on us and started blasting," Black said and thought back to seeing Wanda getting shot and hitting the ground as he took cover. "It all happened so fast. They were gone before I could get a shot at them."

"We'll find who did this."

"I know. I was thinking about the BBKs. You find Montel Rigby yet?"

"No, but I sent Angel and Bowie to follow his girlfriend, Amanda Lindsay, and hope she leads us to him."

"When you find him, kill him." Black paused. "And let's stop fuckin' around with these niggas. Kill them all."

"You got it," Jackie said, and she gave the order to wipe out the BBKs.

Chapter 14

Amanda Lindsay was fine as hell. Her ambition in life was to be an Instagram Influencer. She'd heard about influencers who became millionaires, started their own companies, and some who became actors and hosts in mainstream media. That was the life for her, so she lived her life online, posting images and videos of herself and the exciting life she was living. She'd usually talk about the hot-button topics of the day, but mostly, it was about her and her passion: shopping and how good she looked in her clothes.

"All right, girl, my Uber is here, so I'm gone," Amanda said to Olishia that afternoon as she started for the door.

The night before, Amanda, Olishia, and her friend Qwanisha, all three would-be Instagram Influencers, hit the clubs. Since she had drunk more than her share of martinis, she decided to crash at Olishia's apartment instead of driving drunk.

Getting locked up for DUI is not a good look and might cost me followers.

When she got to the door, Amanda took out her phone and took a picture of herself dressed in the Alexander McQueen cutout, one-shoulder bandage midi-dress she had on the night before.

"You're not gonna post that, are you?" Olishia asked as she followed her to the door.

Amanda looked at the image. "I sure am. I look cute." She put the phone away. "Nobody's gonna know if I took this before or after last night." She hugged Olishia and then left her apartment.

When she arrived home, she took a shower and changed into a pair of Veronica Beard Leena high-rise bootcut raw hem jeans and an NZT NIC+ZOE Sweet Dreams long-sleeve crewneck tee that she thought would look cute with her Allegra James Mandi metallic slingback sandals. She chose an Ippolita 18K diamond pendant necklace and a Michael Kors Marilyn medium metallic leather satchel bag. She took twenty pictures of herself in different poses before she left the house to indulge in her favorite pastime: shopping.

"There she is," Angel said to Bowie when Amanda came out of her building and walked to a waiting Uber.

Bowie started the car. "I hope she's going to see Rigby and not her usual bullshit," he said and followed the Uber.

Angel shook her head. "I don't think so. Girlfriend is probably going to have lunch with her fake-ass friends. Either that, or she's going shopping."

"Like I said, more of her usual bullshit," he said and followed the Uber to Herald Square, a major commercial shopping intersection in Midtown Manhattan at the intersection of Broadway, Sixth Avenue, and Thirty-Fourth Street.

She'd taken pictures of herself looking at phone accessories in the Apple Store before she got some great shots of herself picking out a pair of L'agence Marguerite high-waist skinny jeans at Nordstrom Rack. Amanda made a video of her flirting with male followers as she shopped and then selected a Limited Edition Maude vibe and shine flutter-tip vibrator and organic lubricant set and a L'Occitane nourishing shea butter body cream duo at Sephora.

"I know all of you want to be the one to caress my body with this shea butter," she said suggestively, holding the set up to the camera. Then it was off to Macy's, where she tried on a Focus by Shani Ponte keyhole dress and modeled it for her audience.

"What do you think? You think this looks good on me?" she asked and watched as hearts, flames, and other emojis scrolled up her screen.

Meanwhile, back uptown, Marvin and Baby Chris saw one of the BBKs coming out of the Jamaican meat patty store. Marvin took out his gun and was about to fire, but there were too many civilians around, so he got out of the car and walked up to him. When the BBK saw him coming, he took off running, made it to a car, and sped away with Marvin running behind him and firing shots. Baby Chris started the car and rolled up on Marvin. He got in, and they gave chase.

As Baby Chris closed the distance, Marvin fired at the car and hit one of the rear tires. The vehicle went into a spin and ended up crashing into a telephone pole. Baby Chris brought his car to a screeching halt and jumped out as the shaken driver got out of his vehicle and ran into a nearby building. He ran through the lobby to the stairwell with Marvin and Baby Chris on his tail. They exchanged gunfire as they ran up the stairs until he got to the roof and ran out. The BBK ran to the edge of the building and stopped. He considered jumping to the next building, but it was too far. He turned around and raised his hands as Marvin and Baby Chris approached. Marvin grabbed him by the shirt.

"Where's Montel Rigby?"

"I ain't telling you shit."

"Wrong answer," Marvin said and pushed him off the roof. Marvin and Baby Chris leaned forward and looked at the BBK sprawled out on the ground in a pool of his own blood.

It was about that time when Axe and Press had gotten a tip about where they could find two BBKs hiding out. They went to the house, covered the peephole, and rang the bell.

"Who is it?"

"It's Bucker," Axe said, using the name of a gang member that he'd killed the night before. When the door opened, Axe immediately shot the man in the head. Press rushed in and put his gun to the head of the other BBK as he went for his gun.

"Don't even think about it," Press threatened, and the man moved his hand away from his gun. "Smart man."

"Now, give me your phone," Axe demanded.

As Press got his gun and continued to cover the man, Axe made him get on his knees.

"Call your boys and tell them you need them to come here," Axe instructed. The BBK made the call. "On speaker."

"What's up?" a voice answered.

"It's Damar. I need you to come through. I got something I need to tell you."

"I'll be through there," he said, ending the call.

Then Axe made him call two other men and told them the same thing. Once he had made the calls, Axe gagged and put plastic handcuffs on him and then made him stay on his knees while they waited for his friends to arrive. Over the next hour, members of the BBKs showed up at the apartment. When they arrived, each was disarmed, gagged, handcuffed, and made to kneel until all four had arrived before Axe got started.

"Now, one of you niggas are gonna tell me where Montel Rigby is hiding, and just to show you how serious I am—" Axe raised his gun and shot one in the head.

The other three BBKs flinched, squirmed, and struggled to escape their bonds to no avail. When one tried to get to his feet, Press kicked him in the chest, and he fell over.

"Fuck you think you're going?" he asked as Axe stepped to the man next to him and took the gag out of his mouth.

"Go on and kill me muthafucka! I ain't telling you shit."

"Okay," Axe said calmly and shot him in the head. "Two down, two to go, and I still haven't heard what I wanna hear." He put the barrel of his gun to the next man's head. "Choose wisely. Where the fuck is Montel Rigby?"

"I don't know," the BBK shouted the second the gag was out of his mouth.

"Nope. Bad choice," Axe chuckled and shot him in the head.

With his eyes wide open, the last man struggled, squirmed, and tried talking through the gag.

"I think he wants to tell us something," Press said, jerking the gag out of his mouth.

"He's at a house on 225th, down the street from the park," he said quickly.

"Thank you," Axe said, shot him in the head, and took out his phone.

"What's up, Axe?" Marvin answered.

"I know where Rigby's hiding."

"Where?"

After shopping for the day, Amanda Lindsay took an Uber and headed back uptown with Angel and Bowie in pursuit. When the Uber driver turned and drove down 225th, Angel saw Marvin and Baby Chris in a car parked down the street. Bowie parked his car as Amanda exited the Uber and waited until one of Rigby's men came out to help her carry her bags into the house. It was then that Axe and Press arrived on the scene. Angel and Bowie exited their vehicle and walked to where Marvin and Baby Chris were parked. Axe and Press joined them there.

"What y'all doing here?" Marvin asked Angel and Bowie.

"We followed his girl here," Angel said.

"She's been shopping," Bowie added.

Baby Chris laughed. "We saw the pack mule."

"So, what's the plan? We going in there?" Axe asked as the front door opened and two BBKs stepped out. Once they had looked around the street, one signaled for Rigby to come out. He exited the house surrounded by six men.

"There he is," Angel said, taking out her guns as Rigby and his men walked toward their cars.

"Let's end this," Marvin said, and as soon as they were close enough, they opened fire.

Rigby's men were ready for them, and they were immediately confronted with gunfire. Rigby took cover behind a van and fired. His men exchanged shots. One man fired and ducked behind a car for cover. Baby Chris hit the ground and fired at the men. He shot one of the men in the back as he turned for cover. Axe hit another with two shots to the chest and moved closer to the house. Baby Chris got up and began firing as Marvin reloaded his weapon and fired as the BBKs backed toward the house. Two men made it inside before Press took aim and shot one man in the leg. He limped into the house.

"On your nine, Angel!" Bowie yelled as a man raised his weapon.

Angel dove for the ground and watched Bowie drop him with a shot to the head. Just then, Montel Rigby ran out from behind the van, blasting. He continued firing until his gun was empty, and then he took off running.

Angel saw him and fired several shots. "I got him!" she yelled and went after him.

"Angel, wait!"

Bowie was about to go after her when they fired at him, and he ducked behind a car. He stood up and fired twice and hit one of the BBKs with a shot to the chest, and then he went after Angel.

As Press and Baby Chris exchanged fire with the BBKs and killed them, Marvin and Axe ran into the house. They stopped and looked around but didn't see anybody. They began moving slowly through the house but stopped when they heard a noise. Suddenly, the man that Press shot came out of the dining room, opened fire, and kept firing until he ran out of ammo. He limped back into the room, turned over a table, took cover, reloaded, and then readied his weapon, prepared to fire at them.

Marvin and Axe rushed to the archway and opened fire. When he returned their fire, Marvin and Axe took cover behind the couch. Marvin rose up to return fire as Axe crawled to the edge of the couch and fired a shot that hit the man in the chest. Then he was forced to take cover as the last two BBKs began firing. When Marvin and Axe returned fire, the men retreated. One ran up the stairs, while the other ran toward the rear of the house. Marvin fired a shot that hit him in the back before he made it to the back door.

Marvin and Axe ran up the stairs and started down the hallway. The last BBK reloaded his weapon. With his gun loaded, he fired a few shots down the hall at Axe and Marvin. He fired once and quickly ran toward the door to take cover in the room. Marvin fired and hit him with a shot in the back before he could make it to cover.

Meanwhile, Angel chased Rigby down the street, firing shots until he reached his car. He quickly unlocked the door, reached inside, and came out with an AK-47. He opened fire. She dropped to the ground and crawled behind a vehicle. Angel got to the hood of the car and returned Rigby's fire. When Bowie caught up, he stayed low behind the cars parked on the other side of the street, took aim, and killed Rigby with several shots. Then he rushed to Angel.

"You all right?"

"Yeah, I'm OK." Angel reloaded her guns. "You know I had him, right?" she asked as they walked away.

Chapter 15

It was after four in the morning before the hospital seating got too uncomfortable for Bobby, and he told Pam that once he checked with the nurse for any updates on Wanda's condition, they were going home. During the time that they were there, Barbara, RJ, and other members of The Family had heard the news and came to see if she would be all right.

It was late in the afternoon before Bobby opened his eyes. The first thing he did was call the nurse's station to see if there were any changes to Wanda's condition. Once the nurse told him there was no change, Bobby called Black and told him he was on his way to pick him up.

"I'll be here waiting for you," Black said, ending the call. He and Shy were at the hospital the first thing that morning. They only left when the doctor told them Wanda was doing well, but she felt it best to keep her in a coma for the time being.

"There's nothing for you to do here," she told Black and Shy. "I promise to call you if anything changes." They had only recently made it home before Bobby called.

"How'd it go last night?" Bobby asked when Black had entered the car just after the sun had gone down.

"I didn't find out who was behind it, but I turned Jackie loose on the BBKs."

"You think they were behind it?"

"Not really, but we been fuckin' around with them for too long."

"I get it. You were mad, so somebody had to die over it. I understand, and you're right; we've been fooling around with those kids long enough."

Black chuckled because he knew that Bobby was correct. "Rigby is dead, and our people are hunting down whoever's left and shows their face in public."

"That's all well and good, but if they had nothing to do with it, it doesn't move us any closer to finding out who did it. And I agree with you. I don't think that they did."

"You heard about the robbery at Mama's?"

"Yeah. RJ told me. What about it?"

"Rain said that some nigga they call Big Frenchie was the one who did it, and the word is that he's down with Kendrick Nance."

"You think he's behind it?"

"I don't know. Trying to kill us might be his opening move to take over the market."

"That's a big step, and I'm not disagreeing with you, but if that's the case, why not go hard at Kojo's crew?"

"I thought about that too." Black smiled. "By the way, Kojo is also dead."

"You had a busy night."

"He had a date at the parlor with Edwina a couple of days ago. I just forgot to tell you," Black laughed, and so did Bobby.

"It was just a matter of time."

"That's what Joey said when I told him."

"He was doomed in your eyes the second you heard he was with Johnny Boy."

"That's what I told him before I shot him twice in the head."

Bobby shook his head. "Did the deadly deed yourself, huh?"

"I did," Black said, and Bobby could hear the satisfaction in his voice.

"That Johnny Boy hate ran deep. I get it."

"It did."

"So what now?"

"I wanna ask around, see if anybody knows where we can find this Big Frenchie, and see what he knows."

"And if he's with Kendrick Nance and them and ordered the hit, you think he'll tell us?"

"Not really, but it never hurts to ask. Besides, what else we got to do? I can't just sit around and do nothing."

"I hear you. Sitting around the hospital with nothing to do but thinking the worst was not what I needed to do. I should have been out in the street with you."

"But I understood why you thought you needed to. And I know what you mean about thinking the worst. I'm trying not to think that way, but that coma shit is fuckin' with me."

"Me too. But the doctor said it will give Wanda the time she needs to heal and get stronger."

"I know that, but still, just the word 'coma' makes you think that way."

"I say we go find somebody to kill. That will take our minds off that shit." Bobby paused. "At least for a little while."

"That's the problem. As soon as it's over, those thoughts come creeping back."

"Wanda is strong. She survived getting shot once, and she'll make it through this too."

"I've been thinking a lot about Vickie since this happened."

Their childhood friend Vickie Payne died of an overdose smoking cocaine in Black's apartment while he was sleeping in the next room. Although everyone reminded him that Vickie was on a path of self-destruction and it wasn't his fault, Black held himself responsible.

"Understandable." Bobby glanced over at Black as he drove. "You don't feel like you're responsible for Wanda getting shot, do you?"

"You know I do." Black dropped his head. "Because it *is* my fault. This isn't her world anymore. She just got married, and I'm supposed to protect her, but I lay on the ground like a coward and watched her get shot."

"I know how you feel. Remember, I was lying on the ground next to you."

"I should have done something."

"Like what?"

"I don't know. Something other than lying on the ground and watching James get murdered and her getting shot over some shit The Family is into that has nothing to do with them."

"Trust me, I know exactly how you feel. I say let's just go find who's behind this shit and kill them."

"Slowly and painfully, Bob. Slowly and painfully," Black repeated, and Bobby nodded in agreement.

"So what you wanna do?"

"A part of me wants to go to the hospital to see Wanda." Black paused. "But I don't wanna see her like that. Too many memories of the last time."

"I know what you mean," Bobby said and thought back to the night he and Black arrived at Cuisine in time to watch as Wanda got shot and her body fell to the floor.

Nado Benitez sent men to kill Wanda for interfering in his business. He would never forget standing over her as Keisha cried and tried to stop the bleeding.

"Where you wanna go?"

"Let's see what Sherman's talking about."

Bobby drove them to the house, and when they arrived, they got out of the car, and Black rang the bell. Sherman's wife, Ester, opened the door. She hugged Black.

"I am sorry about Wanda," she said and hugged Bobby. "How is she?"

"She's still in ICU," Bobby said. "I talked to her doctor this morning. She's stable."

"I'm praying for her," Ester said as Sherman came and stood in the doorway.

"Ahh, shit!" he staggered back and grabbed his chest.

"What's wrong?" Ester rushed to him.

"This is the big one." he looked up. "I'm coming to join you, Howard."

"He's having a heart attack!" Ester said frantically.

"Yes!" Sherman cried out as if he were in pain. "I can't believe Bobby Ray is in my living room."

"Stop it," Bobby said, and everybody but Ester laughed. Her fists hit her hips.

"Not funny." She took a playful swing at him and walked away.

"You okay, old man?" Black asked.

"Yeah, just haven't seen this nigga out of the house and in my house in years, that's all."

"Stop it. You saw me at the wedding," Bobby said and followed Sherman to his spot. He went to the bar, poured himself a drink, held up the bottle, and asked, "Anybody else drinking?"

"Stupid question," Black said as he and Sherman sat down.

"How's Wanda?" Sherman asked as Bobby brought the bottle and glasses.

"She's gonna be all right, but they put her in a medically induced coma."

"I heard. You know who did it?" Sherman asked.

"We're here to see if you heard anything," Bobby said.

"Nothing."

"Tell me about Mama's and Big Frenchie," Black asked.

"All I know is the nigga's name is Chet French, and people say he's connected to Kendrick Nance."

"Connected how?"

"Not sure. RJ's on it."

"You know where to find him?" Black asked.

"You remember Classics?" Sherman replied.

"Yeah," Bobby said. "Club that only played classic rap."

"It's called Ten Ninety-Seven now," Black said.

"That's right. RJ heard that he likes to hang out there."

"He check it out?" Bobby asked.

"Him and Judah went by there." Sherman shook his head. "Rihanna said that he had a mask on, so she couldn't tell RJ what he looked like. But here's the thing. Right after the robbery, Kirk and Dawkins showed up."

"What was he doing there?" Black asked.

"Apparently, he was there looking for French," Sherman informed.

"You wanna ride by there, see if they're open?" Black asked.

Bobby shot the rest of his drink. "Fuck else we got to do?"

Black shot his drink and stood up. "We're gone."

Club Ten Ninety-Seven was owned by Cyrus Ruffin and operated by Hal Davis. The club had just opened for happy hour. Therefore, only a few people were there when Black and Bobby arrived and sat at the bar.

"What can I get you, gentlemen?" the bartender asked.

"Rémy Martin XO if you got it," Bobby said.

"I got VSOP."

"That will do," Black said, and the bartender went to get their drinks.

When the bartender returned, both men shot their drinks, and Black put a fifty-dollar bill on the bar.

"Big Frenchie here?" he asked.

"Who's asking?"

"Mike Black and Bobby Ray," Black said.

"I haven't seen him." The bartender picked up the bill. "But I'll check," he said, coming from behind the bar. He went into the office. Cyrus Ruffin and Hal Davis were in there. "Hey, Hal. You seen Big Frenchie?"

"Who's asking?" Hal asked.

"Mike Black and Bobby Ray."

"Mike Black?" Ruffin questioned.

"Yeah. He's at the bar."

"That muthafucka." Ruffin turned the security monitor to display the bar. "That muthafucka," he repeated and opened the desk drawer.

Like Kendrick Nance, Ruffin used to work for Robert King back in the day. Before he went to prison on weapons charges, King was like a father to him. He was Ronald and Rona King's godfather. He held Black responsible for their deaths. Ruffin looked at his right hand. He still had the ring that King gave him for his twenty-fifth birthday.

"That muthafucka dies today." He took the gun out of his drawer and ensured one was in the chamber. "You go back out there and you tell that muthafucka that Frenchie ain't here, and then you get out of the way."

"Okay," the bartender said and went back to the bar. He picked up the bottle and returned to Black and Bobby. He poured them another round. "Sorry. Nobody's seen Big Frenchie in a minute," he said, walking away.

Bobby picked up his glass. "What now?" He was about to take a sip when he saw Hal standing at the end of the bar. He raised his weapon. "Gun!" he shouted, pulling Black to the floor as Hal began firing. Ruffin appeared at the other end of the bar and opened fire.

Both men got their guns out, and Bobby fired off a few shots in Hal's direction. When he ducked for cover, it gave Black and Bobby a chance to find cover. Black turned over a table and returned their fire.

Hal fired a couple of shots and stepped out from the bar. When he did, Bobby shot him in the chest. Hal got off another shot as he fell to the floor. Ruffin was firing at Black from behind the bar and pinned him down. Black raised his gun and blindly returned fire. Bobby stayed low to the ground and went to the other end of the bar without being seen. When he had a clear shot, he fired and hit Ruffin with two shots. He dropped the gun on the bar, and his body slid to the floor.

"You all right, Mike?"

Black stood up. "Yeah, I'm all right. Thanks." He walked over to Hal's body. "You know him?"

"Never seen him before," Bobby said, and they went behind the bar to check out Ruffin.

Black kicked over the body. "I know him."

"Who is he?"

"His name is Cyrus Ruffin. He used to work for Robert King."

"Like Kendrick Nance," Bobby said as they came from behind the bar and headed toward the exit.

Chapter 16

The last few days have not been good for Drew Mack. His brother Rodney, a.k.a. Truck, had gotten in a beef with Ryder, and despite everyone telling him that he should back off and let it go, Truck pushed it, costing him his life. Once Drew realized Kojo would only pay lip service to the issue, he turned to Montel Rigby.

"He's family. BBK for life. We can't let this go down, and we don't do something about it," was what Drew said to Rigby, and he, some would say foolishly, sent men to run a drive-by at The Playhouse one night after the club closed, and the employees were coming out. Rigby's thought was that he and the BBKs could take on Barbara. He hadn't considered that his declaring war on Barbara would make the killing captain his adversary. Nobody was killed, hurt, or injured in the drive-by, so it was unsuccessful, but it did have the effect of bringing the full force of Jackie's crew of assassins and killers down on them.

Since war is bad for business, the war with The Family was interfering with his drug revenue. For that reason, Kojo had been coming down hard on him. Kojo was trying to rebuild after taking several devastating blows to his business. Ryder killing Truck, finding out that Shanice Hardaway was an undercover police officer and killing her, as well as the murder of Arron Copeland because he was the one that brought Shanice in, had all taken its toll, and Kojo was looking to Drew to make up that money. But nobody had seen or heard from Kojo in days, so he had some breathing room. But Drew knew he needed to get out in front of the situation and find new ways to bring in money.

And to make matters worse, his woman, Karleshia, had broken up with him because he couldn't satisfy her sexual appetite. Her exact words were, "You got a little peewee dick, and you can't fuck your way out of a paper bag. Only reason I faked it this long is that you got money."

Her words hurt for a while, but Karleshia was right. He did have money, enough money that his new female interest, Trissa Winslow, quickly learned her lines: *It's so big, daddy. Fuck me hard with that big dick.* But she had a different agenda.

That night, Drew had gotten a call from Amanda Lindsay asking if he could meet her at a reggae bar called One Love. The place was crowded when Drew arrived, so Amanda wasn't easy to find.

"You seen Amanda tonight?" he asked a waitress.

"She's sitting at a table in the back," the waitress replied, pointing him in the right direction.

He pushed through the crowd and found Amanda dressed in a black ATM Anthony Thomas Melillo slub jersey mixed media peplum top, and slacks. She wore dark sunglasses, and her head was tied with a black scarf. Drew sat down at the table.

"What's up, Amanda?"

"Montel is dead."

"What?"

Tears ran down her cheeks. "He was ambushed and murdered in the street."

When the shooting started, Amanda had the presence of mind to run out the back door. She hopped the fence and kept running until she could no longer hear the sounds of gunfire.

"When did this happen?"

"Yesterday."

"I hadn't heard about that."

"That's because most, if not all, of the rest of the Kays are dead too. And I wanna know what *you're* gonna do about it."

"Nothing," Drew said quickly.

"Nothing? What you mean *nothing*?"

"Nothing," Drew said firmly. "Look, I made a mistake when I asked Montel to get revenge for my brother getting killed. We should have never fucked with them niggas. Montel would still be alive if we had backed off and let it go. So, no, Amanda, I ain't gonna do shit but stay outta these niggas' crosshairs and hope that they don't want to kill me over this shit. And if you have any sense, which I doubt, you'd back off and let this shit go too. Live your best life."

"You're a fuckin' coward."

"Maybe, but I'm a coward who plans to live a long life." Drew stood up. "Good to see you, Amanda," he said, fighting his way toward the exit to leave One Love.

Once he got outside, he walked away from the club to his car. Then he stopped, took the pack of cigarettes from his pocket, and lit one up. Drew had just taken a drag of his cigarette when he saw the silhouette of a woman walking quickly toward him. It was dark, but she looked good from where he stood, wide hips swinging, so he stopped to admire her. He smiled when she got closer, but that smile didn't last long.

"I thought you were—" he got out before she raised her nine and shot Drew in the forehead. She stood over him, fired her weapon, and put three more in his chest before she walked away quickly.

Chapter 17

Khalil Patterson loved the life he was living. Some might even say he was living his best life, but he really didn't like what he was about to do. He was on the Bronx River Parkway on his way to White Plains to the home of Julianna Verrett. She used to play the woke Black girlfriend in the sitcom *Neighbors* and had a few bit parts in movies. Now, she did some work off-Broadway—but that was rare—and the occasional commercials, but those parts were hard to come by as well.

But her struggling acting career was of no interest to Khalil. In fact, he didn't even like her. To him, she was a stuck-up bitch who had an overinflated sense of her own importance. Maybe she used to be somebody twenty years ago.

Now, she's just a drug dealer's woman with a bad cocaine habit.

The only upside to coming there was the view. He was going there because that was where Kendrick Nance was that night. He had called to tell him that Cyrus Ruffin and Hal Davis had been killed at Club Ten Ninety-Seven, something that he knew Nance wasn't going to like.

"Not over the phone. I'm at Julianna's. Come on out."

Fuck, he said to himself. "On my way" was what he said instead, and he left Club Ten Ninety-Seven to make the drive.

When he arrived at the house, he parked behind
Nance's Benz and a Lincoln he'd never seen before. He
turned off his car, got the bag from his pocket, tapped a
little cocaine on his hand, and took a couple of bumps before he got out of the vehicle and approached the house.
It took a minute or two, but Julianna finally opened the
door.

"Come in, Khalil," she said and stepped aside.

"Thanks," he replied and went inside. He paused as he
passed to take her in.

That day, Julianna was wearing a candy-apple red
two-piece flared lounge set with a bell-sleeved longline
shirt and wide-leg pants that she had knotted in the front
around her waist. Her fake breasts were enormous. She
never wore a bra, so her hard nipples pressed against the
shirt. Even though she was well into her forties, Julianna
was still an extremely attractive woman.

"He's in the back," she said and turned to walk that way.
Julianna had a big, pretty ass too, so Khalil got an eyeful.
As much shit as he talked about her, the truth was that he
wouldn't mind fucking her.

"What's up, Khalil?" Nance asked when Julianna led
him into the room. She sat beside Nance and picked up
her drink. He was in the living room with Jack Dandridge.
Like most of the people who sold for him, Dandridge
used to deal for Robert King. He did some time in prison
for possession with intent to distribute and got out five
years ago.

"What's up, Boss?" he said and nodded in Dandridge's
direction.

"I hope you ain't come out here to tell me some shit I
don't wanna hear. I heard enough bad news from this
nigga," Nance said and pointed at Dandridge.

"Better you hear that shit from me instead of the cops."

"True." He picked up his drink and put his arm around Julianna. "What you got to tell me?"

"Cyrus Ruffin and Hal Davis are dead."

Dandridge laughed and stood up. "I know you didn't wanna hear that shit either," he said and went to the bar to pour himself a drink.

"No, I didn't. How'd it happen?"

"They were at the club when Mike Black and Bobby Ray came in."

"Mike Black? Fuck was he doing there?"

"They were looking for Big Frenchie."

Dandridge chuckled. "That nigga," he said, and Julianna just shook her head.

"Why were they looking for him?"

"I don't know, but Danny said when he told Ruffin that he was there, him and Hal tried to kill them."

Nance nodded his head and looked at Khalil. "You find Big Frenchie and bring him to me. And see if you can't find out why Black and Bobby are looking for his ass," Nance ordered, and Khalil nodded in acknowledgment.

"Knowing that nigga, he probably robbed somebody he shouldn't have," Dandridge said.

"You're probably right." Nance leaned forward. "Fuck!" he shouted and banged his fist on the coffee table. "Go make me a drink."

"Sure, baby," Julianna said and got up.

"Why would Ruffin wanna kill Black?" Dandridge asked.

"He blamed Black for Robert getting shanked in prison."

Nance thought about what, if anything, he should do about it. He was deep into expansion mode, and dealing with Mike Black and Bobby Ray was the last thing he wanted or needed to do. At one point, he was sure he would have to go to war with Kojo, but their organization was falling apart, and he'd heard nobody had seen Kojo in days. He was making expanding easy, which was good for him.

"What you gonna do?" Dandridge asked because he'd wanted to get revenge for the Kings too.

"About Black and them?" he paused. "Nothing for the time being. At least until I talk to Frenchie and see what's up. In the meantime, I need you to reach out to Newton. He's got ties to some of their people. He used to fuck with—" Nance snapped his fingers a couple of times. "What's that bitch's name—Rhianna McGrew." He shook his head as he thought about her legs. "See if she can't tell us why Black is looking for Frenchie."

Nance sat back. He was worried about Black. He thought it must be something if Black and Bobby were out personally looking for him. Dandridge glanced at Nance and knew that something was bothering him.

"What is it?"

"Nothing. I'm just thinking." He looked up at Khalil. "Didn't I give you something to do?"

"Yes."

"Then why you standing here?"

"No reason. I'm gone."

"Show him out, Julianna."

"Sure, baby," she said and put down her drink. "Come on."

Once they had left the room, Nance stood up. "Let's ride."

Dandridge shot his drink. "Where we going?"

"To talk to Bulletproof."

"What about?"

"Money, muthafucka. Fuck else we got to talk about?"

His name was Benny Thomas, but everybody called him Bulletproof or just Bullet. He got the name when he was the only survivor of a wild shootout without getting so much as a scratch. He was Nance's best earner, making inroads into Kojo's business. When they arrived at his apartment and knocked on the door, there was no answer, so Nance knocked harder.

"Who is it?" a soft and sultry female voice asked.

"Nance and Dandridge."

The door opened, and they stepped inside. When the door closed, Nance turned and saw that the woman was naked.

"Hello," Nance said and tapped Dandridge on the shoulder. He turned to look.

"Damn."

"She fine as shit, ain't she?" Bullet asked, and Nance turned toward him.

He was standing in the doorway to his bedroom without a shirt. When he entered the room, the woman went back to the bedroom.

"Thank you, Yazmeen," he said and grabbed a hand full of ass as she passed.

Nance and Dandridge watched her as she went into the room and could see that another woman was lying naked on the bed.

"Damn," Dandridge said as she closed the door behind her. "Freaky fuck," he said softly.

Nance leaned closer. "Jealous?"

"What can I do for you, gentlemen?" Bullet asked, and the three sat down.

"Tell me what's up with Kojo."

"Nothing," Bullet said.

"Nothing?" Dandridge questioned. "What you mean, nothing?"

"Exactly what I said. There ain't nothing going on with Kojo because ain't nobody seen him in days."

Nance thought for a second or two. "What's up with that?"

"I heard that either he's lying low or he's dead."

Nance chuckled. "Either way, that's good for us. What about the white girl?"

"What about her?"

"What's she talking about?"

Bullet looked at Nance like he was stupid. "Like I said, that the nigga is either lying low or dead. She got what's left of her people out looking for that nigga."

"What I wanna know is why would he be lying low?" Nance asked, and since he didn't believe in coincidences, he wondered if it had anything to do with Black.

He'd heard from several people that there was bad blood between Kojo and The Family. But if that were the case, what did Big Frenchie have to do with it? He was a small-time stick-up artist not involved in the dope game.

"I have no idea," Bullet said.

"You need to find out."

"I got Trissa Winslow on that." Bullet got up and started toward the kitchen. "I got her fuckin' Drew Mack for information," Bullet said and laughed as he thought about what Trissa told him about Drew having a little dick.

Nance stood up, and so did Dandridge. "Let me know what she finds out."

Bullet walked them to the door. "Of course."

"We'll let you get back to what you were doing," Dandridge said, fist-bumping Bullet.

"I'll get with y'all later," Bullet said and shut the door.

"What you think?" Dandridge asked as he and Nance walked down the hall to the stairs.

"I don't like this."

"What?"

"Black and Bobby at Ten Ninety-Seven looking for Frenchie, and Kojo being ghost. I don't know. None of this shit may have anything to do with the other, but I got a bad feeling about this."

Chapter 18

Black sat in the hospital waiting room, waiting for Bobby to come out. He had already been in to see Wanda and had spoken to her doctor about her prognosis.

"She's in stable condition this morning, and her vitals look good. Minor cases of brain swelling due to a slight concussion often resolve within a few days. However, it can take weeks and sometimes months for the brain to resolve the chemical imbalance."

"I understand. I like a few days better than I do 'weeks and sometimes months.'"

"I don't think that will be the case here."

"Let's hope."

"I'm going to continue the medically induced coma for another twenty-four to forty-eight hours until the swelling subsides."

He shook the doctor's hand. "Thank you."

When Bobby came out of the ICU and went into the waiting room, Black stood up, and they left the hospital. There were no words spoken by either man until they got outside and made it to the car. As one could expect, both men were deep in thought about Wanda. The rush of memories, both good and bad, flooded their minds.

"What you wanna do now?" Bobby asked when they got in the car.

"Let's roll by Mama's. I wanna have a look at the surveillance video, and I wanna talk to Rhianna."

Bobby smiled. "You know there was a time when I would have gone hard at her."

"She is your type . . . rail skinny, nice ass, amazing legs. But I hear from more than one person that she's the type of woman that once you get to know her, you don't wanna fuck with her no matter how fine she is, and aren't you retired?"

Bobby chuckled. "I wouldn't go that far. I'm more like that grizzled veteran on the bench."

"You mean the one whose skills have diminished and should retire unceremoniously?"

"That's the one. And I heard that about her too, but back in the day, I wouldn't have given a fuck. I would have fucked her a couple of times before I got ghost."

"I remember running that program."

"For years." Bobby paused and glanced at Black. "Truth be told, I really don't have the heart for all that."

"All what?"

"All the shit I got to go through to cheat on Pam and not get caught or hear a bunch of shit."

"I hear you." Black paused. "After we leave Mama's, I wanna go to the office to see Monika and Carla. I wanna get all the surveillance videos from The RH Rooftop Restaurant."

"They need to check traffic cams to see if they can't track the van."

"That's exactly what I had in mind."

When they arrived at Mama's and went inside, Bobby stopped at the door and inhaled deeply. Then he went to have a look at what was on the buffet.

"Hey, Bobby, Mike, how's it going?" Evette asked. She wasn't just the restaurant manager; she was the cook as well. She cooked everything at Mama's, or it was prepared under her supervision.

"It's going. Everything smells delicious."

"Can I get you gentlemen something?" she asked from behind the counter.

"Nothing for me, thank you," Black said.

"He'll get in trouble if he goes home full," Bobby joked. "But I'll have some of that shrimp mac and cheese."

"You want a pint or a quart?"

"Pint." Bobby took out his phone and called Pam.

"Hey, babe. What you cook for dinner?" he asked as Evette handed him the pint of shrimp mac and cheese and a plastic fork.

"Nothing. Venus is gone somewhere with the baby, and since I wasn't expecting you, I was gonna have something delivered. Why?"

He took off the top. "I'm at Mama's," he said, got a forkful, and shoved it into his mouth.

"Ooh, I haven't had Mama's in a while."

"You want me to bring you something from here?"

"That depends. I know you're with Mike, so when were you planning on coming home?"

He glanced at Black and got another forkful. "I'll bring it to you as soon as we leave here," Bobby said. Black nodded and went to sit down. "What you want?" he asked with his mouth full.

"What you eating?"

"Shrimp mac and cheese."

"Is it good?"

"It's swingin'," he said and ate some more.

"Do they have any meat loaf?"

"They do," he said, telling his wife what was on the buffet.

"Okay, okay. I want the meat loaf, mashed potatoes and gravy, cabbage, and candied yams."

"Corn bread or a biscuit?"

"Corn bread," Pam said, and Bobby told Evette what she wanted.

"What you want, Bobby?"

"I'll have a leg and a breast."

"Fried or baked?"

"Baked. I want some more shrimp mac and cheese, collard greens, corn on the cob, and corn bread," he said as one of her employees brought out a pan of ribs. "And let me have a couple of bones."

"You didn't say that they had ribs."

"They just brought them out."

"Get me a couple of ribs too."

"Throw a couple of bones in Pam's."

"Y'all want any dessert?"

"I'll have a slice of that cherry cheesecake."

"I'll have some cheesecake too."

"Make it two."

"You got it," she said, putting the to-go boxes on the counter. Bobby put a twenty-dollar bill in the tip jar and grabbed the boxes. Black stood up. "Thank you, Evette."

"Enjoy," she said, and Bobby followed Black to the office and knocked on the door.

"Come," Rhianna shouted. When the door opened, and Rhianna saw who it was, she got up.

"Mr. Black, Mr. Ray."

"How are you tonight, Rhianna?" Black asked.

"I'm good. What can I do for you, gentlemen?"

"I want to look at the surveillance video from the night you got robbed," Black said, and Rhianna began to access the video. "And tell me about Kirk and Dawkins."

"They seemed to show up outta nowhere."

"You know why they were here?"

"I don't know for sure. But I heard them talking, and Dawkins asked Kirk if he thought that was their boy, and he said he was sure of it."

"So they came here looking for Frenchie?" Bobby asked.

"Seemed that way to me, and yesterday, they returned with a warrant for the surveillance video." Rihanna turned the monitor toward Black and Bobby. "There you go."

They sat quietly and watched the video. "Who was your security?" Black asked.

"Percy was my security."

"That's it?" Bobby asked.

"From now on, you have two people to provide security," Black said.

"Yes, sir." She paused. "How's Wanda?"

"We just left the hospital. The doctor said that she was stable and her vitals look good, so we'll see," Bobby said.

"What I wanna know is if Frenchie's connected to Kendrick Nance, and did Nance have anything to do with what happened to Wanda," Black said.

"I might know somebody I could reach out to for that."

"Who?" Black asked.

"His name is Billy Newton. I hear that he's dealing for Nance."

"Do it." Black stood up. "Let me know what you find out."

"I will," Rhianna said, and Bobby stood up and followed Black out of Mama's Country Kitchen.

"You in for the night?" Black asked when they got in the car.

"No. I'm in and out like a robbery. I wanna see the footage from the shooting too."

Bobby started the car and relaxed in his chair. "Knowing Carla, she's already got the video."

As promised, Bobby was in and out like a robbery. He gave Pam her food, put his in the refrigerator, kissed his wife, and was out the door.

"That didn't take long," Bobby said when he got back in the car.

"No, it didn't. I'm just surprised, that's all."

"Why?"

"There are usually questions that need to be answered."

"Her mouth was full of a rib," Bobby said. Black laughed, and they headed for Nick's office to talk to Carla and Monika. However, when they got there, the office was empty.

"Carla! Monika! Anybody here?"

Fantasy came out of the control room. "Just me."

"Fantasy," Bobby said, exhaling deeply as he looked at her. She wore a black Brunello Cucinelli hoodie and sweatpants, and her hair was pulled back in a ponytail.

"Good evening, Mr. Black, Mr. Ray. Please excuse my appearance. I wasn't expecting anybody."

"That's all right. Where is everybody?" Black asked.

"They are all still in Burundi. They all went back after the wedding."

"That's right. I was hoping they'd be back by now," Black said. "I wanted Carla and Monika to get the surveillance videos from The RH Rooftop Restaurant and any cameras in the area. And I needed anything they can get on Kendrick Nance and his crew."

"I am, by no means, as good as either Carla or Monika, but they have trained me. I will attempt to get the information you need, and if I cannot do so, I will call Carla and seek her guidance."

"Thank you, Fantasy. Please let me know what you come up with," Black said, and he left the office with Bobby.

"Always a pleasure to see you, Fantasy," Bobby said, walking backward until he was out the door.

Chapter 19

"They already fixed the damage," Kirk said to Dawkins when they walked up to the entrance to The RH Rooftop Restaurant.

The detectives had gone there after they talked to Black at the hospital. Kirk always liked to revisit the crime scene to get a fresh perspective when he didn't have anything to go on. They didn't have anything to go on, so he was there, reexamining the scene and not gaining any new perspective.

"What were you expecting? Bullet holes and blood are bad for business," Dawkins said.

"I know." He scratched his beard. "Nothing to see here."

"So, what do you want to do now?"

"You feel like riding out to New Roshelle?"

"Not really, but let's go. We're not going to find anything here. Might as well go talk to the man. He and Bobby are the only witnesses."

Kirk and Dawkins walked back to their car and made the drive. When they were almost there, Dawkins got a call that they were granted a warrant to search Big Frenchie's apartment.

"Wish we had got that before we rolled out here," she said.

"No worries. We can roll by there when we get back to the city. The way our luck is running, we won't find anything there."

"Come on. You need to think positively. You never know. French may be there when we arrive."

"Right," Kirk said as he parked in the lot at Prestige Capital and Associates. The detectives exited their vehicle and went inside.

"Welcome to Prestige Capital and Associates. How can I help you?" Vandy asked. When Lenecia got promoted to executive assistant to Gladys Gordan, the head of the Big Night Record label, Vandy replaced her at the desk and got a big raise.

"Good afternoon." Dawkins and Kirk showed their badges. "Detectives Dawkins and Kirkland to see Mike Black," she said.

Vandy dropped the welcoming smile. "Mr. Black is not in today," she said coldly. She didn't like cops and had no use for them.

"How about Erykah Morgan? Is she in today?" Kirk asked.

"Yes, Ms. Morgan is in today. Do you mind sitting while I see if she's available?"

"Thank you," Kirk said, and he and Dawkins went to sit down.

Vandy waited until the detectives were seated before she called Erykah.

"What's up, Vandy?" Erykah asked when she answered.

"I have two cops out here looking for Mr. Black," she said, contemptuously gazing at the detectives.

"Detectives Miller and Riley again?"

"No, it's two different ones this time. Detectives Dawkins and Kirkland."

"I've been expecting him." She laughed lightly. "I'm surprised it took him this long."

"You want me to tell them that you're not available?"

"No, I'll be out soon. But I want you to do your best to treat Kirk with respect. You understand, Vandy?"

"Why?"

"Because Mr. Black likes Kirk, and he pays your salary."

"In that case, I will treat him like he's not a cop. What about the other one? Do I have to show her respect too?"

"Yes, Vandy, you do."

"Only for you and a paycheck."

"So, put a smile on your face and in your voice, and let me hear you tell them I will be right out."

"Erykah will be with you shortly, Detectives," Vandy said with a smile on her face and in her voice.

"Thank you," Dawkins said.

"That actually sounded sincere. Good for you."

"It wasn't easy, trust me," she said. "I got another call. Bye." She paused. "Thank you for calling Prestige Capital and Associates. How may I direct your call?"

When Erykah got off the line with Vandy, she called Black on his cell phone.

"What's up, Erykah?"

"Kirk is here. What do you want me to tell him?"

"Tell him that I'm home."

"Yes, sir," she replied. She got up from her desk, left her office, and headed for the lobby. Kirk and Dawkins stood up when they saw her coming.

"Good afternoon, Detectives."

"How are you, Erykah?" Kirk asked and shook her hand.

"I'm awesome. Mr. Black said to tell you that he is at the house."

"Thank you, Erykah," Kirk said, and the detectives left Prestige Capital and Associates. When they arrived at the house, they stopped at the gate. Kirk saw the men rushing toward the car. Once all the men had gathered at the entrance, Kirk rolled down the window as Ronald approached and looked in the car.

"State your business."

Kirk and Dawkins showed their badges to Ronald. "Detectives Kirkland and Dawkins to see Mike Black," he said.

He lowered his weapon and nodded. When he did, the gate opened, and everybody returned to their post.

"I see they've upgraded their security since the last time we were here," Dawkins said as they drove toward the house.

"Somebody tried to kill him and Bobby. What were you expecting?"

Kirk drove to the house and parked out front. Chuck came out of the house as Kirk and Dawkins got out.

"Afternoon, Detectives," Chuck said as he came toward them with his hand out. He shook hands with Kirk and nodded toward Dawkins as he turned toward the house. "Follow me," he said, leading the detectives to the media room. He opened the door. "Kirk and Dawkins are here to see you."

Black and Shy stood up when they came in. "Detectives," Black said, and he shook their hands. Kirk looked at Shy.

"How are you doing, Mrs. Black?"

"I'm fine, Kirk," Shy said to him like Dawkins wasn't there. She was Jada's friend, and even though she and Jada were on better terms, she still had no use for Dawkins. "Now, if you'll excuse me, I'll let you talk to Michael."

"Actually, Mrs. Black . . ." Dawkins said. She knew that Shy didn't like her, and she knew why. "I believe that you were at The RH Rooftop Restaurant with Mr. Black the night that James Austin was murdered and Wanda Moore was shot."

"Yes, Detective Dawkins, I was there that night, but I didn't see anything. Mrs. Ray and I ducked back into the building for cover when the shooting started."

"All the same, I'd like you to stay," she said just to be aggravating.

"Sure," Shy frowned and sat down.

Black and Kirk glanced at each other and shook their heads before sitting.

"How can I help you, Kirk?" Black asked.

"How's Wanda?"

"Still in the medically induced coma," Black said, and he saw the genuine look of concern in his eyes. "The doctor said that she's stable."

Kirk nodded. "That's good to hear."

"You find out who did it?" Shy asked, glaring at Dawkins.

"Not yet." Kirk took a deep breath. "You have any idea who's trying to kill you, Black?"

"No. I've got no idea."

Kirk appeared frustrated. "Look, Black, I know you and Bobby aren't sitting around waiting for me to find who's trying to kill you."

"This time," Dawkins added, and Shy rolled her eyes.

"So, let's put our cards on the table."

"You tell me what you know, and I tell you what I know?"

"Yeah," Kirk agreed.

"Honestly, Kirk, I got nothing."

Kirk chuckled. "Neither do we."

"What about Rain?"

Black shook his head. "Ms. Robinson said she's been playing nice. She's cracking the whip to ensure that nothing is going on that she's unaware of."

"Anything going on with you and Kojo?" Dawkins asked. "My sources tell me that he has a problem with you."

"I heard that too, but no. I can assure you that as far as I'm concerned, the only issue is in his mind."

Kirk covered his mouth to chuckle. "We'll take a run at him anyway."

Good luck with that, Black thought. Dawkin's phone rang. She glanced at the display and saw that it was Detective Miller calling.

She stood up. "Excuse me," she said and headed toward the door. "Dawkins." She reached for the doorknob, opened it, and stepped out into the hallway.

"We finally got the surveillance video from the restaurant."

"Have you watched the footage?"

"Not yet. We just got it a few minutes ago," he said.

"We'll be there as soon as we can." Dawkins ended the call and turned to see Michelle standing there.

"Hello, Detective Dawkins."

"Hello."

"I'm Michelle Black," she said with her hand out.

"Nice to meet you, Michelle." Dawkins shook her hand and then went back into the media room.

"What's up?" Kirk asked.

"We need to meet Miller and Riley."

"Maybe they have something." Black stood up.

"Maybe they do." Kirk rose and walked toward Dawkins. "Thanks for taking the time to talk to us." He and Black shook hands.

"I guess it's pointless for me to ask you to let me know if you hear anything."

Dawkins shook her head, smiled, and left the media room.

"Honestly?"

"We go too far back for it to go any other way." He leaned closer. "I want to get these guys bad. I'll let you know, but that door has to swing both ways."

"You have my word," Black said. They shook on it, and Black saw the detectives go to the door, passing Michelle, sitting on the steps.

"Have a nice day, Detectives," she said.

Kirk and Dawkins waved. "Is that Michelle?" Kirk asked Black.

"It is."

"She's grown since the last time I saw her."

"She's 18. Going to Columbia in the fall."

"Wow. I know you and Shy must be proud."

"We are." They got to the door. "I'll let you know if I get something you can use."

"I hope you do," Kirk said and left the house with Dawkins.

When Black shut the door, Michelle stood up. "Daddy."

"Yes, Michelle."

"The detectives are on their way to see the security video from Aunt Wanda's shooting."

"Thank you, Michelle."

"Just thought you needed to know," Michelle said as the doorbell rang, and her father turned to see who it was.

When Kirk and Dawkins arrived at the Ninth Precinct to review the footage, Detectives Miller and Riley had already watched it.

"And?" Dawkins asked.

"We'll let you draw your own conclusions," Riley said as Kirk and Dawkins sat down.

When he pressed play, they watched as Wanda walked out of the restaurant, laughing and holding hands with James while Black and Bobby trailed a few feet behind them. Then the black van came to a screeching halt in front of James and Wanda, and the shooting began. They watched as the newlyweds were shot and Black and Bobby hit the ground. After that, the van drove away fast.

Kirk and Dawkins looked at each other. "Black and Bobby weren't the targets," Kirk said.

"No," Riley said. "We were thinking that Austin and Moore were just collateral damage."

"So were we," Dawkins added.

"But it's clear they were the target," Miller said. "That, or the shooters were lousy shots."

"Anything's possible, but I doubt it," Dawkins said.

"We weren't able to get a license plate number from the video, but we're canvasing the area to see if another camera caught a better image," Riley reported, seemingly more interested in the case now that the targets of the shooting were civilians and not two notorious gangsters.

"Thanks for calling," Dawkins said, and Kirk stood up and walked out of the squad room. "Let us know if you get anything on the van," Dawkins said and rushed to catch up with her partner, who hadn't said a word since he saw that Black and Bobby weren't the targets.

"You all right?"

"Yeah," he said, but it was clear to Dawkins that he was shaken. "But this changes everything."

"I know." They walked out of the precinct. "You gonna tell Black?"

"What do you think Mike Black and Bobby Ray will do when they find out Wanda was the target?"

"Kill everybody they think might be involved."

"And that is exactly what we're trying to avoid, so, no." Kirk opened the car door for Dawkins, and she got in. "At least not yet anyway," he said when he got behind the wheel.

"We need to get on top of this quickly before they turn the streets red."

Chapter 20

Black stood and watched as William went to see who was at the door.

"What's up, Bobby?" William said, smiling, because Bobby being there meant that he was getting off early that night unless Mrs. Black needed him for something, and she never does because Chuck was her guy.

"What up, William? Where's Mike?" Bobby asked as he stepped inside the house.

"Right here."

"Hey, Uncle Bobby."

"Hey, Michelle. How's my favorite niece?"

"I'm your only niece, Uncle Bobby, and I'm fine."

"Wasn't that Kirk and Dawkins I saw leaving?"

"It was," Black said as he walked to the media room with Bobby. Michelle trailed behind them.

"What were they talking about?" Bobby asked as the three sat down.

"That they don't have anything."

"Like us."

"But they were on their way to check out the surveillance video from the restaurant, so we'll see what's up with that."

Bobby chuckled. "You think he'll tell you?"

"He said he wants to catch these guys too, so like I said, we'll see what's up with that."

Just then, someone knocked at the door. M stuck her head in. "Excuse me, Michael. Oh, hey, Bobby, I didn't know you were here. How are you?"

"I'm fine, Miss Black."

"Dinner is ready, Michael. Have you eaten, Bobby?"

"No, ma'am, I haven't, and I'm starving."

M let out a little laugh. "Pam didn't cook today?"

That night, M had cooked curry goat with rice and peas, sweet potatoes, fried plantains, and saltfish fritters for dinner.

"No, ma'am. The day that the twins left for college was when Pam announced that she was done cooking every day."

"Well, you're welcome to stay for dinner."

"Thank you, Miss Black. You don't have to ask me twice."

After dinner, Black and Bobby left the house and got in Bobby's car. They were out of the gate before Bobby asked, "Where we going?"

"To find who shot Wanda and kill them. But I'll let you know in a minute." Black took out his phone and called Jackie.

"What's up, Black?"

"Where are you?"

"Conversations."

"Me and Bobby are on our way there," Black said, ending the call.

"Where?"

"Conversations," he said and made another call.

"This Rain."

"Meet me at Conversations."

"On my way," Rain said, and Black ended that call.

It was still early when Black and Bobby arrived at Conversations. They made their way through the happy hour crowd and went to Jackie's office. When they walked through the door, Fiona rose to her feet, looking hot in her red Zeynep Arçay stretch leather minidress and black Stuart Weitzman lucite croc-embossed leather wedge boots.

"Damn," Bobby said softly.

"Good evening, Mr. Black, Mr. Ray."

"How are you, Fiona?"

"I'm fine, Mr. Ray. What about you?"

"I'm great," he said, and she sat down as Black tapped on Jackie's door and walked in. Rain was already in there.

"What's up, Black?" Rain asked.

"Tell me something I wanna hear," he said and sat down. Black could tell by the dejected look on their faces that neither Rain nor Jackie had anything.

"Sorry, Black, but I got nothing." Rain got up to refill her drink. "I've been out there pushing hard, but nobody knows anything about it."

Jackie nodded in agreement. "It's almost like it didn't happen."

"You want me to pour y'all a drink?" Rain asked.

"Thank you," Black said and sat down.

"You want one too, Bobby?" Rain asked as she poured Black's drink.

"Stupid question."

Rain grabbed another glass to fix him a drink, and Bobby went to the bar to get it.

"Thanks," he said and shot the drink. She poured him another and then came from behind the bar to take Black his drink.

"Thanks." He took a sip. "Somebody out there knows something."

"I miss the days when Sherman knew everything about everybody," Bobby commented.

"Him not being at the bodega anymore where everybody came in and told him what's up is the reason for that." Black finished his drink, stood up, then went behind the bar, poured his drink this time, and refilled Bobby's glass.

"You told Rihanna to reach out to a guy named Billy Newton," Rain said.

"Yeah, she get anything?"

"Not really. But she said he reached out to her before she reached out to him."

"Really?" Bobby questioned.

"They're trying to feel us out," Black offered, and everyone nodded in agreement.

"You think they're the ones who did it?" Jackie asked because she did.

"Or it might be because we killed those two assholes at Ten Ninety-Seven," Bobby said.

"Cyrus Ruffin and Hal Davis," Black said.

"I remember Ruffin," Jackie announced. "He used to be with Robert King, right?"

"That's him."

"I can tell you that many of Nance's people used to be with the Kings," Rain added.

"So were you," Bobby said. "Can't you make that work for you?" he asked.

"No, they blame me for killing Ronnie."

"What about Rona?" Jackie asked. "You killed her too."

"Nobody throws that in my face. I guess they think Rona died of whatever fucked-up shit was wrong with her."

"Stay on that anyway. Somebody knows something, and they're talking to somebody about it," Black said and shot his drink. "Let's go, Bob."

"What you want me to do?" Jackie asked as Bobby followed Black to the door.

He stopped. "All the BBKs dead?"

"If there are any still breathing, they're either lying low or not wearing colors."

"Have Marvin and Baby Chris take a run at Sienna Petrocelli. Even though I don't think she sent somebody to retaliate for Kojo, I wanna be sure."

"Understood."

"It doesn't need to be a polite conversation."

"Understood," Jackie acknowledged, and Black left her office with Bobby.

"Where to now?"

"Let's go see Eddie Domingas."

Black had known Eddie since when Black worked for Andre, and he was always a good source of information. They went to a salsa bar off of Grand Concourse, looking for Eddie, and went inside. Black took a look around for Eddie but didn't see him.

"You see him?" Bobby asked.

"No."

"I could use a drink," Bobby said.

"You drink too much."

"Since we were 16."

They found a table, and then the waitress took their orders and brought their drinks.

"Eddie here tonight?" Black asked.

"Yup," she said. "Who's asking?"

"Mike Black and Bobby Ray. And we just need a minute of his time."

While they were drinking, Black saw Eddie come out of the back. Once Eddie made eye contact with Black, he came to their table and sat down.

"Sorry to hear about Wanda," was the first thing out of his mouth.

"What can you tell me about that?" Black asked.

"Sorry, Mike, but the streets are quiet. A lot of shock and surprise, a lot of people waiting for you two to unleash holy hell, but nobody's talking."

"What you know about Kendrick Nance?"

"Nance?" Eddie looked across the table at Black and Bobby and saw the angry looks on their faces. "You think he's behind it?"

"I don't know. But I wanna talk to him about it anyway."

"You know where to find him?" Bobby asked.

"Not really. Nance is a paranoid fuck, so he moves around a lot. Never the same place two nights in a row."

"I see."

Eddie signaled for a waitress, and she quickly placed the drink in front of him. "I know somebody that might know how to find him."

"Who's that?" Black asked.

"Her name is Shaunta Elias."

"Who's she?"

"One of the hoes he fucks with sometimes."

"Where do we find her?" Bobby asked and shot the rest of his drink.

"Tracey Towers."

Black stood up and started for the exit. "Thanks, Eddie," Bobby said, reaching into his pocket and dropping a couple of hundred-dollar bills on the table.

Eddie scooped up the money. "Always a pleasure seeing you two," he said, holding up a bill in each hand.

Tracey Towers are two twin buildings located on Mosholu Parkway in the Jerome Park neighborhood of the Bronx. When they arrived at her apartment, Black and Bobby announced themselves.

Shit, she cursed when she looked in the peephole. "Just a minute. I gotta put something on," she said even though she was wearing a Cinq à Sept, Twill Amia jumpsuit. Shaunta walked away from the door and grabbed her phone. Nance didn't answer, so she called Dandridge.

"What's up?" Dandridge asked, happy to hear her voice.

"Mike Black and Bobby Ray are at my door."

"Shit."

"That's what I said."

"What they want?"

"I didn't ask."

"Shit."

Dandridge paused to think about what Nance would want him to do, but since he was fucking Shaunta behind Nance's back, there was really only one thing he could do.

"I'll send somebody over there."

"Do it fast."

Shaunta put the phone down and went to the door. As the banging began again, she stopped in front of the full-length mirror by the door and took one last look at herself before she opened it. Bobby pushed his way into the apartment.

"You can't just come up in here like that," she protested.

"Yes, we can," Bobby said and sat in the living room.

"We're looking for Kendrick Nance. Where is he?" Black asked.

"I don't know where he is."

"Call him."

"I just did, and he didn't answer."

"I don't believe her, Mike."

"Neither do I."

"We haven't hung anybody off a balcony in a while," Bobby said, and Shaunta's eyes got big.

"We haven't."

Bobby stood up. "How much do you weigh?"

"What?"

"Doesn't matter. We can each hold a leg."

"That works for me," Bobby said, and Black picked her up.

As Shaunta hit him in the chest, Black carried her to the balcony door. Bobby opened the door, and they stepped out. Bobby grabbed her leg, Black grabbed the other one, and they hung her over the rail.

"He's with Julianna!"

They pulled her up and back onto the balcony.

"Who's that?" Black asked.

Shaunta's heart was racing, and she tried to catch her breath. "You muthafuckas are crazy!"

Bobby picked her up again.

"Okay! Okay!"

"Who's Julianna?" Black asked, and Bobby put her down.

"Julianna Verrett—his other woman."

"Where do we find her?"

"She lives on Broadview Avenue in White Plains."

"Thank you," Black said and went back inside.

Bobby stood there looking at Shaunta for a second or two, and then he flinched like he would pick her up again, and she screamed. Bobby laughed and went back inside. Black was waiting by the door, and he was laughing too.

Shaunta followed Bobby to the door. "You mutha-fuckas are crazy," she repeated as they left her apartment and went toward the elevator.

When the doors opened, two of Nance's men got off with their guns drawn. When they arrived, they saw Black and Bobby hanging Shaunta off the balcony and rushed into the building to rescue her. As Black and Bobby reached for their weapons, Nance's men began shooting. They ran back to Shaunta's apartment, and Black rammed his shoulder into the door.

"What the fuck!" Shaunta shouted.

Black stuck his gun out the door and fired blindly down the hall before he stepped out and began firing with both of his weapons. The two men pressed their backs to the wall, returned fire, and started backing down the hall. Bobby began firing shots from the doorway. Black shot one in the back as he turned to run. Bobby hit the other with two shots to the chest to clear the hallway.

"You all right?" Bobby asked.

"I'm good. You?"

"I'm okay," Bobby said as they walked down the hall to the elevator.

Shaunta stuck her head out of her apartment and saw the two men lying dead in the hallway. "You crazy muthafuckas," she shouted as the elevator doors closed.

Chapter 21

Sienna Petrocelli drove her blue Maserati GranTurismo away from Joey Toscano's private club in Yonkers. The world she was working so hard to build was falling apart on her. First, Ryder took out Truck, whose real name was Rodney Mack. He and his brother, Drew, controlled the BBKs, which accounted for a large part of their business. Now, they were both dead and what was left of the BBKs was scattered and in disarray.

She'd had Arron Copeland killed because he brought undercover Officer Veronica Isley into her house. That was the right thing to do, but it started the dominoes falling. Since she sent Brendon to kill her, Detective Sergeant Marita Bautista and her strike team had been all over her. And now, to make matters worse, Kojo was MIA. Nobody had seen him or Brendon in over a week. She'd come to see Joey about it.

"I don't think you'll see him again."

"You know what happened to him?"

"No," Joey lied. "It's your house now, Sienna. Angelo is counting on you."

She left there thinking that maybe Joey had something to do with his disappearance. At the very least, he knew something he wasn't telling her. But it didn't matter. At least, not anymore. Kojo was gone. And like the man said, it was her house now, and it was up to her to rebuild the drug operation. Kojo had moved into gambling, prosti-tution, extortion, and protection rackets, and now, those were the strongest parts of her business. When Jerome Dorsey, who ran their gambling operation, went to prison for possession with the intent to sell, Kevin Franklin, who ran the extortion and protection rackets, stepped up and took over that part of the house. Jackson Hill ran their prostitution houses and had just added gambling in those houses. Now, Sienna planned to push Franklin and Jackson to get involved in moving the product.

When she arrived at what was now her office at Action, the dancehall reggae club that Kojo was part owner of, she began thinking about pushing out his partners.

It's your house now, Sienna. Angelo is counting on you.

That meant starting to bring in money or suffering the same fate as Kojo.

"Not happening," Sienna said as she walked into the office. Jackson and Franklin were there waiting for her.

"What's not happening?" Jackson asked.

Sienna ignored the question and sat down at what was now her desk.

"Thank you, gentlemen, for coming."

"You heard anything from Kordell?" Franklin wanted to know.

"No." Sienna paused to think about what, if anything, she would tell them. "Nobody has heard from him, so we have to move forward. That's why I asked you, gentlemen, to meet me tonight."

"What's up, Sienna?" Jackson asked.

"I need the two of you to step up and start moving product in your spots."

"No problem," Jackson said.

He had wanted to get in the game for a long time, but Kojo wasn't trying to hear that. *Stay in your lane,* was what Kojo would tell him. *You're a pimp. You pimp hoes; stick with that.*

"Whatever you need me to do, I'm there."

"I knew I could count on *you*." Sienna looked at Franklin.

Franklin leaned forward, and Sienna put her hand on her gun.

"What's that supposed to mean?"

She and Franklin never got along. They merely tolerated each other.

"Exactly what I said. I knew I could count on Jackson."

"But not me?"

"Well, *can* I?"

Kevin Franklin used to run his extortion and protection businesses out of Club Constellation, but since he had forced his way into Dorsey's gambling operations, he had been getting pushback from Dorsey's sister, Julia. Neither of them had any interest in the dope game.

"Julia's gonna be a problem," he said, blaming it on her.

Jackson laughed. "If you can't handle her, I will."

"I'll talk to Julia. She won't be a problem," Sienna informed them. "Then I can count on you?"

"I'll let you know."

"Why you gotta let me know? I don't see a problem if that was your only issue."

Franklin stood up. "I *said* I'll let you know," he reiterated and started for the door.

"Don't take too long."

Franklin left the office to the sound of Jackson's laughter. "Bitch nigga."

He pushed his way through the packed house at Action and headed for his car, cursing Jackson's arrogant ass and knowing that he didn't have much of a choice. Julia was scared to death of Sienna and would do whatever she wanted.

"I guess I'm a fuckin' drug dealer now," he said as he stopped at a red light.

Just then, a car pulled up alongside him at the light. The last thing Kevin Franklin saw was the gun before the driver of the vehicle opened fire. He was struck by four .40-caliber rounds, one in his arm, two to the chest, and the kill shot to the head.

He died instantly.

Chapter 22

Marvin and Baby Chris sat patiently outside of Jackie's office. She had sent for them over an hour ago, and they'd been sitting there ever since. At least the wait was a pleasure to their eyes because Fiona was looking hot in the dark orchid satin Versace cutout minidress with a revealing slash cutout at the bodice that barely contained her breasts.

"She needs to stand up, Money, and let us see what she's working with tonight," Baby Chris whispered.

"Patience, my nigga; patience."

When the office door opened, Jackie stepped out with a man neither Marvin nor Baby Chris had seen before. Fiona stood up, and they exhaled at the sight of her because it was worth the wait. As Fiona looped her arm in his and escorted the man out of the office, Jackie laughed at the sight of her men as they watched Fiona until she was out of sight.

"Sorry to keep you waiting. Come on in."

Marvin and Baby Chris stood up, followed Jackie into the office, and closed the door behind them.

"Have a seat," she said as the office door opened, and Fiona came in and went to the bar.

"I need you two to take a run at Sienna Petrocelli."

"No problem," Baby Chris said with his eyes glued to Fiona as she poured their drinks.

"Black doesn't think that she sent somebody to retaliate for Kojo, but he wants to be sure, and so do I."

"Understood."

"He said it doesn't need to be a polite conversation." Fiona handed Marvin a glass of Chivas 12.

"Even better," Baby Chris said, practically holding his breath as Fiona stood in front of him and leaned in to hand him a glass of Beefeater Burrough's Reserve. "Thank you."

"How's Aunt Wanda?" Marvin asked.

He had gone by the hospital to see her, but they wouldn't let him in. He was waiting for a chance to speak to the doctor, but he had to leave before the doctor was available.

"Black said that she's still in a coma. But the doctors say that her vitals look good, and she's stable."

"You think she'll be all right?" Marvin enquired.

"All we can do is hope and pray," Jackie said, and they stood.

"You know where to find her?" Baby Chris asked, and he shot his drink.

"No." Jackie stood up. "But I'm sure you'll find her. And I wanna know what she says."

"We're gone," Marvin said and started for the door.

"We'll be back," Baby Chris said, and Fiona escorted them out of Jackie's office.

They rolled by her house and didn't see the Maserati GranTurismo parked in its usual spot in the parking garage in her building, but they rang the bell and banged on her door until Marvin was satisfied that she wasn't there before they moved on and headed for Action.

When they got there, they found her car parked in what used to be Kojo's reserved spot. After a quick check-in with the club's security, they went through the packed club to the office. When they arrived, Baby Chris was surprised that Brendon Walker wasn't guarding the door as he was every other time they'd been there.

"Ain't you heard?"

"Hear what?"

"Big boy had a date with Edwina."

"No, I hadn't heard that," Baby Chris said, knocked once on the door, and they walked in.

"What the fuck?" Sienna said and started to reach for the gun in her desk drawer.

Marvin and Baby Chris drew their weapons. "Don't do it," Marvin said as they approached the desk. Baby Chris went around the desk and got the gun from her drawer.

"What do you want?"

"To talk."

Sienna sat back and ran her fingers along her Mikimoto diamond and pearl lariat necklace. It was a nervous habit of hers, and at that moment, she was *very* nervous. She knew who Marvin and Baby Chris were—Jackie Washington's enforcers. Whatever they wanted couldn't be good.

"Okay, let's talk."

Marvin and Baby Chris sat down in front of her desk. "A couple of days ago, Wanda Moore was shot, and her husband was killed," Marvin began.

"I heard."

"Mr. Black wants to know if you had anything to do with it."

"Wait a minute. You think *I* had something to do with that?"

"Did you?" Baby Chris questioned.

"No. Why would I have anything to do with that?"

"I don't know. You tell me," Marvin answered.

"You're Nick's son, aren't you?" She had seen Marvin once years ago at Angelo's social club when he came there with Nick.

"I am." Marvin raised his gun and pointed it at Sienna. "What does that have to do with anything?"

"Nothing. It's just that I know how far back your father and Mr. Black go with her."

"And?" Marvin lowered his gun.

"So you have to know that Angelo would kill me and my entire family if I had anything to do with it." Sienna paused. "Maybe Kordell might know something about it," she said, thinking that maybe that's why she hadn't seen him in days.

"Where's Kordell?" Baby Chris asked sarcastically since he knew Kojo was dead.

"I haven't seen him in days."

Marvin glanced at Baby Chris. "Kordell didn't have anything to do with it." He pointed the gun at Sienna again. "So, I'm asking you. Did *you* send men to kill Mr. Black and Mr. Ray?"

Sienna's eyes got big. "Hell no," she stated emphatically.

Marvin and Baby Chris stood up. "For your sake, I hope you didn't," Baby Chris said.

"If you did, I'll be back to kill you," Marvin assured her, and he walked out of Sienna's office with Baby Chris.

When the door closed, Sienna relaxed. She was about to pick up the phone to call Joey, but then she thought about what he said to her earlier that evening.

"I don't think you'll see him again."

Couple that with Marvin's confidence that Kordell had nothing to do with it, and Sienna was left to assume that somebody in The Family killed Kordell. Now, what Joey said made perfect sense.

"It's your house now, Sienna," she said aloud, and that made her smile.

Chapter 23

When Black and Bobby left Shaunta Elias's Tracey Towers apartment, they headed straight out to White Plains to look for Julianna Verrett, hoping to find Kendrick Nance, but they should have driven faster.

Julianna's hands were in her hair, and she was screaming incoherently about how hard she was coming before she rolled off his face, shaking and moaning into the fetal position. Nance quickly pulled her up, grabbed her by her hips, and entered Julianna in one hard thrust. She began to squirm a little but took in every inch of that thick dick. Once she had taken all of him inside of her, she bucked harder and harder, and then Nance grabbed her by the shoulders and began to hit it as hard as he could.

"Get it," Julianna screamed as she worked herself back and forth.

The phone next to the bed rang. Nance glanced over and looked at the display and saw that it was Dandridge calling.

"Shit."

Nance let go of her shoulders and began squeezing a tittie with one hand, and then he reached between her legs. The phone rang again.

"Do that shit," Julianna shouted as Nance fingered her clit.

Nance slowed his pace and began to long stroke her as he reached for the phone.

"What the fuck are you doing?" Julianna shouted.

"Shut up!" he shouted and kept slowly easing himself in and out of her. "What you want?"

"Mike Black and Bobby Ray just left Shaunta's apartment."

"What they want?"

"Stop playing with this pussy and fuck it hard."

"Quiet."

"They're looking for you now."

"Fuck."

"What did Shaunta tell them?"

"She said they hung her off the balcony until she told them where you were."

"What did she tell them?"

"They're on their way out to Julianna's now."

"Shit," he shouted, and his dick came out of Julianna.

"Put that dick back in and fuck me."

"What you say?" Dandridge asked.

"Nothing."

"That's not all."

Nance sat down on the bed. "What else?"

"I sent a couple of guys over there. They're dead."

"What the fuck you do that for?"

"So they wouldn't kill her."

"Fuck I care if they killed her." Nance paused. "I'll talk to you later," he said and ended the call, thinking he was right. Dandridge was fuckin' Shaunta behind his back every chance he got. Nance got out of bed and began dressing.

"What's wrong?" Julianna asked.

He sat on the edge of the bed and put on his shoes. "Mike Black and Bobby Ray are on their way here." But he also wondered what else Dandridge was doing behind his back.

"How do they know where I live?" she demanded to know.

"I don't know."

Julianna hopped out of bed and followed him to the door. "One of your other hoes told them, didn't they?"

"I told you I don't know." Nance turned around and grabbed her by the shoulders. "What I tell you about asking me fuckin' questions?"

She calmed down and said nothing. Although she was quiet, you could see the fear in her eyes.

"That's what I thought." He opened the door.

"What do you want me to tell them when they arrive?"

"That you haven't seen me." Nance took her in his arms and kissed her. "I'll make this up to you, I promise."

Julianna kissed him. "You better," she uttered, and Nance left her house.

He got in his car and drove away. Nance took out his phone and called Dandridge back. When he didn't answer, Nance angrily tossed the phone in the passenger seat. Then the phone rang, and Nance answered.

"Why the fuck they looking for me?" he shouted.

"I just talked to Newton to see what he got from Rhianna."

"What she say?"

"Nothing, but he heard that it's about Kojo."

"Kojo? What he got to do with Black and Bobby hunting me?"

"You know Kojo's backed by the Italians, right?"

"And?"

"Word is that Black and Angelo Collette go back years, and he got Black to go at us," Dandridge explained.

"That don't make no sense." Nance thought for a second or two. "I can see The Family doing that cracker's bidding, but Black and Bobby personally? I don't buy it." He paused. "They were looking for Frenchie, and now, they're looking for me. No, there's something else to this to get them out in the street. Anybody heard from Frenchie?"

"Yeah. That nigga robbed one of their joints. When he heard that Black and Bobby were looking for him, he went to L.A."

"Damn it." Nance thought about what to do. "Where are you?"

"Ten Ninety-Seven."

"I'll be through there, but I need you to have Newton get with Rhianna and arrange a meeting."

"Why?" Dandridge demanded to know.

"Why the fuck you think? I need to get them off me."

"You not thinking about backing off of Kojo and them, are you?" he asked. He had invested much of his resources in taking Kojo down to see it all go to waste.

"If that's what it takes to get them niggas off me."

"I think that's a bad idea."

"That's because it ain't you them niggas is hunting. Just do it," Nance ordered Dandridge and ended the call.

Dandridge put his phone down and looked around the room. "What he say?" Khalil wanted to know.

"He wants to talk."

"To who?" Poole asked.

"To Black and Bobby. He wants Newton to get with Rhianna to arrange a meeting." Khalil took out his phone to call Newton. "Who you calling?"

"Newton to set up the meeting."

"Ain't gonna be no damn meeting." He looked at Poole. "I'm gonna end this and them niggas. I want you to get as many men as you can and go to the warehouse. When Black and Bobby show up, kill them."

"You sure about this?" Khalil questioned. "That's not what Nance wanted."

"He'll thank me later. Go," he shouted and picked up the phone. Dandridge always thought that Nance was weak, and this just proved his point.

"Hello," Julianna answered.

"Black and Bobby get there yet?"

"Not yet, why?"

"When they get there, Nance wants you to tell them that he's gonna be at the old plumbing supply place on Zerega Avenue."

"Okay," she said and paused because she had a question. "Who told Black and them where I lived?"

"Detra Finney," he said quickly, saving Shaunta from Julianna's wrath. "You know she's always been jealous of you."

"That bitch. I oughta kill her muthafuckin' ass."

"Whatever, Julianna. You just do what Nance needs you to do."

"I'll do it," Julianna promised, ended the call, and got dressed to receive her guests. "I'm tired of his shit," she spit out as she opened her closet. "Fuckin' all them other bitches. I'll show that nigga I ain't the one to be fucked over."

Julianna wanted to extract some measure of revenge, and what better way than to fuck his enemies. She stood there thinking about what to put on. She wanted to wear something sexy and tempting, so she chose an Amanda Uprichard Sandrine silk halter dress and poured herself into it.

Less than five minutes later, her doorbell rang, and she went to answer it.

"Who is it?"

"Mike Black and Bobby Ray. We're looking for Kendrick Nance," Black said.

Julianna opened the door wide and stood there smiling. Black and Bobby looked at her and then at each other.

"You just missed him."

"How long he been gone?" Bobby walked by her and looked around the living room.

"About twenty minutes."

"Mind if we have a look around?" Black said when he walked in. Julianna closed the door.

"Go ahead; knock yourselves out."

"Watch her," Black said and went to search the house.

"Can I get you something to drink?" she asked and swung her hips going to the bar.

"No." But he did enjoy the view.

"You don't mind if I have one?"

"Knock yourself out."

Julianna poured a drink and sat down on a bar stool. She crossed her legs slowly to be sure that Bobby saw that she wasn't wearing any panties. He smiled and shook his head at how she tried to set it out for him. He thought that in their younger days, he and Black would have given her what she wanted and fucked the shit out of her.

"Where is he?" Black asked when he came back into the room.

Julianna uncrossed and then recrossed her legs so Black could see the show too.

"He said he was going to the old plumbing supply place on Zerega Avenue."

"Really?" Black skeptically asked.

"That's what he said." She stood. "Anything else I could help you with?" she asked alluringly.

Black and Bobby looked at each other. "No," they both said simultaneously and turned to leave.

Since she thought she was irresistible, Julianna looked surprised as they walked to the door and left without a word.

Chapter 24

"Don't say it," Black laughed as they returned to their car.

"I won't, but you know, back in the day, I'da had her ass bent over, and your dick woulda been in her mouth," Bobby laughed, and they got into the car.

"That was a long time ago."

"You wanna go to the spot on Zerega Avenue?"

"Yeah, let's go."

"You know it's a trap, right?"

"Of course, it's a trap."

"Then why you wanna go?"

"What else we gotta do?"

Black took out his phone.

"Who you calling?"

"Just inviting someone else to the party."

"This Rain."

"Where you at?"

"The Rock. What's up?"

"Stay there, and I'll tell you when I see you." Black ended the call. "We're going to Purple Rock first."

When Black and Bobby arrived at Purple Rock, the place was packed, and Roselyn Pierce, last season's *Breakout* winner, was on stage. They were escorted to the office and told Rain what was going on.

"I don't know. It sounds like a trap to me."

"That's what I said," Bobby responded on his way to the bar in Rain's office.

"Of course, it is," Black said.

"Then why you still wanna go?"

"You don't know?" Bobby poured him and Black a glass of Rémy. "Wanda got shot, and Vicious Black needs to kill somebody."

Rain looked at Black, and when he didn't deny it, she got up and went to the bar. "Pour me one too."

Bobby picked up a bottle of Patrón and poured one for Rain.

"What we need is Monika and the tactical van so we can see how many men are in there waiting for us and where they are," Black said as Bobby handed him his drink and sat down. "But they're still in Burundi."

"That's not a problem. When Nick upgraded the tactical van, I took the old one. It's in the garage at my safe house."

"You know how to use the equipment?" Black asked.

"No, but both Jackie and Fantasy do."

"That's right. Jackie was a part of Colonel Mathis's little band of assassins for a while," Bobby remembered.

"So was she," Black commented.

"What happened?"

"The Colonel said that I had a very volatile personality, and I introduced an unstable element into the team." Rain recalled that night in a border town called McAllen, Texas.

Colonel Mathis had the team rob a bank to recover information from a safe deposit box that could embarrass the government. When Rain entered the bank, Monika had been shot in the leg, and Nick and Xavier were pinned down and taking heavy fire.

Omega! We're in trouble! I need you to drive the van through the front door!

Repeat your traffic, Delta.

Drive the fuckin' van through the fuckin' door now, Jackie!

"What did you do?"

"I broke radio silence during a job."

"You saved the team." Black thought for a second. "Call Jackie," he said, and Bobby snapped his fingers.

"What?" Rain asked.

"He just wants to see Fantasy again, that's all," Black informed her. "Call Jackie."

Rain rolled her eyes as she returned to her desk and picked up the phone to make the call.

"Fantasy's busy trying to get the surveillance video from the restaurant."

"More important," Bobby agreed.

"We need to check in with her later," Black said, and Bobby nodded and smiled.

"Jackie, this Rain. Meet me at my safe house as soon as you can."

"On my way."

When Jackie arrived at Rain's safe house, they got in the old tactical van and headed for the ambush at the old plumbing supply place on Zerega Avenue. Bobby parked across the street from the warehouse.

"It's been awhile since I used any of this stuff." Jackie switched on the equipment. "But it's like riding a bike."

"What you see?" Black asked.

"I got eight, no, ten heat signatures spread throughout the building."

Bobby looked at Black. "You still wanna go in there?"

"And kill them all," Black nodded and checked his gun.

Rain smiled. "There's an easier way to kill them all."

"I'm listening."

"Let me check something first," she said, making sure the C-4 and detonators were still stored in the van.

When Jackie saw what she was doing, she smiled. "We can blow the place."

Bobby laughed. "Your usual 'Kill everybody and burn the muthafucka to the ground.'"

"It's simple, but it's effective," Rain replied.

"I like it," Black said.

"Come on, Jackie," Rain said, and they got what they needed and left the van.

Black and Bobby watched on the van's monitors as Rain and Jackie planted the explosive devices around the warehouse and then returned to the truck.

"They're all set," Rain said when she closed the van door.

"Blow it," Black ordered, and Jackie pressed the detonator.

The four sat and watched as the cascade of explosions all but leveled the building. Bobby looked at Black.

"Happy now?"

"Yeah, it just wasn't as satisfying."

"I hear that," Rain said as Jackie got in the driver's seat and drove the van away from the ambush at Zerega Avenue.

Chapter 25

Once they arrived back at Rain's safe house, they separated. Jackie went back to Conversations, Rain returned to Purple Rock, and Black got into Bobby's car.

"Where to, Mr. Happy?"

"Let's go to the office and check on Fantasy."

When they arrived at the office, it seemed empty, as it was their last time there.

"Fantasy!" Black called out to her.

"I'm here, Mr. Black. I'll be out in a minute," she shouted back, and Black and Bobby sat down to wait. It was a minute or so later when Fantasy emerged from the control room wearing the shit out of a matching set of Year of Ours heathered stretch crop sweatshirt and sculpted high-rise stretch leggings.

"Hello, Fantasy," Bobby said breathlessly as she walked toward him.

"I'm here too," Carla announced, following Fantasy out of the control room.

"Carla!" Black said, excited to see her. "I thought you were still in Burundi with the rest of the team."

"I got in a couple of hours ago. When Fantasy called and told me what was happening, I told Nick I needed to be here, and I caught a military transport immediately."

"Well, I'm glad you're here." He glanced at Fantasy. "No offense to you, Fantasy."

"None taken. Carla was who you needed." She paused. "Her trying to talk me through hacking into the NYPD would have taken forever."

"Don't be so hard on yourself. You're just learning the system, and it is a lot." She turned to Black. "How's Wanda?"

It was a question that he was tired of hearing but one that he knew needed to be answered whenever he was asked. "The doctor said that she is going to continue the medically induced coma for another twenty-four to forty-eight hours until the swelling subsides."

"Glad to hear that." Then Carla turned toward the control room; Fantasy did too. "Follow me, and I'll show you what I got."

"Right behind you," Bobby said, anxious to see what she had.

"I know you just got here a few hours ago, but were you able to get the video of the shooting?" Black asked.

"I was able to access what the NYPD had."

"Why the NYPD? Wouldn't the restaurant have been easier to access?" Bobby wanted to know.

"By the time I got to it, the restaurant video had been deleted. And besides, where's the fun in that?"

"What'd you get?" Black needed to know.

"Here it is," Carla said, throwing it up on the big monitor in the control room.

When the video appeared on the screen, they watched Wanda walk out of the restaurant with James. Then Black and Bobby appeared, walking a few feet behind them. Immediately afterward, they saw a black van stop right in front of James and Wanda. The panel door opened, and one man armed with an automatic weapon opened fire. All four watched in horror and saw Black and Bobby hit the ground, and Shy and Pam ran back into the restaurant as Wanda and James took multiple shots, and then the van drove away fast.

Fantasy looked away from the screen.

"Play it again," Black ordered. "Slow."

"Yes, sir," Carla replied, running the video again at half the speed.

"I can't." Fantasy got up and rushed out of the room.

When it was over, Black asked, "Do you have another angle?"

"I do." Carla accessed the video, and it appeared on the screen. "This is from the street camera. It isn't as good a view."

"Run it anyway, slower than the last one. Frame by frame if you have to."

Black watched Wanda take each shot and its effect on her body. The shots took her off her feet, and then her body hit the pavement hard as she lay motionless on the ground next to Bobby.

"Turn it off," Bobby said. "I've seen enough."

Carla looked at Black. "Mike?"

"You can turn it off," he said softly, leaving the room.

When Bobby came out, Black was standing by the window. He went and stood next to him.

"You okay, Bob?" Black asked.

"No, Mike, I'm not. That was hard to watch."

"Yeah," Black paused. "It was."

"Then why did you want to watch it again?"

"I wanted to be sure of what I was seeing."

"They weren't shooting at us, Mike."

"I know. Whoever they are, they were aiming for Wanda and James." He took out his phone to make a call.

"This Rain."

"Where you at?"

"Back at the Rock."

"Me and Bobby are on our way there now. When I get there, I wanna see all the captains."

"What's wrong?"

"I'll tell you when I see you." Black ended the call. "Let's go."

"What now?" Rain questioned as she called Sherman.

He answered. "You know what fuckin' time it is?"

"No, and I don't care. Black called a captains' meeting at Purple Rock."

"When?"

"Now." Rain ended the call and called Jackie.

"Twice in one night. Something must be up," Jackie said, smiling as she answered.

"Something's up, so meet me at the Rock. Black called a captains' meeting."

"When?"

"Now." Rain ended the call. Her calls to Ryder and Carter went pretty much the same way.

By the time Black and Bobby arrived in the office at Purple Rock, all of Rain's captains were there wondering what was happening.

"We here," Sherman said as they walked through the door. "You wanna tell me why you interrupted my beauty sleep?"

Black waited until the laughter ended. "Me and Bobby weren't the targets of the hit."

"Wait—what? Then who?" Ryder asked breathlessly.

"From what I can see from watching the video, Wanda and James were the targets."

"Oh shit," Sherman mumbled because he knew what that meant.

"I want every member of this family out breaking bones until I find out who's behind this. Understood?"

"Understood," each of them said in unison.

"Wanda's been in Nassau for the longest," Rain commented.

"I'll talk to Jada about that," Black replied.

"You going to Nassau, Black?" Jackie asked.

"Jada is still in the city." Black paused and looked around the room at the stunned faces. "Fuck y'all sitting around for?"

Everybody stood up and left the office without saying another word.

Jada West had been living and doing business at the Forbes Five Star-rated and AAA five Diamond-award-winning Peninsula Hotel for years. Its location in the heart of the city's most prestigious shopping, entertainment, and cultural district made it perfect for Jada's purposes.

"Well, this is a pleasant but certainly unexpected surprise. To what do I owe the honor?"

"Where are you?"

"At the Peninsula."

"We need to talk."

"Since you're calling now, I imagine you'd like to talk now."

"You know me too well."

"For reasons we do not need to get into, yes, I know you all too well, Mr. Black. I'll be in the Salon de Ning when you get here."

"I'm here waiting for you now."

"I'll be up in a minute."

Jada got out of bed. Once she explained to Clayton that she was meeting Black in the Salon de Ning, the rooftop bar in the hotel, she dressed in a Beet Red Zuhair Murad Shelby layered tulle midi-dress and a pair of Jimmy Choo bing-embellished patent leather mules. She wore a Fabergé Imperial 18K rose gold, ruby, and diamond Mosaic Egg pendant necklace and was on her way to the door when Clayton rolled over.

"You look nice."

"Thank you." Jada picked up her Jimmy Choo Varenne quilted velvet clutch.

"You always dress like that to meet your ex?"

Jada came back to the bed and kissed Clayton on the cheek. "I always dress like this." She kissed the other cheek. "But fear not. Mr. Black is a man of few words." She glanced at her rose gold Baume & Mercier watch. "I won't be gone long."

And with that, Jada left the Superior Suite. She entered the Salon de Ning and looked around.

"Good evening, Ms. West. Your usual table?" the host asked.

"No, I'm meeting somebody, and they are already seated." Jada scanned the room. "I see them. Thank you, Oscar," she said, heading for the table where Black and Bobby were waiting. They both stood up when they saw her coming.

"Mr. Black *and* Mr. Ray. I am truly honored."

Bobby bowed at the waist and kissed her hand. "Hello, Jada."

"How are you, Ms. West?" Black asked and pulled out the chair for Jada to sit down.

"So, tell me, what's going on?" Jada asked.

"Looks like Wanda and James were the targets of the shooting," Bobby said.

"I came to ask if you knew if she was into anything that might lead to this," Black said.

"Not in Nassau." Jada paused. "But you may want to speak with Fantasy about what Wanda had her doing in Aruba."

Bobby sat back and picked up his drink. "The secret mission."

"You know what it was about?" Black asked.

Jada smiled as a waitress arrived and placed a glass of French 75 in front of her. "Thank you."

"Will there be anything else, Ms. West?"

"No, thank you. That will be all." Jada picked up her glass and waited until the server was out of earshot. "You know she has a thing about trafficking young girls."

"I do."

"I don't know the particulars, but that's what it was about."

"Why didn't she tell me?"

"Because she didn't want to hear your, 'You can't police the world, Wanda,' speech."

"That's because she *can't* police the world," Bobby said.

"And she didn't try to. From what I understood, she just created the conditions for that part of their organization to fall apart."

"So, we have no idea if they know what she was doing?" Bobby asked.

"No, Mr. Ray, we do not."

Chapter 26

Nance was at Ten Ninety-Seven when Khalil arrived to tell him about what happened earlier that evening at Zerega Avenue. As one could expect, he was not happy about it.

"I told that muthafucka to arrange a meeting with them."

"That's not what happened."

"Stop fuckin' around and tell me what you came here to tell me."

"Instead of getting with Newton to arrange a meeting with Black and Bobby, Dandridge had Poole arrange a trap for them."

"He did *what?*"

"He set up a trap."

"I heard what you said, nigga. Tell me what happened."

"He had Julianna tell Black and Bobby that you were at the old plumbing supply warehouse," Khalil explained.

"And?"

"I guess they knew it was a trap because they blew the place up."

Nance threw his glass against the wall. "Fuck!" he shouted. "Now them niggas think *I* set a fuckin' trap for them."

Khalil said nothing because that was probably what was happening, and he wanted no part of it.

"How many men did the bomb kill?"

"Ten that I know of."

"Where's that nigga now?"

"I don't know."

"You find Dandridge and bring him to the club."

"Yes, sir."

"But don't tell him that you told me, understand?"

"Yes, sir."

When Khalil left, Nance thought about calling Newton to contact Rhianna to see if he could find out how they were taking the assassination attempt. But then he thought about it. Thinking that the damage had already been done, Nance began to think about his position in the game and his moves to push Kojo out. He knew that for appearance' sake, he had to do something in retaliation for the deaths of his men. He knew that if he did nothing in response it would make him look weak.

"I gotta do something," he said aloud and signaled for a server. "Bring me another drink and send Cha'relle over here."

It wasn't long before Cha'relle appeared at the table with his drink. "Here you go, baby."

Nance put a fifty-dollar bill on the table. Cha'relle quickly picked up the money, dropped down, and crawled under the table. Nance picked up his drink and took a sip as she hurried to unbuckle his pants and made quick work of getting his dick to the back of her throat.

While Nance thought about what he was going to do, Cha'relle worked her mouth up and down on his hardening length, slobbering and bobbing and working her jaws as if her life depended on him coming hard in her mouth.

As Cha'relle teased his head with her tongue, Nance knew that whatever he did would only escalate the situation, and that was the last thing he needed. Then she slowly worked her soft, wet lips and tongue up and down his length and used the roof of her mouth to apply a little pressure.

"Damn . . ."

He grabbed her head with both hands and pumped in and out of her mouth. Once she had made him explode in her mouth, Nance tapped her on her head, and Cha'relle crawled out from under the table as Khalil approached the table with Dandridge.

"Let me know if you want the whole show," Cha'relle said as she walked away from the table.

"Look who I found," Khalil said.

"Dandridge, my nigga."

"What's up, K Dog," he said, smiling and chuckling. "I see you took advantage of the headmaster's skills."

"You know it relaxes me. It helps clear my mind."

"I hear that."

"Come on; have a seat." Dandridge sat down. "You want a drink?"

"No, I'm good, but I'll have what you just had."

Nance laughed hard. "I'll call her back over in a minute, but business first."

"Sure, sure," Dandridge nodded.

"Tell me, did you get with Newton about arranging a sit-down with Black?"

"Not exactly."

"Fuck is that supposed to mean?" Nance asked and put his hand on his gun.

Khalil's smile grew larger as Dandridge squirmed in his seat.

"I did. I mean, I thought we should end it instead of talking."

"Nigga, stop fuckin' around and tell me what you *did* instead of doing what I *told* you to do."

"I thought—"

Nance chuckled. "That's usually what gets you in trouble."

"Yeah." Dandridge laughed nervously, but he was getting really tired of Nance talking down to him. "I thought that we should end it instead of talking," he repeated more confidently, demanding the respect he thought he was entitled to. "So, I called Julianna and had her tell Black and Bobby that you were at the old plumbing supply joint."

"But not a meeting to settle this misunderstanding?"

"No. I had Poole get as many men as he could and kill Black and Bobby when they showed up."

"So, Black and Bobby are dead?"

"No. Somehow, they must have figured out it was a trap and blew up the place."

Nance put his gun to Dandridge's head. "How could you be so fuckin' stupid?"

"I just thought—"

"There's that word again. You don't think. You do what the fuck I *tell* you to do."

"I fucked up."

"Fuckin' right you did." Nance took the gun away from his head. "Because you had a 'thought,' ten of my best men are dead, and Black probably thinks we wanna go to war with them. Over *your* bullshit."

"I'm sorry, I just thought—"

Nance put the gun back to Dandridge's head. "If you say that you 'just thought' one more fuckin' time, I swear I will end you right now."

"Backing off Kojo was a bad idea," Dandridge said, speaking his mind and not caring about the consequences. "Killing them niggas would have strengthened our position."

"You're right. It would have strengthened our position, but Black is still alive, thinking I want war. *Not* you—*me*." Nance took the gun away from his head. "Now, because of you, I gotta do something, or everybody will think I'm both stupid and weak."

"What you gonna do?"

"I don't know." Nance drained his glass and signaled for another. "But whatever I decide to do, you need to do exactly what I say—*not* improvise. You hear me?"

"I hear you."

"Now get the fuck outta here before I change my mind and kill you."

Dandridge got up from the table and left the club, wondering how much further he would let Nance push him before he did something about it.

Chapter 27

It was after two in the morning when Black and Bobby got to the office to talk to Fantasy about the project that she was doing for Wanda. Once again, when they arrived at the office, it was quiet.

"Fantasy," Black called out to her.

"I sent her home for the night, Mike," Carla said while exiting the control room. "What do you need?"

"I need to talk to her about what she was doing for Wanda."

"You think whatever she was doing had something to do with Wanda and James getting shot?"

"I don't know."

"Well, I could access some cameras, but I couldn't get a license plate for the van. I tracked it for as long as possible but lost it."

"If you could access those cameras, so could Kirk," Bobby said. "Leave that shit for the cops to work. I need you to do a deep dive into the bank and see if anything raises a red flag for you."

"I'm on it," Carla promised.

"Fantasy coming in tomorrow?"

"Afternoon."

"Tell her I need to talk to her and have her call me when she gets here."

"Will do."

"Good night, Carla," Black said and turned to leave the office.

"See you tomorrow," Bobby said to Carla, following Black out.

When Bobby dropped Black off at his house, he tried, as he always did, to quietly make it into their room and get in bed with Shy.

"Did you find out anything?" she asked as she usually did when he came in as soon as he sat on the bed.

"I don't know why I even bother."

"I don't either. Did you find out who's trying to kill you this time?"

"I don't think they were trying to kill me and Bob."

"Oh no," Shy said, anticipating what he was about to tell her.

"I think that Wanda was the target, and it might have something to do with whatever it was that she had Fantasy doing for her."

"The secret mission." Shy sat up in bed and hugged her husband. "Did you talk to Fantasy about what she was doing?"

"Not yet. She was gone when Bob and I got to the office. I told Carla to have her call me when she gets in tomorrow."

"I thought the team was still in Burundi."

"When Fantasy told Carla what was happening, she returned as fast as possible." He got in bed next to her. "She doesn't have the hacking skills to do what I needed."

"I'm sure Fantasy has other talents."

"She does."

Black stretched out in bed and lay his head on the pillow. He looked at Shy. She was looking very sexy in the ivory Fleur du Mal lily-embroidered babydoll. He closed his eyes. But instead of seeing visions of her beautiful body and them making love, he was consumed with thoughts of Wanda. In his mind's eye, he could see each bullet hit her in slow motion. He rolled over and tried to force the images out of his mind but couldn't.

It was as if he had pressed the rewind button, and it all began again. Black could see her and James walking out of the restaurant, holding hands and laughing. He remembered thinking at that moment how happy they looked and how glad he was for them. And then the van stopped in front of them, and the first bullets struck James. He could see himself diving for the ground and taking out his gun. Then watching helplessly as each of the three bullets hit Wanda, the impact taking her off her feet and her body hitting the ground.

Suddenly, his eyes sprang open, and he sat straight up in bed.

"What's wrong, Michael?" Shy asked and put her arm around him.

"When I close my eyes, I see Wanda getting shot." Black lay his head on her chest. He could be vulnerable with Shy, but she was the only one. "I felt so helpless. I still do."

"It's all right, baby. I can't even imagine what you're feeling now . . . the pain you're feeling." She kissed his head. "Just know that I'm right here for you, always."

"I know. And I love you for it. I don't know what I would do without you."

"I love you," Shy said and kissed his head again.

"I love you too."

"Try to get some rest."

"I will." He pulled away from her embrace and sat on the edge of the bed. "I'm gonna get something to drink."

"I'll be down in a minute to keep you company," she said as Black got out of bed and walked toward the door.

When he stepped out into the hallway, Black saw Michelle quietly tiptoeing up the stairs with her shoes in her hand.

"Oh no, you ain't just getting home," he said softly when she reached the landing.

Michelle froze, and her eyes got big. "Uh-oh."

"Get in your room before your mother comes out, and we'll talk about this in the morning."

"Yes, Daddy."

Michelle rushed past him and closed her door just before Shy opened her door and came out of their room. But Michelle noticed the look on her father's face and knew that something was bothering him.

"You didn't have to wait for me," Shy said, holding out his hand.

Michelle stuck her head out the door. "Is everything all right?"

"Yes, Michelle, everything's fine," her mother told her.

"Then why does Daddy look like that?"

"We'll talk about it in the morning. Now, go to bed," her father said sternly and went down the stairs with his wife. She sat with him while he had a glass of Rémy and talked about Wanda, and then they went back upstairs to bed.

When Black woke up, Shy was gone. He looked at the clock by the bed and saw that it was going on one o'clock in the afternoon. He reached for the phone and saw that he had a message from Carla that Fantasy was in the office. Then he called Bobby to tell him William would drop him off in about an hour. Black got out of bed and hit the shower. When William dropped him off at Bobby's, Black got in the car with Bobby, and they headed back downtown to Nick's office to talk to Fantasy.

"Good afternoon, Mr. Black, Mr. Ray," Fantasy said as she came out of the control room to greet them. That day, she looked gorgeous in her Markarian Nicolette jacquard metallic floral sleeveless midi-dress, finished with a petaled neckline.

"You look amazing," Bobby commented, looking at her.

"I have an appointment this afternoon with Ms. West, and I want to look my best."

"I see," Black said, thinking it was beyond time for her and Jada to kiss and make up.

"Carla said that you wanted to speak with me."

"Yes. Please, have a seat."

When Fantasy sat on the couch, Black sat down next to her, and Bobby leaned on the desk in front of them.

"I wanted to ask you about what you were doing for Wanda," Black began.

"The secret mission," Bobby said, making air quotes.

"Ms. Moore asked me to go to Aruba to infiltrate a drug and human smuggling operation."

"For what purpose?" Black asked.

"My job was to destabilize it by making suggestions and starting rumors that led the human trafficker, a man named Arturo Gael, to cooperate with the FBI."

"Was it successful?"

"Yes, very. Once I infiltrated the organization through a woman whose name was Mashawn Putney, I used her to spread the rumors and create doubt designed to make Arturo Gael believe that Ignacio Tomas, the head of the organization, had turned on him. He eventually talked to the FBI."

"Do you have any reason to believe that they were on to you or knew of Wanda's involvement?"

"No, Mr. Black, I don't. The operation was totally successful. And there was no way they could have known I was working for Ms. Moore."

"How can you be so sure?" Bobby questioned.

"Because I stayed in Aruba for a month after FBI agents and the Aruba Police Force raided the compound and arrested Arturo Gael and Ignacio Tomas. I wasn't killed when the new head of the organization, Joaquín Alejandro, killed everyone who he thought might have been involved," Fantasy said confidently. "I was still on the island when Ignacio Tomas was released on bail, and I experienced no repercussions for my actions on Ms. Moore's behalf."

"You have any idea how she got on to these guys?"

"I am not sure of the particulars. However, I know Mr. Austin had been spending a great deal of time in Aruba on business."

"Wanda told me that she thought James was having an affair because he was spending so much time on the island," Bobby mentioned.

"Do you know who Mr. Austin was working for in Aruba?"

"I do not. To my knowledge, Mr. Austin was there doing some consulting, but Ms. Moore never told me anything about that."

"Need to know," Bobby commented.

"It was my understanding that when Ms. Moore went there to visit was when she discovered the trafficking operation," Fantasy informed them.

"I want to check them out. Thank you, Fantasy. You've been a big help," Black said.

"No need to thank me, Mr. Black. Anything I can do to help you end the individuals responsible for it is my honor and privilege."

"But it doesn't tell us what she was into that got her shot and James murdered," Bobby said.

"No, it doesn't." Black stood up. "Please give Ms. West my best and apologize to her for us interrupting her evening last night."

When Black walked away, Fantasy stood up.

"Always a pleasure to see you, Fantasy," Bobby said, bowed at the waist, and kissed her hand.

"Believe me, Mr. Ray, the pleasure is all mine," Fantasy said, looping her arm in his, and they left the office.

Chapter 28

When Dawkins opened her eyes and glanced over at the clock on the nightstand by the bed, she saw that it was just after two in the morning. She rolled over and found that she was alone. She shook her head, assumed that he had left, and tried in vain to go back to sleep, but it wasn't to be.

There was too much on her mind.

She tossed and turned but couldn't escape the concepts and theories filling her inner thoughts. Sure, the attempted murder of Wanda Moore and the murder of James Austin was on her mind. However, that was not the dominant thought.

The former lieutenant was thinking about how the NYPD treated her in general and Deputy Inspector Cavanaugh in particular. She was sure that he had tipped Kojo about her unauthorized undercover operative, and he had made sure that she was busted back down to detective and suspended without pay for a month. Despite her partner urging her to let it go, and she promised him she would, revenge was still at the top of the list. She had no idea what that revenge would look like or how she would accomplish it, but she promised herself that she would have her revenge, and she always kept her promises to herself.

That was when she heard the sound and saw the light coming from her living room. She got out of bed, and after a quick stop in the bathroom, Dawkins put on her

La Perla maison lace trim silk blend robe, a birthday gift from Jada, and went into the living room.

"I thought you were gone," she said to Kirk.

He was sitting on the couch, looking at his laptop. "No, I couldn't sleep. I see you can't sleep either."

"What are you looking at?" Dawkins asked and sat down next to him.

"The footage of the shooting."

She leaned closer. "See anything you didn't see before?"

"I think so."

"What you got?"

"We've been operating under the assumption that the target of the hit was Wanda. And that assumption was based solely on her ties to Black and Austin being a civilian. But suppose the target was Austin?" Kirk started the video in slow motion. "This is from the restaurant," he said, and the detectives watched the black van stop and the doors open. "They stop in front of Austin, and they start blasting." He paused the video. "He takes five shots."

"I'm with you so far."

Kirk restarted the video. "There's a brief pause, and the van starts to move off—"

"And that's when Wanda gets shot."

Kirk stopped the video and looked over at Dawkins. "I believe that Austin was the target."

"Play it again and zoom in on the van." Kirk did as she asked, and Dawkins watched it again. "I think you're right. Austin was the target. And if that's the case, what was he into that would get him killed?"

"Let's find out," Kirk said and closed his laptop.

"You coming back to bed?" Dawkins asked and stood up.

"Yeah."

The following morning, the detectives went to the Austin law firm. They approached the reception desk and showed their badges.

"I'm Detective Kirkland, and this is Detective Dawkins. We're investigating the murder of James Austin."

"Yes. How can I help you?"

"We were hoping we could speak to his law clerk," Dawkins asked.

"Yes. Mr. Austin's law clerk, Magdeleine Lavergne, is in the office this morning. If you wouldn't mind having a seat, I will see if she can speak with you."

"Thank you," Dawkins said, and the detectives took seats in the plush waiting area. "This place is nicer than my apartment."

Thirty minutes later, a well-dressed woman entered the reception area, and the receptionist pointed in the detectives' direction. "Good morning," she said as she approached.

Kirk and Dawkins rose to their feet. "Good morning, I'm Detective Dawkins, and this is Detective Kirkland."

"My name is Magdeleine Lavergne. I am Mr. Austin's law clerk. How can I help you?"

"As we explained to your receptionist, we're investigating the murder of James Austin, and we'd like to ask you a few questions," Kirk said.

"I've already talked to the police."

"We won't take up much of your time," Dawkins added.

"Of course. Please, follow me."

Magdeleine Lavergne led the detectives to her office, and they took seats in front of her desk. She sat down, and after she moved a few things around on her desk, she asked, "What can I do for you?"

"We'd like to know if Mr. Austin was having any problems in either his personal or professional life," Dawkins began the questioning.

"I really can't speak to his personal life, but as far as I know, he wasn't having any issues."

"How long have you been with Mr. Austin?" Dawkins asked.

"Fifteen years. I started as a clerk in the Los Angeles office and moved here when he opened this office."

"I imagine after fifteen years you'd have some unique insights into his personal life, and you, better than most, would be able to tell us if there were any changes in his behavior, whether he was worried about anything that might have led to him being killed," Kirk said.

"Wait—what are you saying?" Lavergne asked.

"We have reason to believe that Mr. Austin may have been the target of the shooting."

Lavergne seemed visibly upset but not necessarily surprised by Dawkins's statement. "No. I can't think of anything, and I haven't noticed any changes."

"Any clients he might have an issue with?"

"Does he have any clients in the Caribbean?" Kirk asked, and Lavergne swallowed hard.

"Do you have a warrant?"

"We could get one, but it would be much easier if you'd just tell us whether he had any Caribbean clients."

"As I said," Lavergne began, and Dawkins took out her phone, "I can't release client information without a warrant."

"That's what she's doing," Kirk said as his partner got a judge on the line.

"It's been tried," Lavergne said confidently, sitting back in her chair. "Something about a 'fishing expedition.'"

Dawkins put her call to Judge Peterson on speaker.

"Rachael, how are you doing?"

"I'm fine, Your Honor. How are you and Mimmie doing?"

"I'm fine, thank you for asking. Mimmie is as mean as a rattlesnake. What can I do for you?"

"I need a warrant," Dawkins said, and he listened as she ran down the particulars of her need to search.

"Not a problem."

"Thank you, Your Honor. And if it's not too much trouble, could you have your clerk expedite that, please?" Dawkins looked at Lavergne. "What's your email address?"

"mlavergne@austinlaw."

She protested, but Dawkins had already relayed her email address to the judge's clerk. Then the office door opened, and a woman walked in.

"Hey, Maggie. I left something in his office. I won't be a minute," she said as she passed the desk on her way into James's office.

Kirk pointed. "Who's that?"

"Lisa Austin."

Kirk and Dawkins looked confused.

"His first wife. She's a partner in the firm. She's in from L.A. to transition the office . . . and attend the funeral, of course." Kirk got up to follow her into the office. "You can't go in there."

"Yes, he can. We're the police," Dawkins said. "You should get your warrant in a minute, so you might as well get the information ready to turn over."

Kirk went into the office and closed the door behind him.

"Mrs. Austin?"

She was startled by Kirk's presence in the room. "You can't be in here."

On top of being startled, she was mad. She had just got off the phone with Keisha Orr, Wanda's personal assistant. She was determined not to let James's ex-wife take over the arrangements that she made on Wanda's behalf. They agreed to have a service in New York and another in Los Angeles. However, Lisa wanted to have the body shipped back to L.A., and Keisha had filed a court order to keep her from doing it. Lisa was hot about it.

He flashed his badge. "I'm Detective Kirkland. I want to ask you a few questions."

Lisa frowned. "I see NYPD decided to put a brother on the case." She sat down behind her ex-husband's desk, but sitting there felt funny. "What can I do to help?"

"You know anybody that may have wanted to see your ex-husband dead?"

She sat back, and her expression changed to one of surprise. "I was under the impression that his death was related to his *new* wife and *her* associates."

"I was under that impression as well, but new information has surfaced that has led me to believe that Mr. Austin may have been the target."

"That's not possible, Detective."

"Perhaps, but what I'd like is if you, as his partner, could tell me who Mr. Austin was representing that may have led to him being murdered."

"No, Detective," Lisa said quickly. "I don't know anybody, but I will see to it that this office makes any information you need available."

"We have a warrant on the way."

"No need. As I said, you will have this office's full and complete cooperation." When she stood up, Kirk did as well. "Now, if you'll excuse me, Detective?"

"Kirkland."

"I have an appointment to meet with Keisha Orr about the funeral arrangements she's made."

"When is the funeral?"

"Day after tomorrow," she said on her way out of the office. Kirk followed her out.

"Maggie, see to it that everybody in the office gives the detectives whatever they need."

"I'm waiting for their warrant to come now."

"Don't worry about that. I expect everyone in this office to cooperate with the police to solve James's murder. Is that understood?"

"Yes, ma'am," Lavergne said. She received the warrant as Lisa left the office. "I'll have that client list ready for you in a minute."

"Does he have any Caribbean clients," Kirk asked again. He thought that the Caribbean had been where Wanda had been for more than a year. It stood to reason that even if he were the target, it still may have had something to do with Wanda.

"That would be Private Investment and Equity Solutions."

"What can you tell me about them?" Dawkins asked.

"They are a private equity asset manager that invests worldwide across the primary fund, secondaries, and direct investment channels, covering the entire private equity spectrum. They operate offices in New York, Amsterdam, Hong Kong, and Aruba."

"Thank you," Dawkins said, and she and Kirk both rose to their feet. "We'll be in touch if we need anything else."

Chapter 29

"We were buried therefore with him by baptism into death so that as Christ was raised from the dead by the glory of the Father, we too might walk in newness of life."

That morning, family, friends, and business associates gathered for the funeral of James Austin. Black, Shy, and other members of The Family attended the service, as did Detectives Kirkland and Dawkins and Ninth Precinct Detectives Miller and Riley. When it was over, Mr. and Mrs. Black walked to the SUV.

"There goes Kirk," Shy noted as they walked. "I'm surprised he's not rushing over here to talk to you."

"He has no reason to talk to me. For once, I'm not a suspect." Black thought for a moment. "But I would be interested to know who he *does* talk to." He stopped and waited for Rain to catch up.

"What's up?"

"I wanna know who Kirk talks to."

Rain looked around and saw Baby Chris coming with Payton Cummings on his arm. She wore Michael Kors, and he dressed in KNT by Kiton. Rain waved him over.

"What you need?"

"I need you to hang around and watch Kirk and Dawkins. I need to know who they talk to. Understood?"

"Understood," Baby Chris said, and Rain walked away and caught up with Black just as he and Shy reached their Mercedes-Maybach GLS. Chuck opened the door for Shy, and she got in.

"Baby Chris is on it," she informed them.

"Good. Kirk likes to harass suspects at funerals."

While others paid their respects to James, Carla was looking into Wanda's recent banking activities for anything that might tell them a reason for her getting shot and James's murder. Fantasy was in the office too. Although she wasn't the hacker that Carla and Monika were, she was there to do what she could to help. She was unwilling to accept that her work for Wanda had contributed to what happened.

What if? she questioned, and that thought led her back into the control room. Even though she could barely sit through it the first time she watched it, Fantasy cued up the police video of the shooting and pressed play.

"Carla!" she shouted.

"What's up?" Carla shouted back.

"Can you come into the control room, please? There is something that I need you to see." When Carla entered the room and sat down, Fantasy started the video again.

"What am I looking at?"

"I think we've all been so focused on Wanda getting shot—" Fantasy began, and Carla held up her hand.

"Back that up to just before the van stops," she ordered and watched the van stop in front of James. The doors opened, and the shooting began.

"Are you seeing what I'm seeing, or am I—"

"James takes five shots. The van starts to move off, and then, as they're pulling away, Wanda gets shot." Carla looked over at Fantasy. "James was the target, *not* Wanda. She was just collateral damage."

"We need to tell Mr. Black," Fantasy said, reaching for the phone.

"No!" Carla said louder than she needed to. "Run it again. Frame by frame. We need to be sure before we call Mike." Fantasy ran it again, and once they had watched it three more times, Carla leaned back. "Call him."

Fantasy smiled and picked up the phone to dial.

"Hello."

"Good afternoon, Mr. Black. This is Fantasy speaking."

"Good afternoon, Fantasy."

"I apologize for bothering you."

"No bother at all. What you got for me?" Black asked.

"Carla and I believe we have something you need to see."

"Chuck."

"Yes, sir."

"Take us by Nick's office, please."

"On our way," Chuck said and changed direction.

"We're on our way to you."

When Black and Shy arrived at the office over an hour and a half later, Carla wasted no time showing them what she and Fantasy had discovered. Shy found it hard to watch, but when it was over, and her husband had seen enough, he came to the same conclusion.

"James was the target." He dropped his head into the palms of his hands. Shy wiped away a tear and gently patted his back. He looked up. "I was so focused on Wanda getting shot that I didn't see what was right in front of me."

"We all were," Carla cosigned.

"I need you to start digging into James. I want to know what he was into."

"Way ahead of you. I got into his files on the Austin and Associates server. I remembered Bobby mentioning that James had been spending a lot of time in Aruba, and I learned he had been there consulting for a company called Global Technology Insights."

"Doing what?" Black demanded to know.

"The file had a 128-bit encryption, so it's gonna take me some time to crack it."

"You stay on that." Black thought for a minute about what to do next. "I need to know what he was doing down there."

"Sounds like you're going to Aruba," Shy commented.

There was a time that she would have said, "Sounds like *we're* going to Aruba," but she had too much on her plate at Camb Overseas Importers for a pleasure trip to Aruba. It did, however, reinforce the fact that she needed to settle on one of the many outstanding candidates she'd interviewed to replace Reeva Duckworth.

"I think so too, but there may be an easier way to find out what he was involved in down there."

"What did you have in mind?" Shy asked.

Black paused. "What was the name of the company James was consulting for?"

"Global Technology Insights," Carla answered.

"Who are they, and what do they do?"

Fantasy quickly tapped the keyboard and clicked the mouse a few times. "Global Technology Insights is widely recognized as one of the top providers of advanced technical analysis and intellectual property services."

With that fact in mind, Black had Erykah arrange a meeting with one of their representatives to see if he could find out what James was into on the island.

The following morning at Prestige Capital and Associates, a woman with long, black hair parted in the middle and honey-kissed skin entered the lobby. She was dressed in a Teri Jon by Rickie Freeman floral Jacquard velvet blazer, matching skirt, and a Cinq à Sept Marta silk cowlneck cami top. Her feet were adorned in Bottega Veneta stretch square-toe ankle-strap mesh pumps. She stood for a second and looked around the room before she took off her sunglasses and approached.

"Whatever," Vandy said to herself, and then she smiled. "Welcome to Prestige Capital and Associates. How can I help you?"

"Good morning." The Brazilian-born beauty handed Vandy her card. "My name is Bruna De Souza, with Global Technology Insights. I have an appointment to see Jaila Bell."

"Good morning, Ms. De Souza. If you wouldn't mind having a seat, I will let Ms. Bell know you're here."

"Thank you," Bruna said and went to sit as Vandy called Jaila.

"I have Bruna De Souza with Global Technology Insights to see you, Jaila."

"I don't even know why Mike scheduled this meeting. We are already doing everything she has in her repertoire in-house." She paused, and her tone changed to a less angry one. "Give me ten minutes, and then have somebody escort her to conference room three. And, please, call Jenna and let her know she's here. I'm on my way."

"Will do," Vandy said and called Jenna Faulk, the director of information technology.

Jaila gathered her things for the meeting and left her office, passing the office of Deana Butler, the head of the real estate division, on her way. She considered inviting her to the meeting but felt it would be as big a waste of Deana's time as it was hers.

"Where you going?" Deana asked as Jaila passed her office.

"To conference room three. Jenna and I are meeting with Bruna De Souza with Global Technology Insights."

"Who are they?"

"Somebody Mike wants us to meet with."

"Why wasn't I included?"

"Because it has nothing to do with real estate."

"So?" Deana stood up and began to gather her things. "When has that ever mattered to me?"

"If you wanna come, you are more than welcome," Jaila said, heading toward the conference room area.

"I'm right behind you."

Once security escorted Bruna De Souza to the conference room, she introduced herself and prepared to make
her presentation. Jaila sat through the presentation and
asked questions, most of which were actually directed
at Jenna. Once she discreetly acknowledged that it was
already being performed in-house, she allowed Bruna to
move on. Jenna was listening intently to what Bruna had
to say.

As Jaila warned, everything that was presented
was something that they had already done in-house.
Therefore, like Jaila, she wondered why Black had
arranged the meeting. Although the presentation had absolutely nothing to do with her division, Deana listened
intently to hear if there was a service that might be useful
to her. If there were, she would speak with Jenna about
making it happen.

Bruna was just about finished with her presentation
when the conference room door opened, and Black
walked in. She felt a flush of excitement as she watched
him enter. Although she wasn't expecting it, she had
hoped he'd stop by. Bruna, who believed that information was power, liked to know as much as she could about
everybody she did business with. So, when James told
her he was marrying Wanda Moore, she checked her out.
That was where she first heard of Mike Black, and her
need to know took over from there.

"Good morning, Mike," his department heads said as
he sat.

"Sorry to interrupt," he said and nodded respectfully to
Bruna. "Please continue."

Bruna continued her presentation, only now she was
looking directly at and talking to Black as if Jaila, Deana,
and Jenna were no longer in the room. When she came to
the closing of her presentation, Bruna leaned on the table
directly in front of him.

"Do you have any questions, Mr. Black?"

"Not at the moment, but I'm sure I'll think of something."

Jaila, who had already satisfied herself that there was nothing that Global Technology Insights could do for them, asked a few questions, more because Black was in the room than anything else. Then she leaned close to Black and whispered. "We don't need them, so why am I really here?"

"I'm getting to that. Play nice, and I'll explain later."

"That's all I have, Mike."

"Thank you, Jaila," he said, and Jaila got up, as did Jenna and Deana. "I'll escort Ms. De Souza out."

With that, Deana and Jaila headed straight for the door. "It was a pleasure meeting you, Ms. De Souza," Jaila said on her way out the door.

"Same here," Bruna said, but Black still had her undivided attention.

"Can I get your card?" Jenna asked, and Bruna looked away long enough to hand her a card.

"We'll be in touch," Jenna said, and the last of the department heads left the conference room. But not Black. He was there for a reason. Bruna started packing up but kept her eyes on Black.

"So, tell me." She came across the room and leaned forward on the table in front of him. "I know you only heard a short summary of what I can offer you, but I'm interested in your thoughts."

"I thought your summary was interesting and well presented, but I'll get a full report and recommendations from my department heads in the morning and decide from there."

"That sounds good. I will look forward to hearing from you."

Bruna continued packing, but then she stopped, looked at Black, and smiled. "I have a question, Mr. Black."

"Ask away, Ms. De Souza."

"Bruna," she breathed out. "Please, call me Bruna."

"What would you like to know, Bruna?"

She came, sat in the chair next to him, and crossed her legs.

"I have to say, from what my research about this company and the comments of Ms. Butler and Ms. Bell," Bruna paused and let out a flirtatious giggle, "tells me that there isn't very much I can do for you that you're not already doing. So I was wondering what I'm *really* doing here."

"Ms. Faulk, she's our director of information technology, and she seemed to be very interested in what you had to say."

"Yes, she did appear to be." Bruna smiled and leaned forward. "I've met and had business with women like Ms. Faulk. She will call, and her sole purpose will be to pick my brain for information to improve your process. So, I repeat, what am I *really* doing here?"

"James Austin recommended you."

Bruna leaned back and smiled. "Mr. Austin is one of my favorite clients."

"Can I be candid with you, Ms. De Souza?"

"Please, call me Bruna," she said flirtatiously. "And yes, of course, you can be honest with me."

"I mentioned that James Austin recommended your services."

"Yes, you did. And I'll have to thank James for the referral next time I see him. Has he come back from his honeymoon?"

"James was murdered last week."

"Oh my God." Bruna put her hand on her chest, and then she crossed herself. "I'm so sorry to hear that."

"So, what I'm interested in is if you can tell me who and what business he had in Aruba."

"James worked with David Efrem at Private Investment and Equity Solutions."

After seeing that Bruna De Souza got safely to her car, Black returned to his office and had Erykah arrange for him to fly to Aruba.

Chapter 30

It was a rainy, miserable night, but that didn't stop Sienna from doing eighty miles per hour as she rolled up the Bronx River Parkway on her way to Yonkers. Not that she was in any hurry to get to her destination, but Sienna liked to drive fast, and a little water on the road wasn't enough to change that.

When she parked her Maserati, Sienna was a bit surprised that none of the usual suspects were standing outside as they always did every time she had been there, and she had been coming there since she was a little girl. It began to rain harder, so she hoped somebody would be standing outside with an umbrella.

"Where's the goon squad when you really need them?" she joked, thinking about her outfit.

That night, Sienna was wearing a Balmain studded zebra tweed jacket and knee-length tweed skirt with Prada metallic leather pumps, which she didn't want to get drenched in the downpour. But after sitting there for a while, hoping the rain would subside, Sienna shut off the car, got her Burberry tote, put it over her head, and made a dash for the door. The effort was in vain because she was drenched from head to toe as she knocked on the door.

"What's up, Sienna?" Santino said, holding the door to the social club open so she could come inside. "Looks like it's coming down pretty hard out there."

"Fuckin' cats and dogs."

Santino looked at Sienna from head to toe. "I think you should come outta those wet clothes before you catch pneumonia."

"You're right. I should just strip right here."

"Just trying to help a woman out."

"A real gentleman, that's what you are, Santino," she said sarcastically.

"Living proof that chivalry is not dead."

"In your dreams. He in?"

"Yeah, he's here, but he's with somebody, so it might be awhile before he can see you." Santino smiled. "You might as well come outta those wet clothes." He looked around the room that was crowded with men. "I'm sure one of the guys would be happy to donate the shirt off his back for you, Sienna."

"As I said, Santino, in your fuckin' dreams," she replied on her way to the bar.

"What will it be?" the bartender asked.

"Glenlivet single malt. Make it a double."

"You got it," he said, handing her a towel she used to dry her hair.

Over thirty minutes later, Joey came out of the back of the social club with Rocco Vinatieri. Sienna motioned for Santino, and he came to see what she wanted.

"Change your mind about coming outta those clothes?"

"What's Rocco doing here?" Sienna wanted to know. He was a made man and a captain of his own crew. Sienna had known him for as long as she could remember.

"I don't know. Want me to ask him?"

"I'll find out for myself," she said, leaving the bar.

Rocco threw up his hands when he saw Sienna coming his way. "Sienna, come let me get a look at you."

"How are you, Rocco?"

"Okay for an old man." He hugged her.

"You're not old, Rocco."

"Bullshit." He broke their embrace. "I've been young, and I can tell you for a fact that this ain't it." He shook hands with Joey. "About to get outta here before this guy starts busting my balls. It was good to see you, Sienna." He turned to Joey. "We'll talk about that thing tomorrow."

"Sure thing," Joey said as Rocco left the club. "What can I do for you, Sienna?"

"I need to talk."

Joey extended his hand toward the rear of the club. "What are you drinking?" he asked when they entered his office.

"Glenlivet single malt."

"What can I do for you?" Joey said as he poured.

"I need to ask you a question."

"What's that?"

"Do I have a Mike Black problem?"

He came from behind the bar. "What makes you ask that?" He handed her the drink.

"I was hoping for a definite answer."

"The answer is no, you don't have a Mike Black problem. And I still wanna know what makes you ask."

"In the last week, I've lost Drew Mack and Kevin Franklin."

"What do you mean 'lost'?"

"They're dead, Joey."

"And you think Black had something to do with it?"

"I don't know. That's why I'm asking." She sipped her drink. "Nick's son and his pretty boy sidekick came to see me."

"Marvin and Baby Chris. What they want?"

"They wanted to know if I had anything to do with Wanda Moore getting shot and her husband murdered."

"I wouldn't worry about that. If Mikey really thought you were involved in that, you'd be dead."

"How can you be so sure?"

"Because I asked him."

"You asked him if he had Drew Mack and Kevin Franklin killed?"

"No. I asked him if he had a problem with you."

"And?"

"And he said that he is the least of your problems."

"What's that supposed to mean?"

"What that means is that you got your hands full between Kendrick Nance and Bautista's strike team."

"Then who's murdering my people?"

"My guess is that it's Nance." Joey stood up. That told Sienna that he was done talking to her. "Mikey and them are focused on finding out who shot Wanda. I guarantee you, that is the only thing he's thinking about."

"You mean the shit they asked me at gunpoint if I was involved in?"

Joey chuckled and started for the door. "Like I said, if Mikey thought you had any hand in Wanda getting shot, Marvin would've clipped you when he walked in the door." He shook his head and opened the door for her to leave. "Wouldn't have been any talk."

"Okay, Joey. Thanks," she said, and he walked alongside her.

When she came out, Santino rushed to get an umbrella and escorted Sienna to her car.

"Thanks, Santino," she said as he held the door open for her to get in.

"Anything for you, Sienna," Santino said, closing her car door. "Sexy, fuckin' ass," he said as he went back inside the social club.

Chapter 31

Oranjestad, Aruba

The weather was the only thing that kept the Cessna Citation grounded, but at eight o'clock that following morning, Black and Fantasy boarded the jet. Jake landed at Queen Beatrix International Airport in Oranjestad, Aruba, six hours later. During the long flight, Black found Fantasy to be a brilliant conversationalist.

He had invested a lot in her, so he expected no less.

Erykah made reservations for two Ocean-Front Balcony Suites at the Renaissance Aruba Resort and Casino. Once they had checked into their suites, Black and Fantasy relaxed and enjoyed a fabulous seafood buffet lunch at Aquarius before setting out.

Since Black thought that it was more likely that what happened to Wanda and James had something to do with Fantasy's work, their first stop was the Xanadu Casino. She had reassumed the persona of Constance Phillmore, a personality that she had created when she infiltrated the Walsh campaign in New York. She had chosen it because being a former political insider gave her credibility with Reynelle Rocio and Arturo Gael, who ran the human trafficking operation and had the ear of Ignacio Tomas, the head of the organization.

She wore a Zimmermann Vitali yoke blouse and Vitali floral belted scallop-trim shorts, an appropriate outfit for the very conservative Constance Phillmore. It didn't take long for her to be noticed by Armando Cruz, who knew her from her infiltration of the organization. He was there with Joaquín Alejandro.

"Who is he?" Black asked as they sipped cocktails.

"He was Tomas's number one guy. Now, he runs things. I never interacted with Alejandro, but I know he was aware of the relationships I forged with Reynelle Rocio and Arturo Gael."

Black watched as Cruz discreetly pointed Fantasy out to Alejandro. "We have, or I should say, *you* have their attention."

Fantasy looked directly into his eyes and nodded in acknowledgment. "There is no polite way to say this," she said. "Armando is a vulgar, disgusting, masochistic asshole."

"Yes, but tell me how you *really* feel about him," Black chuckled.

"Every time he would see me, he would ask if he could have sex with me in the most disgusting ways." She shook her head. "And I would ask him if that approach actually worked on other women."

"What would he say?"

"He would just find another disgusting way to ask to have sex with me," Fantasy said as Armando stood up, buttoned his jacket, and started toward them.

"We're about to find out if there are any hard feelings," Black said.

"Yes, Mr. Black, we are. However, I would feel much better about this encounter if we were armed."

"Honestly, I would too."

"Hello, Constance," Cruz said when he reached their table.

"How are you, Armando?"

"I haven't seen you in a while," Cruz said and sat down.

"I decided to go back to New York for a while."

"What brings you back to the island?"

"I'm accompanying my employer. Armando Cruz, Mike Black."

"I thought so." Cruz nodded because he knew that he had seen Black before. Jada's operation on the island and in Oranjestad, in particular, was not only vast but also strong, so the name Mike Black carried weight on the island. "It is good to meet you, Mr. Black."

Black shook his hand. "Good to meet you, Mr. Cruz."

Mr. Cruz looked at Fantasy. "I didn't know you worked for him."

"Why would you know who I work for? And why would that be any business of yours?"

"Right. Mr. Alejandro would like to talk to you," Cruz said, and then he stood there waiting for Black and Fantasy to stand. "Didn't you hear what I said?"

"I heard you," Black said, but he didn't move. "I don't want to talk to Mr. Alejandro. Constance, do you want to talk to Mr. Alejandro?"

"No, not really. I have nothing to speak about with Mr. Alejandro. If Mr. Alejandro wants to talk to me, he must get up and walk over here just like you did."

Cruz looked indignantly at Black and then at Fantasy before he walked away.

They sat and watched as Cruz returned to the table where Alejandro was seated. He listened to what Cruz said, and then he smiled. He stood up, buttoned his jacket, and approached.

"Mr. Black. Forgive me for being rude. My name is Joaquín Alejandro. May I sit?"

"Please do," Black said and graciously extended his arm. Alejandro sat down but when Cruz reached for a chair, Alejandro looked sternly at him, and Cruz moved his hand.

"It is an honor to meet you, Mr. Black. I am," he paused to think about how he wanted to put it, "a business acquaintance of Jada West, and she always speaks very highly of you."

"It is an honor to meet you as well."

Alejandro turned his attention to Fantasy. "And you are Constance Phillmore."

"Yes, Mr. Alejandro. We've never been formally introduced."

"You are good friends with Reynelle Rocio and Arturo Gael."

"I am. I was hoping to see Reynelle here. However, I don't see her."

"It has been some time since I've seen her around." Alejandro looked around and then signaled for a server.

"Shame what happened to Arturo and Mr. Tomas," Fantasy said.

"Things didn't turn out so bad for Arturo. I understand he is cooperating with the FBI," he said as the server arrived. "Can I get you another drink, Mr. Black?"

"Rémy Martin Tercet."

"And for you, Ms. Phillmore?"

"I'll have the same, thank you."

"And for you, Mr. Alejandro?"

"Bring me a Magic Mango," he said, and the server left the table. "What brings you to our island, Mr. Black?"

"Business, mostly. I haven't been here in a while, but a very good friend and business associate spent a lot of time on the island and told me how much it had changed since my last visit. Perhaps you know her. Her name is Wanda Moore."

"I don't believe I've had the pleasure of meeting her." He glanced at Cruz, who shook his head because Wanda's name wasn't familiar to him either.

"Then I'm sure you're not familiar with an attorney named James Austin?"

He leaned forward. "I try as hard as I can *not* to need to know a lot of lawyers," Alejandro joked.

"They do prove their value when you need them," Black said as the server returned to the table with their drinks. He placed the glasses of Rémy in front of Black and Fantasy and then the bottle of Magic Mango, an Aruban beer, on the table.

"I've intruded long enough." Alejandro stood and picked up the bottle. "I just wanted to introduce myself and tell you that if there is anything that you need while you are on my island, please don't hesitate to ask. Ms. Phillmore will know how to reach me."

"I imagine I can reach you through Mr. Tomas," Fantasy said, and Alejandro smiled.

"Ignacio Tomas was extradited to Miami last week due to the treachery of your friend Arturo Gael."

"I was unaware."

"Most unfortunate. However, you can reach me through those same channels," Alejandro said, walking away with Cruz.

"Observations?" Black asked.

"First and foremost, I do not believe they have any involvement in what happened to Ms. Moore and Mr. Austin."

"I agree." One of the things that Black prided himself on was his ability to read people. "He never heard of Wanda or James. Anything else?"

"He wanted to be sure that you understood this was *his* island."

"I picked up on that too."

"And he wanted to point out and make clear that Arturo was *my* friend."

"Seems that he benefited from that. That last bit about how you can reach him was so we know that he took Tomas's spot and runs things now." Black shot his drink. "Unless something happens to change it, I'm satisfied that what you were doing wasn't the reason they got shot." Black stood up. "Let's see if we can get an appointment with David Efrem."

Later that afternoon, when Black and Fantasy arrived at the offices of Private Investment and Equity Solutions, they were told that Efrem was in a meeting and were given an appointment to return at six thirty that evening.

"Six thirty it is," Black said, and he left the office with Fantasy and returned to the Renaissance Aruba Resort.

They were at Papagayo, a beachfront bar & grill in the hotel, having cocktails when Black got a call from Carla.

"I was able to decrypt the file."

"What was he working on with Efrem?"

"According to the file, David Efrem and somebody named Hans Schubert were accused of conspiring to launder $3.6 billion in bitcoins that were stolen from a company called Digital Asset Management's platform after a hacker breached the Digital Asset Management system. The hacker initiated more than 2,000 unau-thorized transactions that were sent to a digital wallet under Efrem and Schubert's control over five years via a complicated money-laundering process. The stolen funds were deposited into financial accounts."

"That's enough to get somebody killed."

"The file also contained the private keys required to access the digital wallet that directly received the stolen funds."

"What was James's involvement?"

"He and Efrem are old friends from college, so James was advising him on what he should do after the criminal complaint was filed."

"What was that about?"

"The criminal complaint alleged that Efrem and Schubert employed numerous sophisticated laundering techniques, including using fictitious identities to set up online accounts utilizing computer programs to automate transactions. It's a laundering technique that allows for many transactions to take place in a short period of time. They also deposited the stolen funds into accounts at various virtual currency exchanges and darknet markets and then withdrew the funds," Carla informed him.

"How'd they leave it?"

"James recommended that Efrem cooperate with the investigation. The case goes to trial next month."

"What do you think?" Black asked.

"I don't see it."

"Reason?"

"Why now? Although the case is going to trial next month, according to his notes, all that happened over a year ago. James had nothing to do with the money-laundering scheme, and he is not defending him at the trial, so I see no reason for them to go after James." Carla paused. "Sorry, Mike, I just don't."

"I don't either." Black exhaled. "Thank you, Carla."

"I'll keep digging if you want, but—"

"No need. I mean, if something jumps out at you, but I don't see it either."

"Sorry, Mike."

"That's all right, Carla. I'll talk to you when we get back." Black ended the call and looked at Fantasy. "You heard that?"

"The important part. Neither you nor Carla sees that there is any connection between Efrem's money-laundering scheme and Mr. Austin's murder. What now?"

"Unless you have a reason to hang around here, we might as well head back to New York."

"I have nothing else," Fantasy said.

Once they finished their drinks, Black and Fantasy returned to their suites. Neither had taken the time to unpack. Therefore, all they needed to do was to get their bags ready to leave. They agreed to meet at Fresco, an Italian restaurant in the hotel, before heading to the airport. They had just about finished their meal when a man and a woman approached the table.

"Excuse me, are you Mike Black?" the man asked.

"Yes. I'm Mike Black."

"I'm Inspector George Walker, and this is Deputy Inspector Pamela Edwards."

"What can I do for you?"

"Would you mind coming with us?" Inspector Walker asked.

"And what reason would I have for doing that?" a defiant Black asked.

"We would like to speak with you about the murder of David Efrem," Deputy Inspector Edwards advised.

Black stood up. "Am I under arrest?"

"No, sir," Deputy Inspector Edwards said. "We just have some questions."

"After you," Black said.

"No, I insist," Deputy Inspector Edwards said. "After you."

Fantasy sat there and watched as the police escorted Black out of the restaurant. She quickly took out her phone and made a call.

"What can I do for you, Fantasy?" Jada asked.

"I'm in Oranjestad, Aruba, with Mr. Black, and the police just took him in connection to a murder."

"I'll be there as soon as possible," Jada said, ending the call.

Chapter 32

After losing ten good men when Black blew up the warehouse where they had set a trap for him, it was clear to Nance that he had to do something, or he'd look weak. At the same time, he knew that he wasn't trying to go to war with Black. Many had gone down that road, and they were all dead now. He was locked up when Rona King went hard at The Family. In the end, Rona was dead, and they were still standing. Therefore, his plan was simple: "One hard hit, and then let's talk."

Bullet and three of Nance's men, Wilson, Taylor, and Green, sat in separate cars outside of Romans. Their target for the night was Carter Garrison. The plan was to open fire at him as soon as he came out, but Bullet knew enough to realize that would be suicide.

"This is where them niggas hang out. We start shooting, and they all come out blasting."

"So, what's your plan?" Wilson wanted to know.

"We let him make it to his car and drive away from here, and then we take him," Bullet told Nance's men. So they waited.

Bullet and Taylor in a Chrysler 300, Wilson and Green in a Dodge truck, waited and watched Laquita Harris walk in Romans.

She had become a nightly fixture at Romans in the past few weeks. Laquita moved through the crowd of sports fans, thugs, and killers watching the Yankees on all the screens on her way to the office. She knocked on the door.

Geno opened it and then looked back at Carter, who was seated behind his desk.

"I'll talk to you about that tomorrow," he said, looking at Laquita. "Hello."

"Hi."

Geno stepped aside and allowed her to enter the office before closing the door behind him.

"Hello, Laquita."

"Hi," she said and walked toward the desk. Carter stood up, came around, and met her in front of the desk.

"You're late."

"I know. So I don't have much time."

"Take it out, Laquita," Carter ordered.

Without another word passing between them, Laquita dropped to her knees and hurried to unbuckle his pants. She fumbled with the zipper before pulling it down and grabbed a handful of dick. He unbuttoned her blouse, took off her bra, and cupped her tits. Her head drifted back as Carter leaned forward and sucked each hard nipple. He licked and made them hard before pulling back long enough to help her out of her skirt.

Laquita quickly moved things aside and jumped up on the desk. She leaned back on her elbows as Carter moved between her thighs and spread them apart. He leaned forward to kiss her gently. Laquita lifted her legs so that her knees were pressed against her chest, and Carter slid into her slowly.

"Oh shit," she moaned softly as his steady, hard, and deep thrusts moved her body back and forth on top of the desk.

"Take this dick," he said, and her pussy grabbed and released his dick.

He just kept pounding her, fucking her so hard that all she could do was hold on before they both collapsed on the desk, breathing heavily.

"That was good," Laquita said as Carter stood and pulled up his pants.

"It just wasn't enough," Carter said, handing Laquita her skirt.

"I'm sorry I was late. You know how much I look forward to this all day, but it couldn't be helped."

"No worries. As long as you made it," Carter said, and the fuck buddies straightened their clothes before leaving the office. They weaved their way through the crowd of gamblers, thugs, and killers, past the pizza counter, and out of Romans. Carter walked Laquita to her car.

"There he is," Wilson said and readied his weapons.

"Be patient," Bullet said and looked on as they approached the car.

Laquita raised her arm and unlocked the car. Carter opened the door for her when she turned quickly and threw her arms around his neck.

"See you tomorrow," she said and kissed him. "And yes, I'll be on time."

"If it couldn't be helped," Carter kissed her, "it couldn't be helped."

After one last, long, passionate kiss, Laquita got into her car, and Carter closed the door. She started the car and then rolled down the window.

"I was thinking about leaving work early, so we have more time. Maybe even get a room where we could stretch out and really do some things."

Carter chuckled. "Sounds good. All you gotta do now is get off early."

"I just might surprise you one night."

"I like surprises," he replied as she rolled up her window and drove away.

Carter stood there and watched as Laquita drove home to her husband until she was out of sight. He turned and headed for his car, thinking that married women were all he wanted to be bothered with these days.

They knew what they wanted: some different dick.

They show up and do what they came to do: fuck.

Then they leave and take their problems, issues, and complaints home to their husbands.

It was another by-product of what he had come to call "The Rain Robinson Experience." It had shaken him to his core when she abruptly ended their sex life, all but stopped speaking to him, and then told him she was pregnant with his baby before she cut him off completely. It left him feeling like he didn't want to be bothered with women—any women—at all. But he still wanted to fuck them, so it had been all about the married women who weren't interested in a relationship. It was all that was on his menu for the foreseeable future.

Carter got into his Cadillac and headed for Major Deegan when the two cars closed in on him, and the shooting began. He looked in his rearview mirror and saw a blue Dodge truck coming up on his right and a Chrysler 300 on the left. Carter sped up and opened the window to fire back wildly at his pursuers, but they kept coming. He weaved through traffic, but they started shooting again once the Dodge and the Chrysler 300 got close enough. Carter gripped the steering wheel tight and dodged several cars before entering the intersection.

"Romans, this is Barry. How can I help you?"

"This Rain, I'm on my way up there, and I want two slices with sausage, bacon chunks, and extra cheese."

"You want a grape Nehi too?"

"You know I do. You want anything, Alwan?"

"Naw, I'm good."

"I'll have it ready for you when you get here, Rain," Barry promised, and she ended the call in time to see the cars speeding in the opposite direction.

"Wasn't that Carter's car?" Alwan asked as the Dodge truck and the Chrysler 300 stayed on his tail and kept firing.

"Yeah, go after them," she shouted, and Alwan made a U-turn that nearly caused an accident.

The light at the coming intersection turned red, and traffic began to slow down in front of them. But Carter sped up and fired a few more shots at his pursuers just as a car that was speeding through the intersection slammed into him. The Cadillac went into a spin and crashed into another vehicle coming through the intersection.

The Chrysler and Dodge came to a screeching halt in front of the wrecked car. Bullet and Taylor, as well as Wilson and Green, exited their vehicles, armed with AK-47s. Although he was dazed by the crash and his chest hurt like a muthafucka from the deployment of the airbags, Carter had the presence of mind to grab his guns and get out of the vehicle. As Nance's men opened fire and civilians ran for cover, Carter made it behind a car.

He rose up and tried to get off a shot, but he was seriously outgunned and quickly dropped back behind the car. He crawled to the front of the car and opened fire with both guns, then promptly dropped back behind the vehicle. Carter returned fire until his guns were empty, and he dropped down for cover, thinking that he was about to die as the shots bounced off the wall in front of him.

Just then, Carter heard another car come to a screeching halt, and suddenly, the shooting began again, but this time, it wasn't coming in his direction. He peeked over the hood of the car and saw Rain firing at Taylor until one of her guns was empty, and he went down. He saw Wilson coming around the car, and then he saw Alwan raise his weapon and fire three times. Each shot hit Wilson, and he fell on the hood of the vehicle.

Bullet kept firing at Carter, keeping him pinned behind the car. Rain opened fire again, and the shot hit Bullet in the back of the head. Finally, the shooting stopped, and Rain rushed behind the car to check on Carter.

"You all right?"

"No. Every bone in my body hurts."

"Did you get hit?"

"No."

"Can you walk?"

"I think so," Carter said. Rain tried to help him up when they heard the sound of police activity moving in their direction.

"We gotta go, Rain," Alwan said.

"Help me get him up," Rain ordered.

"No. Alwan is right. You need to get outta here."

"I'm not leaving you. Come on, Alwan."

"No, Rain. You go with Alwan. I can handle the cops." He let out a little laugh. "I need to go to the hospital anyway."

"Get his guns, Alwan," Rain ordered, and once he had them, she said, "We'll see you at the hospital." Then she rushed away with Alwan.

Chapter 33

Oranjestad, Aruba

Following his detention by the Aruba Police Force, Black was taken to a holding cell with other inmates, and that was where he remained for the rest of the night. It was early the following day when an officer came to his cell.

"Mike Black."

Black stood up and came to the bars. He put his hands through the bars so he could be handcuffed.

"Come with me," the officer said and unlocked the cell.

He was taken to an interrogation room, where he was cuffed to the table and left alone. Thirty minutes later, Inspector George Walker and Deputy Inspector Pamela Edwards entered the room.

"Good morning, Mr. Black. I'm Inspector Walker, and this is Deputy Inspector Edwards."

"I remember. I also remember you saying I was not under arrest, yet I've been here all night."

"On behalf of the Aruba Police Force, please accept my apologies. It couldn't be helped," Inspector Walker said.

"As I said, we just have a few questions that we'd like to ask you in connection with David Efrem," Deputy Inspector Edwards said.

"Before we start, would you like an attorney present during questioning?"

"Why? Do I need one?"

Walker and Edwards glanced at each other, but neither answered directly. "Are you familiar with David Efrem?"

"I know the name, but we've never met."

"What was the nature of the relationship between you and Mr. Efrem?" Inspector Walker asked.

"It was or would have been a business relationship. He was referred to me by James Austin, one of my attorneys."

"You had an appointment with him last night at six thirty?" Deputy Inspector Edwards said.

"That's right."

"What did the two of you discuss?"

"We didn't discuss anything because I canceled the appointment."

Once again, Walker and Edwards glanced at each other. "Why did you cancel the appointment?" Inspector Walker asked.

"Who did you speak to?" Deputy Inspector Edwards questioned.

Black grinned at Edwards. "I canceled the appointment because I received information that made the meeting unnecessary. And I didn't speak to anybody. There was no answer when I called, so I left a message."

"What time was this?" she inquired.

"About five."

"Let's get back to the nature of your business with Mr. Efrem," Inspector Walker said when there was a knock at the door, and another officer entered the room. He leaned in and whispered something to Walker. "Why?"

The officer shrugged his shoulders and left the interrogation room.

"What?" Deputy Inspector Edwards asked.

Walker reached into his pocket and got out his keys. He uncuffed Black.

"You're free to go, Mr. Black."

"Why?" Deputy Inspector Edwards asked, and Walker whispered something to her. "This bites," she said as Black rubbed his wrists and stood up.

"Please escort Mr. Black to the cage to get his belongings."

She bounced up angrily. "Yes, sir," she said, and although she didn't like it, she did as she was told.

Once he had collected his belongings, Black went into the lobby at the Aruba Police Station and was surprised but not shocked to see Jada West sitting on a bench, elegantly and totally overdressed for her surroundings in an Erdem Sage embroidered floral midi-dress and Jimmy Choo Saeda 100 crystal-embellished pumps.

"Good morning, Mr. Black."

"Good morning, Ms. West. I take it that I have you to thank for the abrupt end to the interrogation?" Black extended his hand for Jada to get up.

"Yes, Mr. Black, you do." She looped her arm in his, and they left the police station. "I had a little chat with Roland Rasmin, who is the chief commissioner."

"And a client, I take it," Black commented as they approached the limo. The driver opened the door.

"One of our *better* clients."

"I'm going to assume that I am not a suspect since they gave me back my passport."

"Of course not. I assured the chief commissioner that you could not have possibly had anything to do with a murder."

"Thank you, Jada."

"My pleasure. I had just returned to Nassau when Fantasy called, so I came immediately. Had I still been in New York, you would still be a guest of the fine men and women of the Aruban police department."

"Thank you again, Jada."

"Were you able to ascertain whether Fantasy's involvement with the traffickers was responsible for Wanda and James?"

"I'm fairly confident that it didn't. And I'm basing that on instinct and the reception that Fantasy and I got from the new regime."

"You've trusted your instincts this long, and they have served you well."

"They have. I just hope that I'm right. But tell me what you know about Joaquín Alejandro."

"There is no polite way to say this," Jada shook her head, and a look of revulsion spread across her face. "The man is an absolute pig. Only certain ladies will have anything to do with him, and they tend to charge him triple for their services."

"I see."

"However, if he thought that Wanda had any involvement in Arturo Gael speaking with the FBI and Ignacio Tomas being arrested, he would have made that known."

"That was my assessment as well," Black said as the limo pulled up in front of the Renaissance Aruba Resort and Casino. The driver got out and opened Black's door. "You're not coming in?"

"I have a pressing matter that I must deal with here on the island. But I will join you this afternoon. Perhaps we can have lunch?"

"That would be excellent," Black said and exited the limo.

After watching Jada drive off, Black entered the hotel and returned to his suite. Once he showered and changed clothes, he called Fantasy.

"You're free."

"Yeah, Jada got me out. Thank you for calling her."

"I know that Ms. West has great influence here on the island. An influence that I would not be able to wield effectively. Fortunately, she had returned to Nassau and could come right away."

"Yes, otherwise, I'd probably still be there." Black paused. "Have you eaten yet today?"

"I had coffee and grapefruit this morning after I ran."

"Would you like to join me for drinks at Solé at poolside? Ms. West said that she'd be back to have lunch."

"I'll meet you at Solé in about twenty minutes," Fantasy promised.

"See you there."

Black hung up the house phone. He reached into his bag and took out the satellite phone.

"This Rain."

"It's Mike. What's going on up there?"

"Carter had a little problem I'll tell you about, but other than that, everything has been quiet since you left. You find out anything?"

"No, but I'm convinced that Fantasy's secret mission wasn't the reason for the hit."

"I checked with Carla, and she said nothing was going on at the bank that she can point to."

"Who did Kirk and Dawkins talk to at the funeral?"

"He talked to James's ex-wife and Garry Amarantos."

"Who's that?"

"He's a partner in the firm. And before you ask, I got Carla digging into him."

"Look into the ex-wife too."

"I'll get her right on that."

"You talk to Bobby?"

"Last night. He said that the doctor wanted to continue the coma for another couple of days, and she told him that the swelling was going down."

"That's good to hear."

"Everything else good down there?"

"I got arrested last night."

"You bullshittin'?"

"No."

"Can't stay outta trouble," she laughed. "What they lock you up for?"

"I'll tell you about it when I see you."

"When you coming back?"

"We were gonna leave last night before I got arrested." Black chuckled. "But we should be back sometime tomorrow. I'll let you know what time."

"You want me to meet you?"

"No. I'll talk to Bobby before then. He can pick me up. I'll call you when I get on the ground."

"Talk to you later," Rain said, and they ended the call. Then Black left the room to meet Fantasy for drinks at Solé.

"By the way, how did your chat with Jada go?" Black asked Fantasy over drinks when they saw Jada coming toward the table.

"It didn't. When I arrived, Ms. West had another engagement, so I was asked to reschedule for the following day, but that was not to be either because I made this trip with you."

"Unfortunate. But I will ensure the conversation occurs before we leave the island."

"Thank you, Mr. Black."

When Jada sat down at the table, she suggested they leave the hotel and have genuine Peruvian cuisine at Asi Es Mi Peru, a local restaurant she'd become fond of. She recommended they try the Sudado de Pescado and Pescado a lo Macho while she had the Escabeche de Pescado. They were nearly finished with their meal when Black picked up his glass and turned to Jada.

"I understand it's my fault that you ladies haven't had an opportunity to speak."

Jada put down her fork and dabbed the corners of her mouth. "Yes, Mr. Black." She picked up her drink. "We were scheduled to talk, and then you whisked her away."

"I was hopeful we could have that conversation before I returned to New York with Mr. Black."

"I am quite sure that could be arranged." Jada put down her cocktail and stood up. "Would you excuse me?"

"Of course," Black said, and he and Fantasy rose.

While Jada was away from the table, Black saw Bruna De Souza enter the restaurant wearing a Carolina Herrera floral cutout strapless midi-dress. She waved flirtatiously when she saw him.

"If you don't mind me asking, who is that?"

"That is Bruna De Souza with Global Technology Insights. She's the one who told me about Efrem."

"What is she doing here?"

"I don't know."

"That is quite the coincidence." Fantasy picked up her drink. "Her having a late lunch here."

"I don't believe in coincidences." Black waved and invited her to join them because he had a question. "What brings you to Aruba?"

"I have a client here on the island. And when I heard that Efrem was murdered, I came right away," she said as Jada returned to the table. The way that Bruna was looking at Black made Jada feel some kind of way.

"Am I interrupting something? I hope so," she said and reclaimed her seat at the table.

"No," Black said quickly.

"Bruna De Souza with Global Technology Insights," she said with her hand extended toward Jada.

"Jada West."

"I was just telling Mr. Black that I had a client here on the island, and when I heard that Mr. Efrem was murdered, I came right away."

"Who is your client, if you don't mind me asking?" Black enquired.

"Hans Schubert."

It raised an eyebrow for Black because he remembered from Carla's report that the name Hans Schubert was involved with Efrem in the money-laundering scheme. It left him to wonder if she had dropped her client's name to gauge his reaction, and then she answered his question.

"I was wondering if you had an opportunity to speak with Mr. Efrem or Mr. Schubert?"

"Unfortunately, no. Mr. Efrem was murdered before I had an opportunity to talk to him. I wasn't aware that Mr. Schubert was somebody that I needed to talk to, Ms. De Souza."

"Bruna, please," she flirted, and both Jada and Fantasy rolled their eyes.

"As I said, I wasn't aware that Mr. Schubert was somebody that I needed to talk to. Perhaps if you have time, you could tell me what I need to know regarding Efrem's involvement and how it relates to Mr. Schubert."

Bruna looked nervously at her watch, and then her smile returned. "How much longer do you plan on being on the island?"

"I don't know. I'll leave sometime tonight or tomorrow."

"Where are you staying?"

"The Renaissance Resort."

"I'm meeting associates for lunch, but I am certain that we can set aside some time to talk," Bruna said as a man and a woman entered Asi Es Mi Peru. She acknowledged their presence. "That's them now." She stood up. "But I will contact you at the hotel this evening."

"Sounds good," Black said and rose. He shook her hand. "Enjoy your meal."

He looked at Jada and Fantasy as Bruna De Souza walked away from the table. "There is something about that woman that rubs me the wrong way," Jada said and stood up.

Black glanced at Bruna as she sat down with her associates. She waved when she saw him looking.

"Do you trust her?" Fantasy asked as they followed Jada out of the restaurant.

"No, Fantasy, I don't trust her at all."

Chapter 34

Jackson Hill had finally reached the spot where he always saw himself. He had raised himself up from a chilly pimp that had to beat his one ho to get her to do what he wanted to a boss who had a stable of twenty hoes working out of two locations and a crew of crackhead streetwalkers. He had branched out into gambling at both spots and wanted to expand. And now that Sienna had put the product in his hands, Jackson knew that the world had opened up for him, and this was just the beginning.

"I was nobody, came from nowhere. Ain't nowhere to go from here but up," he said aloud as he tried out the newest edition to his stable. She dropped and knelt in between his thighs.

"And I'ma be right there with you," she said and stroked his dick before pulling him into her hot mouth. His hands went to her head, encouraging her to go with his flow.

"Top of the world," he shouted.

She licked and sucked that dick in and out her mouth until she gagged. Jackson pulled up her head to allow her to regain control. Then he tapped her on top of her head.

"Concentrate."

He eased her head down, and she put that dick back into her mouth as he grabbed her hair with both hands and guided her head.

"You gonna be a good, dick-sucking ho for your daddy, ain't you?"

"Yes, daddy."

"Say it."

"I'm gonna be a good, dick-sucking ho for you, daddy," she all but sang and took it to the back of her throat once again.

She kept her eyes locked on his as she felt him begin to swell in her mouth. Jackson came, and she swallowed his cum. Then she took his twitching dick out of her mouth.

"That was good. Now get out and go make me some money."

"Yes, daddy," she said and exited the car.

Once she was out and had walked back to her corner, his three bodyguards got in the Jeep Wagoneer that he had just paid cash for. Jackson may have thought he was on top of the world, but his eyes were wide open. In the last couple of weeks, he had seen the Mack brothers and Kevin Franklin get murdered, and he had no plans on being the next one.

With them getting popped, it created opportunities for him. It only took an hour after he heard that Franklin was dead before Jackson showed up at the gambling houses that he had taken when Dorsey went to prison and forced his way in. He had reached out to and was doing business with what was left of the G-40s. Now that the Mack brothers were dead and the BBKs had all but vanished from the streets, the G-40s had gotten bold and were taking back what was once theirs.

"Where you wanna go now, Jax?"

"Let's hit the gambling spot and then take it to the house. Everybody getting some pussy tonight," he shouted, and his men joined in.

Their first stop was the gambling spot that Julia Dorsey ran. She was his partner until he went to prison for possession. Then Kevin Franklin showed up and pushed his way in. At least he was smart enough to know that he didn't know shit about running a gambling club and let her run it how she saw fit. But he was dead, and now, she had Jackson Hill and his goon squad to deal with, and they played rough. He too knew nothing about gambling. He was a pimp, and on their first meeting, he tried to treat her like one of his hoes. Julia called him a fuckin' fool, and he slapped the shit out of her.

"Nobody talks to me like that."

But then Jackson made the mistake of walking away and letting Julia get anywhere near her gun. With a gun in hand, she walked up to Jackson at the bar and put the gun to the back of his head.

"If you ever touch me again, you won't see it coming. I'll just blow your brains out."

"Take it easy now, sexy," Jackson said with his hands raised.

"Do we understand each other better now?"

"Yeah, sexy, we understand each other."

Julia pushed the gun to his head harder. "And don't call me sexy."

That established their relationship, and now she always carried her gun with her. But Jackson had only been there for a few days, and she was already planning how to get rid of him.

"What's up, Julia?" Jackson all but shouted when he and his men came into the office.

"Nothing," she replied and kept looking out of the two-way mirror at the club.

"Business looks good."

"It is."

Jackson went and stood next to her. "You know, if you gave it some effort, you'd find I ain't a bad guy."

Julia turned and looked at him like he was a fuckin' fool. "I gotta put up with you because Sienna says I have to. She said nothing about putting forth any effort to *like* you."

He walked away from the mirror. "I'm just saying." He sat behind her desk and put his feet up. "It would be easier for you to work with me if you were a little nicer."

"Fuck you, Jackson." She turned and faced him. "I'm not here trying to make it easier for you. And get your fuckin' feet off my fuckin' desk," she said, and Jackson's men chuckled until he looked in their direction. However, he took his feet off the desk and stood up.

"You need anything from me?"

"Never gonna." Julia turned around and returned to staring out at the club, wondering if it would ever be just her club.

"Then we out," Jackson said, leaving the office with his men.

"Muthafucka," Julia said when the door slammed.

After making their way through the spot, Jackson and his men returned to the Jeep.

"Where you wanna go now, Jax?"

"Take it to the house."

"Everybody getting some pussy tonight!" one of his men shouted, and the other men joined in the excitement.

When Jackson's phone rang, he looked at the display and saw that Sienna was calling. "Y'all kill that noise," he shouted over the music and enthusiasm for getting their choice of women for the night. "What's up, Sienna?"

"I need to see you."

"Where you at?"

"I'm at my apartment."

"I got a couple of stops that I need to make, and then I'll be through there."

"No, Jackson. I'm calling you now because I want to see you now. Not in two or three hours. *Now*."

"See you in twenty minutes," he said angrily, ending the call.

That white bitch gonna fuck around and make me put a bullet in her brain.

"Roll me by Sienna's," he said, which killed the enthusiasm.

When they arrived at Sienna's building, they parked in the garage, got out, and walked to the elevator. He didn't know what Sienna wanted but hoped she'd be quick about it. Jackson stood behind his men, waiting impatiently for the elevator doors to open. When that happened, Jackson saw the woman standing there . . . with her silencer-clad weapon raised.

"Oh, shit," Jackson said and ran.

She fired three shots. Each shot hit one of Jackson's men in the head. She leaped over them and went after Jackson. He turned and fired several shots wildly on the run and didn't come close to hitting anything. When he got to the Jeep, he reached into his pocket and pulled out the keys. But before he could press the button to unlock the door, his pursuer stopped, assumed a firing position, and pulled the trigger.

The bullet hit Jackson in the neck, and blood sprayed from the wound. He grabbed his neck and fell to his knees, looked up, and saw her walking toward him. He tried to raise his weapon, but she began firing as she walked, hitting him with five shots to the chest.

Chapter 35

It was well after two in the morning when Jake was cleared to take off from Queen Beatrix International Airport. Black sat in the cabin looking out the window as Jake lined up the aircraft with the runway before accelerating to full power. He taxied down the runway and then accelerated to an airspeed that provided sufficient lift for the jet to become airborne.

Once Jake reached cruising altitude, Black got up, fixed himself a drink, and reclaimed his seat. Earlier in the evening, he did have an opportunity to speak with Bruna De Souza. She reached out, and they met for drinks at Blue, an open-air bar in the hotel renowned for its Blue Martinis.

"I don't see why you want to speak with her when you already know what she's going to tell you," Jada told him when he was getting ready to meet Bruna. They had been sitting on the balcony of her suite, talking.

"I'm sure she'll have something interesting to say that I didn't know. You wanna come with me?"

"I certainly do *not* want to go with you."

"Good. Then you have time to talk to Fantasy." Black paused and smiled at Jada.

"Why are you smiling at me like that?"

"Because you're going to talk to Fantasy, and you already know what she wants to talk to you about."

"Touché." Jada stood up and went back into the suite. Black followed her in. "Has she talked to you?"

"No. But that doesn't mean I don't know what she wants, and so do you."

"And what might that be?"

"She's finished with Wanda, and now, she's ready to do something else. But like I said, you already know that."

"I do."

"And?"

Jada walked to the door and opened it. "And we'll see how it goes."

"I'll let you know how it goes with Ms. De Souza," Black said as he passed Jada.

"And I will let you know how it goes with Fantasy," she said as he walked down the hall.

When Black arrived at Blue, Bruna was already there waiting for him. She stood up and waved when she saw him come in. She had selected a black and gold Naeem Khan embroidered strapless midi-dress, and her feet were adorned in a cute pair of Platino Prada leather slingback logo pumps. As he walked toward her, Black took a second or two to acknowledge that Bruna De Souza was not only a very attractive woman but also a very attractive woman who was openly, if not discreetly, flirting with him. It caused him to think briefly about Susan Beason and how she moved him in ways that only Shy and Jada West had in the past.

Which is why you stay away from her, he thought and thought about the commitment, the unbreakable bond, and the intense love he had for Shy and what that meant to him.

Monogamy is hard.

"Hello, Mr. Black."

"How are you tonight, Ms. De Souza?"

She put her hands on her hips. "Bruna. Please, call me Bruna," she giggled, and that made him think back to the days when Jada's giggle made him want to be deep inside her. He shook it off.

"Mind if I sit?"

"Please do," Bruna said, signaling for a server as they sat down.

"How did your lunch meeting with your associates go?"

"Not well, to be honest with you. I'm anxious to conclude my business here on the island and return to New York."

"What can I get for you, sir?" the server asked when she arrived at their table.

"Rémy Martin neat, XO, if you have it."

"We do. And another Cranberry-Jalapeno Martini for the lady?"

"Please."

"I'll be back with those shortly," the server said, walking away from the table.

"So, while we're waiting on our drinks, why don't you tell me what you haven't told me about Hans Schubert and David Efrem?"

"I mentioned that I had a client on the island."

"You did."

"Mr. Schubert is my client."

Her head dropped to her chest, and her hair drifted across her face. Then Bruna raised her head and slung her hair back.

"I assumed as much."

"For several years, five to be exact, and without my knowledge, of course, Mr. Schubert and Mr. Efrem conspired to launder the proceeds of stolen bitcoin."

"Is that what James was involved in, money laundering?"

"No. Efrem and James were friends from college, and he went to James for advice."

"That's good to know," Black said as the server returned with their drinks and quickly disappeared. "What happened?"

"I'm not sure how they got caught, but the courts authorized a search warrant for their online accounts. FBI special agents obtained access to files in an online account controlled by Hans, and the agents were able to seize and recover more than 94,000 bitcoins."

"Not being well versed in bitcoin valuation, I'm curious about how much money that is."

"The recovered bitcoin was valued at over $3.6 billion."

"That's enough to get somebody killed," Black said and sipped his drink. "But you say James wasn't heavily involved in that, right?"

"Not on any level. He was just trying to help out an old friend." Bruna sipped her martini. "I have a question, and please feel free to tell me that it is none of my business."

"Trust me, I will."

"You're not, by any definition of the word, a cop?"

Black chuckled. "No, I'm not."

"But yet, you are here trying to solve a murder."

"I wouldn't put it like that."

"How would you put it?"

"I am trying to find out who's responsible for a lifelong friend getting shot and in a coma."

Bruna picked up her glass and leaned forward quickly. "What will you do to the responsible party if and when you find him?" She sat back. "And yes, that was the part where you could feel free to say, 'Bruna, you need to mind your business.'"

"I plan to turn them over to a detective I know to face justice."

"From all I've learned about you, that answer surprises me." She paused. "But then again, it doesn't."

"How much do you think you know about me?"

"Only what I've read online."

"You shouldn't believe everything you read on the internet."

"I don't. I take it all with a grain of salt." Bruna picked up her glass and took it to her lips. "But according to what I read, you control one of New York City's most notorious criminal organizations."

"Honestly?"

"I'd appreciate it."

"Once upon a time, that was true. But now, I am a legitimate businessman."

It was then that Bruna's phone rang. "Excuse me. I need to take this." She swiped talk. "Bruna De Souza." She paused to listen to what the caller had to say. "Say that again, please." Bruna sat up straight. "Thank you for letting me know," she said, ending the call.

"Is everything all right?"

"No. Hans Schubert was just arrested for the murder of David Efrem, and I have to go."

"I understand."

Bruna finished her drink and rose to her feet. "I apologize for having to cut our evening short. I was looking forward to getting to know you better."

Black stood up. "Unfortunate, but I understand."

"How much longer are you going to be on the island?"

"I'm leaving tonight."

"Perhaps I'll call you when I return to the city."

"Perhaps you will."

"Have a safe flight," Bruna said and walked away, taking out her phone to make a call.

Black thought about something that Shy said to him. *If you are not doing anything to discourage her, all you're doing is encouraging her.*

As he looked out the window, he thought that perhaps he should have done something, said something to discourage Bruna, especially now since their business was concluded. Of course, there was the possibility that she might become a valuable business contact, but that was a stretch. The truth was that he had no more use for Bruna De Souza, so why not simply say, "No. Your calling me when you return to New York isn't a good idea because I am desperately in love with my wife."

But he left the door open for her, and Bruna will call when she returns to New York. He emptied the glass and got up to make another drink, thankful that she would have to get by Erykah, and that wasn't happening.

Black looked around the empty cabin and thought for a second or two about joining Jake in the cockpit. Fantasy did not make the trip back to New York with him. After Black left her suite to meet Bruna, Jada called Fantasy and asked her to come by to talk. When she reached the suite, Fantasy got right to what she wanted.

"I wanna come home, Jada. I wanna come home with you to Paraíso. I've enjoyed the work that I've done for Monika and the team, but I believe that my talents could be put to better use than they are on monitor duty."

"I cannot disagree with you. In that position, your unique skills are of no value." Jada paused and smiled. "I have to say that I have been very impressed by your work for Wanda and in the Walsh campaign for Mrs. Black. I have taken some pride in the small part that I played in the woman you've become."

"I am the woman that you made me to be."

"Are you?"

"Yes, Jada, I am."

Jada looked at Fantasy for a while without speaking. "Have you learned anything since our last conversation?"

"I have. When you left, and I went with Monika, I had a lot of time to think about what you said to me, why you said it, and why you were so disappointed in me. It wasn't just that my behavior was deplorable. It was that I had not ordered my priorities, and because of that, I was completely undisciplined, and I allowed my passion to dictate my actions. You trusted me to represent you in your absence, and I failed you."

"As I said to you that night, you weren't ready to represent me because I hadn't adequately prepared you. I'm the one that failed you because of my expectations. They were unrealistically high, and my judgment was far too rigid." Jada smiled. "As I tend to be at times. You had a lot more to learn."

"And now I am ready for you to teach me."

"Go pack your things, and I will explain to Mr. Black that you will return to Nassau with me."

Black had no problem with Fantasy going back to Nassau with Jada. In fact, he expected it. So he settled into his seat and relaxed for the six-hour flight back to New York.

Chapter 36

"This Rain."

"It's Rhianna."

"What's up?"

"I'm here with Billy Newton, and he says he got Kendrick Nance on the phone."

"What he want?"

"Says he wanted to sit down with Black."

Rain laughed. "Niggas love to scream peace after they start some shit."

Rhianna looked at Newton and shook her head. "They do, don't they?"

"Black's out of the country. Tell him that I'm the one he needs to be talking to."

"Tell him that it's Rain Robinson he needs to be talking to," Rhianna relayed.

"You need to meet with Rain Robinson," Newton told Nance, and he said, "That's fine. When and where?"

"He said that's fine and wants to know where and when."

"Tell him that I'm at Purple Rock," Rain said, and Rhianna relayed her response to Newton.

"He said he'll be there in an hour," Newton advised.

"He said he'll be there in an hour," Rhianna told Rain.

"Thanks, Rhianna."

"Anytime," she said and ended the call.

"What he say?" Dandridge demanded to know when Nance ended the call with Newton.

"I'm gonna meet Rain Robinson at Purple Rock in an hour."

"Rain Robinson?" Dandridge questioned.

"That makes sense," Poole commented. "She runs things for him now."

"So, no sit-down with Black, huh?" Dandridge said. The look and sound of disgust were apparent.

"No," Nance said.

He was tired of Dandridge questioning his every move and knew that he would have to deal with him sooner or later. At that moment, Khalil came into the office at Ten Ninety-Seven.

"What's up?" he said to everybody and went and sat next to Nance. "I know why Black and Bobby wanted to talk to you."

"You gonna keep that shit a secret or what?" Nance asked.

Dandridge moved closer so he could hear what Khalil had to say.

"Wanda Moore and her husband got shot in a drive-by. He's dead, and she's in the hospital."

"And they think I had something to do with that?"

Khalil shook his head. "The way I get it was that they just wanted to talk until Ruffin and Davis took a shot at them." He looked at Dandridge.

Nance looked at Dandridge and pointed. "And then this asshole set a trap for them."

"I ain't gonna be the asshole too many more times," Dandridge said angrily.

"You'll be the asshole as long as you do asshole shit."

"So what you gonna do now that you know? Roll over for these muthafuckas?"

"Ain't nobody rolling over. I'm not rolling over for anybody. Bottom line is, fighting a war with these niggas is bad for business and manpower. Both of them are better spent pushing Kojo out than fighting Black."

"So, that's it? Fuck the men we lost; you just roll over for them. That shit ain't right," Dandridge said, and it was in that single second that he decided what he was going to do.

Meanwhile, at Purple Rock, Rain put down her phone and looked at Alwan.

"Nance wants to meet. They're coming here in an hour."

Alwan stood up. "We'll be ready for them."

"I saw RJ in here. If he's still here, tell him I wanna talk to him," Rain ordered, and Alwan went to get her men ready to receive Nance and deliver her message to RJ.

He didn't have to look that hard. RJ was still in the club with Mia Rubio. She had come there that night to see last season's *Breakout* winner, Roselyn Pierce. Mia had heard from some friends that Roz was tearing it up, and the crowd loved her. It was one part curiosity, one part rivalry, and one part jealousy that had Mia in the house that night.

"What's up, Rain?" RJ asked when he and Mia sat down at the table.

"Nance and his crew wanna talk. They're coming here in an hour."

RJ turned to Mia. "You need to leave."

"Why?" she asked as RJ stood up.

"Something might happen here that you don't need to have any part of. Now, come on," he said, and Mia stood up. He handed her his keys. "I'll walk you out." He nodded at Rain. "I'll be back."

She nodded and picked up her phone to call Jackie.

Once RJ had Mia safely in the car, he took out his phone.

"What's up, RJ?"

"Where you at, Money?"

"At Honey's. What's up?"

"I need you at Purple Rock. Nance wants to talk here in an hour."

"I'm coming," Marvin said, and he and Baby Chris left Honey's and headed for Purple Rock. RJ's next call was to Judah, and he said that he was on his way.

While RJ rounded up the troops at Purple Rock in anticipation of Nance's arrival, the tension between Nance and Dandridge continued to build at Ten Ninety-Seven.

"What mistake am I making?" Nance got in Dandridge's face to ask.

"Same mistake King made." Dandridge took a small step back.

"What he got to do with it?"

"I watched Robert bend over backward to stay outta Black's way. Fuckin' around with Mike Black is bad for your health. I heard him say that shit plenty of times."

"I remember him saying that shit too," Nance admitted, thinking that it was good advice.

"And what that shit get him, huh? What it get him? Robert King got shanked in prison on Mike Black's order—*that's* what it got him. Dead."

"What you think I should do? Go to war with them like Rona did? What did that dumb shit get her? Oh yeah, she's dead too."

"At least she wasn't weak."

"What you say, nigga?"

"I said you weak, nigga! Like her daddy and Ronnie were weak." Dandridge took out his gun. "And we don't need to be led by no weak muthafucka." He raised the gun and shot Nance in the face. Then he pointed the gun at Khalil. "You got a problem with that?"

"No problem." Khalil put up his hands. "It's all good."

"Anybody else got a problem or something to say?" Dandridge asked as he scanned the room, pointing his gun at each man as he made eye contact. "I didn't think so."

Khalil put down his hands. "So what you gonna do?"

"What I *ain't* gonna do is sit down with Rain Robinson."

"So what *are* you gonna do?" Khalil asked again.

Within the hour, Marvin and Baby Chris arrived at Purple Rock. Judah had arrived shortly before that. "It's been a minute since The Four Kings put in work together," he said, shaking hands with Marvin.

"Only three Kings. Pills ain't here."

"I think I got more claim to that title than Pills ever did," Baby Chris said boldly.

Marvin smiled because Baby Chris had made his case to him, and he agreed.

"What you mean?" RJ stepped to Baby Chris to ask.

"I mean, my father was a member of this Family. He wasn't no boss or even a captain. My father was a straight-up soldier."

"What you saying, BC?" Judah asked.

Baby Chris held up his hands. "I got nothing but respect for Pills, y'alls' friendship, and the work he put in. But if The Four Kings are the princes, the future kings of The Family, then I'm more of a prince in this family than Pills."

Judah nodded. "He's right. What you think, Money?"

"I think he's right too. He's been in my ear about this for a while. Besides, Pills ain't here."

"Probably won't be back either," Judah said, knowing that RJ had only heard from him twice in the year and a half that he'd been gone.

RJ held out his hand to Baby Chris. "Four Kings for life."

They shook hands as Marvin and Judah repeated, "Four Kings for life."

Now that that was settled, all there was to do was to wait for Nance to get there for his sit-down with Rain. By then, Jackie had sent Angel and Bowie and Axe and Press to Purple Rock. However, the time came and went without any sign of Nance. That didn't matter. Nobody left until well after the club had closed.

"I appreciate y'all coming, but it don't look like Nance and them gonna show," Rain said, and she walked out of Purple Rock with her soldiers.

Once they were outside, one by one, each came and said good night to the boss of The Family before heading to their car. As her soldiers drove off, Rain and Alwan were walking to her car when two motorcycles with riders armed with fully automatic Uzis rolled up on them and opened fire. They ran and made it to cover. Rain got out both of her guns and waited for an opportunity to fire back.

When the shooting stopped, she and Alwan returned their fire. The motorcycles rode off quickly, and Rain came out from cover blasting. One of her shots hit the helmet of one of the shooters, who fell off the bike. When the shooter saw Rain and Alwan coming, she took off her helmet and got up. She tried as best she could to escape but was in a lot of pain, so it didn't take Rain long to catch up with her.

"Stop right there!" Rain shouted with her guns raised.

The woman stopped and put up her hands.

"Turn around," Rain ordered, and she did as she was told. "Where's Nance?"

"Nance is dead. Dandridge is calling the plays now."

"That's fucked up." Rain shot her in the forehead.

Chapter 37

After flying all night, Jake landed the Cessna Citation at Westchester County Airport. When Black got off the jet, Bobby was waiting to pick him up. On the way to New Rochelle, they stopped at the hospital, where the doctor told them that Wanda was doing well and that if all continued to go well, she would bring her out of the coma soon. After that, Bobby took Black home. When they arrived at the house, Ronald passed them through the gate, and both men were surprised to see Rain's car parked in front of the house.

"That's not a good sign," Bobby said, pulling in behind her.

"I thought you said it was quiet while I was gone."

"It was when I went to sleep," Bobby said, exiting the car.

When they entered the house, Black heard Rain's voice coming from the dining room, so they went that way. Neither was surprised to find her at the table across from Shy, and they both had big plates of food in front of them. Because it was Rain, M went all out for breakfast. She cooked scrambled eggs with ham, mozzarella, and cheddar cheese, Belgian-style waffles with maple syrup, potato pancakes, sausage, bacon, and flaky and buttery croissants.

"Morning, ladies," Black said, and Shy got up to welcome her husband home. Rain kept eating. After a big hug and a passionate kiss, Shy sat back down and picked up her fork.

"That you, Michael?" M asked, coming out of the kitchen. "And Bobby."

"Hey, Miss Black."

"Hi, Ma." Black went and hugged his mother and kissed her on the cheek.

"Have you two eaten?"

Looking at Shy and Rain's plates, Bobby answered quickly. "No, and we're starving," he said and sat down at the table.

"We are?" Black asked and sat down at the table next to Shy.

"Yes, we are." Bobby looked at M. "I'll have what they're having."

Black looked at Rain, who still hadn't spoken because her mouth was full, and then at Shy. "Kids eat yet?"

Shy's mouth was full, so she just shook her head before replying, "No. My mother and Mansa are doing what they do," she began.

"What's that?" Bobby asked.

"Sleeping," Shy said. "I haven't seen or heard anything from Michelle and Eazy."

"Morning, everybody," Michelle said when she came dragging into the dining room. After hugging her father and mother, she was about to plop down in the chair next to Rain.

"Go let your grandmother know that you're up and then help her with your father and uncle's food," Shy said while she spread the strawberry jam on her croissant.

"Yes, Mommy," Michelle said and went into the kitchen.

"I hate to interrupt you, but what brings you to breakfast this morning?" Bobby asked, no longer able to contain his curiosity.

Rain held up one finger while she chewed. "Dandridge tried to kill me outside Purple Rock a few hours ago," she said as Michelle came back into the dining room with plates for Black and Bobby. Once she put their plates in front of them, she returned to the kitchen to get her food.

"Dandridge? What happened to Nance?" Bobby asked.

"He's dead. Dandridge killed him and took over."

"What did you do?" Black asked as Michelle came back into the dining room and sat down.

"Nothing yet. I knew Bobby was picking you up, so I came here."

"What's going on?" Michelle asked as she sat down.

Rain looked at Black before she answered. He nodded and started to eat. "Somebody tried to kill me."

"You know who it was?" she asked.

"I do."

"I see," Michelle said, nodded, and started eating.

When she and Rain finished eating, Shy said they were going to the media room and got up.

"We'll join you shortly," Black said and continued eating.

When they all were finished eating, Michelle cleared the table, and not wanting to miss anything, she came back quickly. Her father stood up when she came back into the dining room.

"Come on, Bob." Black looked at his daughter. "You too, Michelle," he said, and she followed them to the media room. Both Shy and Rain looked surprised when Michelle closed the door and sat down.

"So, what you gonna do?" Black asked.

Rain smiled. "The Empire is gonna strike back."

Later that night, Carla parked the new Mercedes-Benz Sprinter tactical van down the street from Ten Ninety-Seven. While Rain and Alwan got comfortable, she set up a platform that, using thermal imaging, could detect concealed weapons. A few minutes later, Marvin, Baby

Chris, Angel, and Bowie arrived on the scene and awaited instructions.

"What you got, Carla?"

"The two men at the door are armed. Two men by the bar are armed, two others are mobile, and three stationary targets are in the back."

"Okay, Angel, Bowie," Rain began, "as soon as you get in there, you take out the two at the door and watch for the three guns coming out of the back."

"You got it, Rain," Angel said.

"Marvin and Baby Chris, the two at the bar, are yours, but you need to look out for the two other guns Carla said were mobile," Rain ordered.

"Acknowledged," Marvin said.

"I'll try to give you as much advanced warning as possible," Carla informed them.

"Everybody ready?" Rain asked.

"We stay ready," Bowie commented.

"We're ready," Marvin said, reaching for the door handle.

"Get to it then," Rain ordered.

Dressed head to toe in black leather, Angel walked in the front door with a PLR-22 in one hand and a Beretta in the other because she'd heard that was what Shy carried. When she stepped inside with Bowie, the two men at the door approached them. As Marvin and Baby Chris entered, Angel raised the Beretta and fired at one of them. He took a shot to the head, and then she shot the other in the chest. People in the bar hit the floor. Some took cover under the tables, while others ran for the exits.

As Marvin and Baby Chris rushed past them, Bowie took cover and raised his weapon to prepare for the men coming out of the back. When the men at the bar aimed at the door, Marvin and Baby Chris raised their guns. Marvin shot one, and Baby Chris took out the other.

Just as Angel made it to where Bowie had taken cover, two men came out from the back of the club and opened fire with automatic weapons. She stood up and returned fire with the PLR-22 until the fifteen-shot magazine was empty before she took cover. Angel hit one in the back as she forced them to take cover.

"Two enemy targets moving in your direction, Marvin," Carla advised.

Marvin turned and fired on one man as he prepared to shoot. The shots hit him in the chest, and he went down. The other man returned fire on them as he got to cover. As Angel reloaded the PLR-22, Bowie shot it out with one of Dandridge's men.

"Last shooter coming out of the back," Carla said, and Angel put down the PLR-22 and aimed at the door with the Beretta. "In three, two, one—now!"

The door swung open, a man rushed out, and Angel fired once. The shot hit him in the forehead and knocked him off his feet.

One of the last men stood in the open and sprayed the bar with bullets. Baby Chris crawled along the floor, trying to make it to a spot where he could get a clear shot. When he stopped to reload a fresh clip, Baby Chris fired and hit him with two shots to the chest. The man went down and took cover as his partner began firing at him. While he fired at Baby Chris, Marvin shot him in the back.

Outside in the van, Carla turned to Rain. "All enemy targets eliminated."

Rain stood up. "Let's go, Alwan."

They got out of the tactical van, and he followed Rain inside. When she entered the building, Marvin had a gun to the head of the bartender. Rain walked up to him.

"You tell Dandridge that Rain Robinson is coming for him," Rain said, and then she led her soldiers out of Ten Ninety-Seven.

Chapter 38

"Dawkins."

"This is Officer Short at the hospital."

"Morning, Short. What's going on?"

"Just thought you should know, doctors plan on removing Moore from her coma this morning."

"Thanks. Have they notified the family?"

"That I don't know, Detective."

"Thanks for the heads-up," Dawkins said, and she ended the call.

"Let the family know what?" Kirk asked.

"Doctors plan on removing Wanda from her coma this morning, but he doesn't know if they contacted the family yet."

"We need to talk to her, preferably before Black does."

"That might come down to a matter of timing and luck."

"Tell me about it."

"I should go down there and camp out," Dawkins volunteered.

Kirk thought about it. "No, I'll go. I've known Wanda longer than you have."

"You're right. You do have a better relationship with her than I do. In the meantime, I'll follow up with Magdeleine Lavergne. Now that I've reviewed James Austin's client list, I have some questions I'd like to ask her."

When Kirk arrived at the hospital, the doctors were still working on Wanda. Knowing he might be there for a while, he relieved Officer Short.

"Why don't you go grab yourself some breakfast?" Kirk said, and he waited outside the room.

Wanda was stable and progressing well and was able to come off the respirator after the sedation and the pain medication had been minimized. Once the drugs that kept her in the induced coma had been removed, weaned, and minimized, Wanda slowly woke up. Her first questions to the doctors were about James.

"I'm sorry to tell you this, but Mr. Austin didn't make it."

"No," Kirk heard Wanda say, then she started crying.

Once the doctors and nursing staff had left the room, Kirk gave Wanda some time before tapping on the door and entering.

"Wanda," he said softly.

"Kirk?" she questioned and wiped away her tears.

"How are you feeling?"

"Numb."

"I'm not gonna take up a lot of your time, but I have to ask . . . Is there anyone that might have wanted to kill you or James?"

Wanda didn't answer right away, and Kirk didn't press her. "Mike and Bobby weren't the targets?"

"No. It appears that James was the target of the shooting," Kirk said, and Wanda started to cry again. He couldn't even imagine what she was thinking and feeling. "I'm sorry."

"No, Kirk, I don't know of anybody that would want to kill James," Wanda said through her tears.

"What about clients?"

Once again, Wanda didn't answer right away, and Kirk didn't press her, but this time was different. He had known Wanda long enough to know that his question caused her to think.

"I can't think of anybody." She looked into Kirk's eyes. "I'm tired. Can we do this later, Kirk?"

He stood up. "Sure, we can. I'm sorry to have to bother you. And I am so sorry for your loss," he said, backing out of the room. "You get better," he said and left.

When he exited, Wanda cried and eventually fell asleep. When she opened her eyes again, Black was in the room with her. He had fallen asleep in the chair.

"Mike," she said in a voice that was barely above a whisper, but it wasn't loud enough to wake him. "Mike," Wanda said louder this time, and Black woke up. He stood up and went to her bedside. He took her hand in his.

"How are you?"

"I don't know. Still kind of groggy and numb."

"Did the doctor tell you about James?" Wanda nodded quickly and began to cry. "I am so sorry, Wanda," he said, squeezing her hand tightly.

She wiped away the tears that were cascading down her cheeks. "You know who did it?"

"No, I'm sorry, but I don't. I wish I could stand here and tell you that they're dead, but I can't."

He took his time and walked Wanda through the steps he had taken, without success, to find out who was responsible. She was familiar with David Efrem and Hans Schubert laundering $3.6 billion in bitcoins and the part James played in it, but she was confident that it had nothing to do with the shooting. She laughed a little when he told her about his arrest and release. Wanda quickly ruled out Fantasy's work infiltrating Ignacio Tomas's trafficking operation.

"Fantasy's operation was flawless. I took steps to ensure that nothing could blow back on us." Wanda paused. "But something Kirk asked made me think."

"Kirk's been here already?"

"He came in right after the doctors left."

Black shook his head. "Why am I not surprised."

"He asked if it could have been a client, and I immediately thought about Daryn Chambers."

"Who's he?"

"He's a drug dealer from L.A. that James defended. He was charged with multiple counts of murder, conspiracy to distribute, and money laundering." Wanda was still a little groggy, but she continued. "I remember one day we were in Eagle Beach having lunch at Sunset Grille in the Hilton when Chambers and two of his men arrived. James excused himself and left the table to talk, but I could tell it was a heated conversation. And when James returned to the table, he said it was nothing, but I could tell that whatever they talked about had James shaken."

"Did the case go to trial?"

"It did, and Chambers was found guilty on all counts and was sentenced to thirty years in prison."

"I imagine he wasn't happy about that. You think he might have ordered the hit?"

"I don't know, Mike." Wanda paused and thought for a moment. "I can tell you that Chambers has people in the city, and he was here when they arrested him. He was extradited from New York to stand trial in L.A."

"Where do I find these people?"

"Thomas Gates is his name. I don't know how to find him."

"No worries. I'll find him." Black stood up. "You rest and get better, and I'll be back to see you later."

Chapter 39

Honey's was a gambling club that Honey Rawlins ran. When Glover and Spike foolishly decided to go to war with Barbara, they were quickly eliminated because, let's face it, Barbara Ray ain't no joke. At that point, Honey, who had done every job at Glover's, from bartending and waiting tables to dealing blackjack and poker to running the cashier window, was put in charge when Jackie, Marvin, and Baby Chris arrived. Glover had just been killed, and Jackie had a question.

"Who's running the place?"

"I am."

"And who are you?"

"I'm Honey."

Jackie gave her a message to give Javan, who was on the run for killing Glover, that every member of The Family was out looking for him, and then she issued a warning.

"He needs to come to see me before somebody finds him."

Then Jackie walked away. When she did, Marvin got in her face.

"You *will* do a good job running Jackie Washington's house for me, won't you, Honey?"

"I got you, Money, I promise."

It had been her place ever since that night. However, the place she was given was little more than a hole-in-the-wall bar running a profitable gambling operation in the back room. Now that it was her spot, Honey decided to make some changes.

She had seen what Barbara did when Jackie handed her Sweet Nectar. Since she hated the name, Barbara got Jackie's permission to change the name to The Playhouse, threw out all of the office furniture, had the office sanitized, and bought new furniture. But that was just the start. Barbara ordered the new signage and brought in one of the top interior designers in the city to share her vision for her place.

Well, Honey already had a new sign that said *Honey's,* and now, she was about to make some major changes, with her captain's blessing and support, of course. She bought the building next door. With the extra space, Honey expanded the gambling room and added two more poker tables, a roulette wheel, and blackjack tables. She also added two more bars and built a dance floor. The addition of the dance floor and the bar doubled that revenue, and the expansion of her gambling operation more than quadrupled her gambling revenue.

Honey's was now a big-money gambling spot, which put it on Big Frenchie's radar. He had scoped out the place and knew that with the increased security, it wasn't a job he could do alone. He had tried to get Bullet interested in doing the job with him, but he passed because Honey now had *six* men providing security. Rain recommended it when some of Glover's people tried to push her out.

Then French took the idea to rob Honey's to Dandridge, who ran it by Nance. He had absolutely no interest in it because, as Robert King was well known for saying, "Fuckin' around with Mike Black is bad for your health." And since he thought that it was good advice, he passed. But now that Nance was dead and Dandridge was looking for a way to bust back at Rain, hitting Honey's seemed like a great idea to him.

"This is the last call for alcohol."

"You don't have to go home, but you need to get the fuck up outta here."

It was almost four in the morning, and the dance club at Honey's was getting ready to close. The lights had just come on, and people began approaching the exits. Two of the bars had already shut down, and the waitresses and waiters had cashed out or were cleaning their sections so they could head for the exits as well. Ross, the head of security, and Patra, the bar manager, were in the count room.

"Tonight was a good night," Patra said as she put another stack of bills in the cash counter and counterfeit bill detection machine.

"It was, and you need to count faster. I got something waiting on me," Ross said as he paced the floor.

"That little skank in the piece of red dress you were hugged up with?"

"That's her. Me and Garland are meeting her and her girl at the diner."

Patra laughed. "You're gonna get there and find two other niggas with them."

"Not if you count faster."

"I'm sorry if counting 999 bills per minute ain't fast enough for you," Patra said, and Ross opened the door and looked out.

That night's crowd had thinned out, and all that remained in the club were the waitstaff cleaning their sections, as well as Pearson, Jamarco, and Tameron. They were moving the stragglers toward the door when four masked men with AK-47s walked in. One shot the doorman the second he stepped inside. Another one sprayed the club with 7.62-mm ammunition. He took out two members of Honey's security with his opening volley.

As they continued firing, Honey ran toward the bar for cover and then dove for the floor when the shooting got too intense. Pearson set up behind some tables and came up firing. Jamarco flipped over a table for cover and fired back, but he was hit by one of the gunmen with three shots. As the gunmen kept firing and made their way toward the cash room, Garland and Tameron ran to seek better cover. When Tameron stood up, one of the gunmen fired twice, hitting him with one to the chest and one to the head. Another gunman fired and hit Garland with two shots. As Honey crawled to the bar to make it to the weapons safe, she watched the gun slip from Garland's hand and his body fall to the floor.

"Fuck," she breathed out and got to work on the combination.

Now that the gunmen had cleared the room, they went straight for the cash room. While Patra hid in the closet, Ross pointed his .45 at the door. When the gunmen began firing through the cash room door, they hit Ross with multiple shots to the head, chest, and stomach, and his bloody body hit the floor hard.

Patra covered her mouth to keep from screaming and tried to stay as still as she could while she watched through the slats in the door. The men filled gym bags with money, and then they turned to leave. She breathed a sigh of relief when she heard the door close . . . and she was still alive.

As the gunmen made their way toward the door, Honey opened the safe and got two guns. She raised her weapons, fired, and hit the last man with several shots in the back. He dropped one of the money bags before going out the door.

Chapter 40

"Aunt Rain!" Eazy exclaimed when she entered the dining room that morning while they were having breakfast. He'd had a crush on Rain for as long as he could remember. He had been crushing on Michelle's friend Tierra, but he was beginning to think she was too immature.

"Hey, everybody."

"Have some breakfast, Lorraine?" M asked and started to get up.

"Yes, ma'am. But I need to talk to your son first." Rain motioned toward the media room with her eyes.

"Excuse me, everybody."

When Black stood up and left the dining room with Rain, Michelle wiped her mouth and started to get up.

"Sit down, Michelle," Shy said without looking up from her food. "Nobody invited you."

"Yes, Mommy."

Dejected, Michelle slumped down in her chair, and Eazy stuck out his tongue. She discreetly gave him the finger and wondered what she was missing.

Once Black and Rain were in the media room, she wasted no time telling Black what happened the night before at Honey's.

"We lose anybody?"

"All six of her men are dead. They killed them and then went for the money."

"How much did they get?"

"She hasn't counted yet. She shot one of them on the way out, and he dropped a bag."

"Honey?"

"Yes, Honey. My girl crawled to the weapons safe, got two 9s, and came up blasting."

"I'm impressed. I'm gonna have to look at her in a whole different light."

"I'm saying."

"So, they rob the place, Honey caps one on the way out the door, but they don't return for the money."

"The money wasn't the point. This was Dandridge hitting back," Rain said as Black's phone rang. He glanced at the display and saw that it was Carla calling.

"Hold that thought." He swiped "talk." "What's up, Carla?"

"Morning, Mike. If you're not busy, could you come by the office today? There are some things that I need to make you aware of."

"I'll see you later." Black ended the call. "What are you getting ready to do?"

"Nothing, why?"

"I need to go see what Carla wants."

"Can I eat first?"

At the same time, Kirk placed a cup of coffee and a honey-pecan cream cheese bagel on the desk in front of Dawkins and went to sit down.

"Thank you, kind sir."

"You're welcome." Kirk sipped his coffee. "What you got?"

"I've been combing through Austin's client list, and the one that jumped out at me was Daryn Chambers."

"Who's he?"

"He's a drug dealer that Austin defended in Los Angeles. He was charged with multiple counts of murder, conspiracy to distribute, and money laundering. He was found guilty on all counts and sentenced to life without parole."

"A motive for murder?" Kirk speculated.

"Maybe." Dawkins took a bite of her bagel. "What flavor is this?"

"Honey-Pecan Cream Cheese."

"It is so good," she said, talking with her mouth full. "I also had Bankston, the forensic accountant, looking into it."

"What did he come up with?"

"He said that Garry Amarantos, one of the managing general partners, has a Key person life insurance policy on Austin as part of their business continuation plan."

"What's that?"

"It describes what happens if a business owner dies prematurely."

"I imagine that's pretty standard, isn't it?" Kirk asked.

"According to Bankston, it is. It's designed to help a company recover from the financial loss caused by the death of an owner or partner." She took another bite. "What isn't standard is that the *ex*-wife, Lisa Austin, has a double indemnity life insurance policy on Austin. He has one on her too."

"Who's the beneficiary?"

"Her and their four children."

"We can take a run at her, but I wanna hear more about Daryn Chambers."

"One of the things that stood out about him was that he was arrested in Scarsdale in a routine traffic stop."

Kirk chuckled. "Who were the arresting officers?"

"Officers Christopher and Murray."

"You feel like riding out to Scarsdale?"

"No." Dawkins finished her bagel and stood up. "But you're driving, so let's go."

"Right."

Kirk stood up and followed his partner out of the unit. After a thirty-five-minute drive on the Bronx River Parkway, the detectives entered AB's Cafe N' Grill.

"Officer Christopher?"

"Yes."

"I'm NYPD Detective Kirkland, and this is Detective Dawkins. Your desk sergeant told us where to find you."

"We'd like to ask you a few questions about an arrest you made," Dawkins said. "Mind if we sit?"

"Not at all. Please sit and tell me what I can do for you."

"You and your partner arrested Daryn Chambers," she began.

Officer Christopher smiled and nodded. "That was a big fish we reeled in."

"What can you tell me about that?"

"It started out as a routine traffic stop. The vehicle that he was driving had no taillights. He gives me a California license in the name of Harold Camp. I run it, and it comes back as one of Chambers's aliases." He chuckled. "I guess he didn't know that LAPD was on to that alias, but anyway, I called for backup. When they arrived, he surrendered. We searched the vehicle and found a gun and cocaine in the console. We arrested him and the woman he was with."

"Woman?" Kirk questioned.

"Car was registered to her, so we took her too. She was charged with possession of a firearm and a controlled substance."

"You wouldn't happen to remember her name?" Dawkins inquired.

"Not off the top of my head."

Kirk and Dawkins stood up. "Thank you, Officer. If we have any more questions, we'll be in touch," Dawkins said.

"Anytime," Officer Christopher said and went back to his meal. Their next stop was to meet with Morris Campbell. He was the detective assigned to the case.

"What can you tell me about the woman Daryn Chambers was arrested with?" Kirk asked.

Campbell checked his notes. "Her name is Carrie Berkley. She's a 42-year-old third-grade teacher from Boise, Idaho."

"Not exactly the ride-or-die chick type," Dawkins mused.

"Not exactly. She claimed that she had no idea who he was. She said that he told her that his name was Byron Joseph." He laughed. "Funny thing was that when it came time to interrogate her, I had just enough time to listen to her tell me about how she knew nothing about Chambers when her lawyer busts in and says, 'Not another word.'"

"What happened to her?"

"By the time her case came up for trial, the lawyer pled the charges down to misdemeanor possession and got the weapons charge thrown out. Then the judge dismissed the case because the prosecution couldn't prove the drugs were hers or that she had any knowledge of it."

"You got an address for her?"

Once they got the address, the detectives made the short drive to Carrie Berkley's home.

"Who's there?"

"My name is Detective Dawkins," she began, holding her badge up to the peephole. "And this is my partner, Detective Kirkland. We want to ask you some questions about Daryn Chambers."

When Berkley opened the door and allowed them to enter, they were surprised to find that Carrie Berkley was a little white woman with dark, beady eyes.

"Definitely *not* a ride-or-die chick," Dawkins whispered as she allowed them into her home.

"Behave," Kirk chuckled. "We're not going to take up much of your time."

"We just have a few questions," Dawkins said and sat down.

"What would you like to know?"

"We talked to Detective Campbell, and he said that you had no idea who Chambers was," Dawkins began. "How did you meet him?"

"We met at the grocery store. He said his name was Byron Joseph, and he was a real estate investor who recently moved here from Los Angeles."

"How long were you with him?"

"Nine months."

"Nine months, and he never gave you any indication that he wasn't who he said he was?" Kirk asked skeptically.

"No clue. He was always so nice and respectful, and he never gave me a reason even to suspect that he was a drug dealer on the run for murder."

"Did he have any friends or people he hung out with that you know of?" Dawkins asked.

Berkley shook her head quickly. "No, Byron, or whatever his name was, pretty much kept to himself."

"I see."

"Did he have a cell phone?" Kirk asked.

"He had one of those temporary phones."

"A burner?" Dawkins inserted.

"Yes. He said that he didn't want to commit to a contract until he was sure that he would stay or go back to L.A."

"Is there anything else you can tell us about him?"

"Not really. As I said, he had me completely fooled." She dropped her head and shook it. "I felt like such an idiot insisting that they had the wrong man, that he couldn't possibly be some murderous drug dealer."

"I understand," Dawkins said, reaching into her pocket to pull out one of her cards. "If you think of anything else, please call me."

And with that, the detectives stood up and prepared to leave. Meanwhile, outside the house, Rain and Black arrived on Scarsdale Street, where Carrie Berkley lived.

Chapter 41

"We're in the right place," Black said.

"Why you say that?"

Black pointed. "Because that's Kirk's car. Pull over here," he said, and Rain parked up the street from the house so they could see the detectives when they left.

Once Kirk and Dawkins came out of the house and drove away, Black and Rain exited her Lexus and walked toward the house. They rang the doorbell, and thinking that it was the police again, Berkley opened the door.

"Who are you?"

"Carrie Berkley?" Black asked.

"Yes."

"I'd like to ask you some questions about Daryn Chambers."

"Are you with the police?"

"No, but I want to know what you told the police about him."

"If you're not the police, I have no reason to talk to you," she said and was reaching to close the door when Rain pulled out her gun and shoved it in her face.

"This reason enough?"

"Can we come in?" Black asked politely. "I promise she won't hurt you, and I'll make the conversation worth-while."

Berkley quickly stepped aside and allowed them into her house. While Rain pointed her gun at Berkley, Black asked her the same questions that the detectives asked, and she gave them the same answers. That was . . . until he asked if Chambers had any friends, and Berkley hesitated before she answered, and her hands shook a bit.

"No, Byron, or whatever his name was, pretty much kept to himself."

Black and Rain looked at each other. "Why don't I believe you?" Rain stated and raised the gun.

Berkley looked between Black and Rain. "He said that he'd kill me if I ever mentioned his name to the police or anybody else."

"Tell me who he is and where I can find him, and *I'll* kill him." Rain smiled a somewhat terrifying smile. "That way, you don't have to worry about him killing you."

Berkley took a second or two to consider her options and chose wisely. "There were two of them. One's name was Thomas Gates, and the other was Larry Bracy."

"Do you know where we can find them?" Rain asked.

"No, I don't."

"You sure?" Rain leaned forward in her seat to ask.

"I did pick him up from Gates house, but it was so long ago, and I've tried to put the entire experience out of my mind. I don't remember where I picked him up." Berkley paused and thought about it. "Wait. When he called and asked me to pick him up, he sent me a text message with the address." She looked at Black. "Can I get my phone? It's in my purse."

"Get her phone," he ordered, and Rain got her purse and handed it to Berkley.

It took her awhile to scroll through the messages, but eventually, she said, "I got it," and handed the phone to Rain. Rain made a note of the address and handed Berkley back her phone.

"Thank you. Now, you wouldn't have a picture of him, would you?" Black asked.

"On Facebook."

Rain took out her phone and opened the app. "Show me."

Black chuckled. "You're on Facebook?"

Rain smiled and said nothing as Berkley went to her Facebook page and found an image of her, Gates, and Bracy. Black stood up, and Rain put away her gun.

"That wasn't so bad, was it?" Rain said. After Black counted five hundred-dollar bills and gave them to Berkley, Rain followed him out of the house.

Their next stop was to check out the address they had just obtained from Berkley.

"We're in the right place," Rain said as she parked the car.

"What makes you say that?"

Rain pointed. "Black van in the driveway," she said, and they both took out their guns and cautiously approached the house.

When Rain banged on the door, they were again surprised when it swung open.

"What the fuck is wrong with you? Beating on my fuckin' door like that!" She got in Rain's face to shout.

Once again, Black and Rain glanced at each other, and then Rain shoved her gun in the woman's face. It changed her entire attitude, and she raised her hands.

"We're looking for Thomas Gates. He here?" Rain asked.

"No."

"What about Larry Bracy?"

"That muthafucka don't live here no more."

"Can we come in?" Black asked gently. "I promise she won't kill you, and I'll make the conversation worth your while."

She held the door open wider and stepped aside. "Fuck y'all want?"

"What's your name?"

"Chaka muthafuckin' Khan. What the fuck y'all want?"

Rain liked her attitude; she reminded her of herself. "When was the last time you saw him," she demanded to know.

"He been gone about a week. Nigga came into some money and bounced. After all his fuckin' talk about what all we was gonna do when he got that money . . ." She shook her head. "That's what I get for fuckin' with a broke-ass nigga."

"You know where he got the money from?" Black asked.

"Nope. All I know is that he was talking to some bitch about it."

"You know where to find Thomas Gates?" he asked.

"Another good-for-nothing, broke-ass nigga. I don't know where that muthafucka live. As far as I know, the nigga was homeless."

"Whose black van is that outside?" Black inquired.

"That's my uncle's van. Why?"

"Where is he?" Rain asked.

"He's in Alabama. And you still ain't told me why you wanna know whose van that is."

"Bracy ever use it?" Black asked.

"Sometimes. Why?"

"Because he used it to kill somebody," Black informed her.

"And since it's sitting in your driveway, that makes *you* an accessory to murder," Rain added.

She pointed at Rain's face. "You know what? Fuck that stupid shit you talkin'. I ain't have nothing to do with no fuckin' murder."

"You know where to find either of them?"

"No, I don't, and I think it's long past time for you two to get the fuck outta here." She started walking toward the door. "I don't give a fuck if y'all got guns." She opened the door. "Talkin' that dumbass shit in my fuckin' house . . ."

Black and Rain looked at each other. They smiled and then headed for the door.

"That's right. Get to steppin'." They left the house and started for their car. "And don't come back," she shouted and slammed the door.

"I like her," Black said as they approached the car.

"I do too." Rain unlocked the doors for them to get in. "What now?"

"Take me to the office." It was then that Black's phone rang. He glanced at the display as Rain pulled off. "What's up, Carla? Me and Rain were just on our way to see you."

"My timing is, as always, perfect," she giggled.

"What you got for me?"

"Come by the office. I got something major to share with you."

"In that case, we are on our way."

Chapter 42

The Conrad Hotel is located on West Fifty-Fourth, a quiet side street in Midtown Manhattan. The luxury Manhattan retreat is five blocks from Central Park and Times Square, and the Theater District is a ten-minute walk down Seventh Avenue. Detectives Kirkland and Dawkins knocked on the door of one of their park-view premium bedroom suites and waited.

"Just a minute," a voice came from the other side of the door. "Oh," Lisa Austin said when she opened the door and saw the detectives. "I thought you were the valet come for my luggage."

Dawkins looked down at the bags by the door. "Heading back to L.A.?"

"Yes. I have a five o'clock flight leaving from Kennedy."

"We won't keep you long," Dawkins said. "We just have a couple of questions for you. Mind if we come in?"

Lisa smiled brightly and stepped aside. "As long as we can make this quick. As I said, I have a flight to catch."

The detectives entered the room, and Dawkins went straight to a chair and sat down. Kirk extended his hand for Lisa to sit in the other seat.

"Have you caught the people who killed James?"

"We haven't made an arrest yet," Kirk said and stood by the table next to Dawkins. "But I'm sure we'll have a suspect in custody very soon."

Lisa folded her hands in front of her. "What can I do to help?"

"Have you ever met Wanda Moore?" Kirk asked.

"No, I haven't had the pleasure. How is she doing, by the way?"

"Her doctors have taken her out of the medically induced coma, and she is expected to make a full recovery," Kirk informed her.

"I know it must be hard on you." Dawkins leaned back in her chair. "I remember how it felt when my first husband remarried." Kirk looked at her strangely since, to his knowledge, Dawkins had never been married. "I never met her either, but I couldn't stand that woman," she chuckled. "I guess it was just feeling like he was mine, that's all."

"*Was* yours," Lisa said. "It's a feeling I had to wrap my brain around." She laughed. "It wasn't easy, but I got there."

"Is that when you decided to have him killed?" Dawkins asked bluntly.

"*Excuse* me?" Lisa asked, although she had heard the detective's question quite clearly.

"Is that when you decided to put a contract out on your ex-husband?"

"No."

"Well, when did you decide to have him murdered?" Kirk asked.

"Are you two serious with this?" she asked, and neither Kirk nor Dawkins said a word. "I did not have the father of my children killed."

Dawkins leaned forward. "Yes, you did."

She removed the folder from her Mollie Tote and placed it on the table.

"You were upset that he was marrying another woman, *and* you had twenty million reasons to want him dead."

"What are you talking about?"

"The twenty-million-dollar life insurance policy you have."

"You're crazy."

"Am I?" Dawkins opened the folder and placed a piece of paper before Lisa. "Are you familiar with CIBC First Caribbean International Bank?"

"Choose your answer carefully," Kirk said, and Lisa said nothing.

"This is a bank statement from CIBC First Caribbean International Bank," Dawkins smiled at Lisa. "*Your* statement, in fact."

Lisa picked up the statement and glanced at it. "Yes. This is my account statement." She let the paper drop from her hands. "What about it?"

Dawkins picked up the statement and held it out in front of her. "You see the line that I highlighted?" She pointed to the line. "It's a transaction for a one hundred-thousand-dollar withdrawal."

"Where did the money go?" Kirk asked.

"I had some major expenses that came up. Kids' tuition, home repairs, that type of thing."

"Try 'paying for the contract on your ex-husband,'" Dawkins said, taking another piece of paper from the folder. She slid it in front of Lisa.

She picked up the paper. "What's this?"

"That is a list of all of the shell company accounts that you ran that money through before it got to the killer."

Kirk dropped an image on the table. "This guy."

"Do you know him?" Dawkins asked.

Lisa picked up the image and glanced at it before she handed it to Dawkins. "He doesn't look familiar."

"He should. His name is Thomas Gates," Dawkins announced.

"You got him off on a murder charge fifteen years ago. He's the half-brother of Daryn Chambers. You know him. Your firm defended him recently for murder."

"That was James who tried that case."

"And Chambers was found guilty. He told Austin that he would see him dead because he thought that he told the police where to find the murder weapon," Kirk said, tired of playing cat and mouse with her. "So let's stop fuckin' around. You were pissed because Austin was getting married, and Gates was pissed that Austin sold out his brother."

"You two were a perfect couple. He wanted revenge, and you wanted money," Dawkins added, and then she slid one last piece of paper in front of Lisa. "In case you're wondering, that is the statement from the offshore account you set up for your old client Gates at the National Bank of Belize."

"You wired the money to his account, and he killed Austin," Kirk said and looked Lisa in the eye.

"We were working things out when he met her. And then I felt him slowly pulling away again until he was gone." Lisa sucked her teeth. "Said she made him feel young again."

"And he was worth more to you dead." Dawkins stood up, and Kirk took out the cuffs. "Stand up, please." He put the handcuffs on Lisa. "Lisa Austin, you're under arrest for the murder of James Austin. You have the right to remain silent. Anything you say can be used against you in court."

"Glad to have you back, partner."

"Glad to be back. I didn't realize how much I missed this," Dawkins said as she escorted Lisa out of the room.

Chapter 43

"Got him!" Carla shouted when a camera picked up Larry Bracy coming out of a convenience store. She watched him walk to a car and get in. It was a late model Toyota Avalon, so she hacked the GPS and tracked the vehicle to the Scarsdale house of Chaka Khan.

"Her real name is Elaine Ellis."

"Me and Rain were there last night," Black said.

"Guess we're going back again tonight," Bobby said.

"Let me know if that car moves."

"I got him," Carla said to Black as he left the office with Bobby.

When they reached Elaine Ellis's house, Black and Bobby spotted the car and waited silently. When Bracy came out, he was dragging a suitcase behind him, and Ellis was standing in the doorway yelling, "You're a fuckin' liar!" as loud as she could.

When Bracy got in the car and drove away, Bobby followed. As they went, both men were quiet and in their thoughts. Mostly about Wanda, naturally. They were glad she had survived the ordeal and would be all right. But thoughts of losing Wanda had caused them to think about Vickie, how that profound loss changed their lives, and how they saw the world. She was the catalyst behind how they shaped the world in which they currently exist.

Imagine a world where Vickie didn't die. Black would have never seen drugs as death. Therefore, when he killed Andre and took over, he would have, more likely than not, continued Andre's legacy and become its new king.

"How are the twins doing?" Black finally asked to break the silence. "I didn't get much chance to talk to them while they were here."

"They're doing all right. Couldn't wait to get back to L.A." Bobby laughed. "They love it out there."

"How do you feel about your girls being so far from you?"

"I don't like it at all. But it was something I had to get used to. We were kinda enjoying being, you know, empty nesters." He chuckled. "But that didn't last long. First Venus, and then the baby."

"How's that going, Granddad?"

"You know I ain't really into that yet."

"Being a grandfather?"

"No. I love *being* a grandfather. I'm just not into being called 'Granddaddy' and shit like that."

"No, you're still a young man."

"Right," Bobby said, and they both laughed. "But it's nice having them in the house after the girls ran out of there."

Black laughed. "You mean after Barbara ran them up outta there?"

"Barbara getting kidnapped scared them straight to the West Coast," he said and laughed. "They wanted to get as far away from this thing we do as possible." Bobby paused. "And what is up with you letting Michelle sit in while Rain talked about Dandridge?"

"Like it or not, it's where she wants to be and who she wants to be. One day, this thing we do will all belong to them." Black laughed. "And she is right about one thing."

"What's that?"

"One day, it might fall to her to be the boss of this Family."

"Did she say that?"

"She did. And because of that, she thinks she needs to know everything that goes on in this Family."

"Who does that remind you of?"

"She *is* my daughter." Black shook his head. "Imagine her if she had, as she calls it, 'grown up in her rightful place at my side'?"

"No," Bobby said flatly. "I have a hard enough time seeing Barbara doing what she's doing."

"We try to protect our little girls, but then they grow up and do what they wanna do."

"Wouldn't it be interesting if our daughters, instead of our sons, take over what we built?"

"Shit, Bobby, that's the way it's gonna be. Eazy got no interest whatsoever."

"You're right. RJ is more businessman than gangster."

"So Sherman tells me."

"Being a father and having two women is kicking the boy's ass," Bobby said as they parked in front of the building they followed Bracy to. He turned off the car and reached for his gun. "How you wanna do this?" Bobby paused. "Or did you wanna call Carla down here with the tactical van?"

Black laughed. "Remember the days when we wouldn't have been worried about who or how many were in there?"

"Those days we would just kick in the door and go in blasting. But we were young and stupid those days."

"No. We didn't have wives, children, or grandchildren, or as much to lose," Black added.

"So what you wanna do?"

Black checked his guns. "Kick in the door and go in blasting," he said, and they got out of the car and walked toward the building where Thomas Gates, Larry Bracy, and three other men were relaxing, getting drunk while they watched the Knicks lose to the Celtics.

The three men in the living room were all startled when Black kicked in the door and rushed in, blasting with Bobby. One man dropped his drink and was reaching for his gun when Black hit him with two shots to the chest. Another was able to get to his weapon, but before he could get a shot off, Bobby caught him with one to the head. The third man jumped up from the couch, firing as he ran to the kitchen, but Black shot him in the back, and he fell over the dining room table. Gates bounced up from his chair and started running toward the back of the apartment, firing shots as he ran.

"I got him!" Bobby shouted and ran after him.

Gates ran out the back door of the apartment and ran down the alley. Bobby fired several shots at him, but he missed when Gates dove for the ground. He quickly got up and started running, firing shots wildly at Bobby as he ran. Gates took cover behind a car and fired more shots before he turned to run. Bobby fired and hit Gates in the leg. He stumbled, fell to the ground, and dropped his gun. Bobby stepped up quickly and shot him in the other leg.

"That's for makin' me run," he said and then shot him in the head.

Back in the apartment, Bracy kept shooting at Black, who took cover in the kitchen. Bracy blasted away until he ran out of bullets. When he did, Black came out from the kitchen and approached him. Bracy dropped to his knees and raised his hands.

"All I did was drive."

Bobby came rushing back into the apartment in time to see Black walk up to Bracy, put the gun to his head, and shoot him twice.

Bobby walked up to Black as he stood over the body. Black looked at him.

"Did you get him?"

"I got him."

Chapter 44

According to Wikipedia, a scorched-earth policy is "a military strategy that aims to destroy anything useful to the enemy. Any assets, weapons, transport vehicles, communication, and industrial resources used by the enemy are targeted."

Well, Rain Robinson had her own scorched-earth policy.

"Kill everybody and burn the bitch to the ground."

But it was pretty much the same thing.

It had been two weeks since his men hit Honey's, and in that time, Dandridge had come to wish that he had followed Nance's example and realized that fuckin' with Mike Black and The Family is not only bad for your health, but it's also bad for business. But it was too late for that now. The streets weren't safe, so it had been two weeks since Dandridge had been seen on them.

In those weeks, Rain disrupted his cash flow by strategically targeting any place he was making money. And then the team came back from Burundi.

"What y'all into, sunshine?" Monika asked, and since she enjoyed blowing things up, car bombings became an everyday thing, and none of the vehicles driven by Dandridge's people were safe.

Once they had taken one of their phones, Carla was up on all their communications, which made it easy to find the warehouse where Dandridge cut and cooked his product.

"We shutting that down," Rain said.

"You gonna let her blow it up?" Jackie asked.

"No. Too many civilians in there."

"I could start a controlled burn to give the civilians time to exit the building before I blow it up," Monika said.

"Gives them time to move some product out too," Jackie pointed out.

"And we have our people waiting for them when they come out," Carter recommended.

"Or we could do it old school," was Ryder's suggestion. "Go in there and kill everybody with a gun. Then Monika can start her controlled burn to give the civilians time to evacuate the building. After that, we blow it up," she said, and Rain nodded because it was what she wanted to do. It was part of her usual, kill everybody and burn the bitch to the ground, policy. Accomplishing her objectives without civilian casualties was better. Rain was evolving into her role as boss of The Family.

But since she involved The Family in the assassinations of Greg Mac and Drum, her judgment had been called into question. Rain questioned her own judgment in allowing herself to get pregnant. The combination caused her to be more thoughtful and cautious in her decisions, not as reckless in her actions, and more conscious of her position as boss of this Family.

"Does anybody want anything else to eat or drink?" Ester asked.

"No, I think we're fine," Sherman said, and she went back into the kitchen.

When Rain called about having a captain's meeting, Ester answered Sherman's phone.

"Dinner is just about ready, Rain. Can't it wait?"

So, Rain asked, "What you cook?"

Once Ester told her what she had prepared and said, "There's plenty. Y'all are welcome to have your meeting here," that settled that.

"What you wanna do, Rain?" Jackie asked.

"We're gonna do it all. Monika is gonna do a controlled burn to get them outta there." She looked at Carter. "We have our people waiting for them when they try to come out with the product." He nodded, and she looked at Jackie. "Our people go in there and kill everybody with a gun," she ordered, and Ryder smiled.

"And then I do what I do," Monika concluded.

"Any questions?" When no one said anything, Rain said, "Make it happen."

On the way out of Sherman's house, when they were on their way to their cars, Rain stopped and waited for Carter.

"I know you, and I got a lot that we need to work out between us," Rain began.

"We do."

"But for now, let's try to get along and work together."

"I never had a problem with that."

"I'm gonna do better, okay?"

"I got no problem with that."

"Okay," Rain said and walked to her car with Alwan.

Monika got enough C-4, timers, and everything else she'd need the following night and infiltrated the warehouse undetected. She headed straight to the ventilation system. Once she was there, she set a fire in the vent that carried the smoke throughout the building. On her way out, Monika set up a couple of explosive devices because she knew the smoke wouldn't be enough to drive them out.

"Is that smoke?"

"Where's it coming from?"

"Go check it out," one of Dandridge's men ordered, and that was when he heard the explosion. "You two check it out. You see about getting the product out of here."

When the naked women who were cutting, cooking, bagging, and packaging the product heard the explosion, they began running to grab whatever clothes they could and ran for the exit.

"Where y'all going?"

When the door swung open, and the women began running out, Marvin and Baby Chris made their way inside. But when they got inside, two men were coming toward them. They opened fire. Marvin and Baby Chris ducked for cover and returned fire. Marvin hit one man with several shots, and he went down.

The other man fired at Baby Chris as he went deeper into the warehouse. When his gun was empty, he made a run to the back. As RJ and Judah came into the warehouse and opened fire, Baby Chris went after him and hit him with two shots.

Outside the warehouse, Alwan found a spot and parked Rain's Lexus. Although she was an adrenaline junkie, Rain wasn't there to get into the action inside.

Learn to delegate, she could hear Black saying to both her and Jackie more times than she could count.

It took a minute, but now, Jackie had no problem sending Marvin and Baby Chris to do the dirty jobs that earned her the name "The Killing Captain."

Rain hadn't reached that point yet, but she was working on it. But she was bored sitting around Purple Rock waiting to hear what was happening, so she went to the warehouse to see for herself. What Rain didn't know was that Dandridge was there that night. When he heard the explosion, he got out of there quickly and made it to his car.

"That's Dandridge's car," Alwan stated.

"Follow him. But keep your distance."

"On it."

Back inside the warehouse, RJ and Judah split up, went in different directions, and continued to sweep through the building. Suddenly, two men with AK-47s came out firing and forced them to take cover. One circled around to the side of Judah, but before he could get off a shot, RJ saw him.

"On your three!" he yelled.

Judah hit him with three shots to the chest. Two men armed with Mini-14s began firing at RJ. They forced him into an office, and he hit the floor as the shooters kept firing. He shot one and then crawled for cover while the other continued firing at him. Judah fired and hit him with three shots before moving to cover. When the shooting stopped, they reloaded their weapons, and a man appeared at the door and prepared to fire. Marvin came up behind him, fired, and hit him in the back.

"You owe me one," Marvin said and moved off.

While the action was going on inside the warehouse, Monika was setting explosive devices around the outside of the building to bring it all down when the shooting was over.

As the gun battle raged on and the fire continued to spread throughout the warehouse, three of Dandridge's men had gotten as much product as they could carry and made it outside. They ran toward their cars with duffel bags in each hand and their weapons around their necks. Angel and Bowie were there waiting for them with raised weapons. The men ran for cover and shot back. Bowie emptied his magazine and put in another one. Angel stood up and fired twice, hitting one man with one to the chest and one to the head. The other man opened fire at Bowie, and he returned fire and hit him with a shot right between his eyes.

When the shooting stopped, Marvin and RJ checked the building to make sure they didn't miss anybody.

Once they came out, everybody left the warehouse and moved to a safe distance. Monika pressed the detonator. Then she got out of the car to watch it burn to the ground.

As Rain instructed, Alwan had kept his distance as he followed Dandridge away from the warehouse. Rain knew exactly where he was going when they got close to Tracey Towers. She sat back and watched as he double-parked the car and ran toward the building.

"Shaunta! Shaunta!" Dandridge shouted when he rushed into the apartment but got no response.

He went straight to the bedroom closet, where he kept a safe. He thought about grabbing his clothes there, but there wasn't time for that. He was getting out of the city, so he was there to get the money from the safe and run.

Dandridge got one of Shaunta's bags and went to work on the safe. Once he had filled the bag, he closed the safe and headed out of the room. When he came into the living room, Rain was standing there with her gun raised.

"You should have locked the door."

Rain's first shot hit him in the chest. The second was to the head. She walked up to Dandridge and stood over him. Rain took the bag from his hand and put two more in his chest before she left the apartment.

Chapter 45

It had been two weeks since Dandridge's men hit Honey's, and in that time, his operations had been all but shut down. Neither Nance nor Dandridge had been seen on the streets in two weeks. During that time, his cash flow had been strategically targeted, their vehicles were being blown up, and his men were dead, in hiding, or left the city.

And for all those reasons, Sienna Petrocelli couldn't be happier.

She zoomed into the parking lot at Action and parked in her reserved parking space. It used to be Kojo's space, and for a while after he disappeared, she respected it, halfway expecting to get there one night and see his Audi R8 in the space. But that was behind her now.

"I don't think you'll see him again," was what Joey told her.

He knew that Kojo was dead when he said that. Sienna wondered why he didn't just come out and tell her, but she really didn't care. She got out of her Maserati GranTurismo, looking confident and stylish in her blue Safiyaa crepe Cara jumpsuit with a draped cowl bodice and trailing back cape.

"It's your house now, Sienna," and those were the only words that mattered to her.

Although she had lost all of her key people in recent weeks, one thing was certain: Somebody was always standing in the wings, ready to fill the void. Sienna assumed that Kojo, Drew Mack, Kevin Franklin, and

Jackson Hill were killed by either Nance or The Family. And now that Nance was no longer pushing, her things were good. Sienna made her way to the bar, thinking things could only improve.

"What will it be?"

"Glenlivet single malt."

"You got it."

She leaned against the bar and looked around the dancehall reggae club she was now part owner of. Sienna thought about her mother. She ran her father's business while he stood out front and took all the credit. It was her time to stand out front now.

The bartender placed the glass in front of her. "Here you go, Sienna."

"Thank you."

Sienna shot the drink and headed toward the stairs to her office. She went up the stairs, thinking about firing the security guard who wasn't at his post by the door again. Now that she was part owner, Sienna thought about how active a role she wanted to play in the club's management. She opened the door and turned on the lights.

"I was wondering when you'd get here."

Sienna stopped and looked at the woman sitting behind her desk.

"I thought you were dead," she said to Veronica Isley, the woman she knew as Shanice Hardaway, an undercover police officer whose murder she ordered.

Isley's gun was pointed at her; Sienna put up her hands.

"No, Brendon tried, but he didn't kill me. And before we go any further, why don't you toss the clutch?"

Sienna tossed the Bottega Veneta leather clutch containing her gun on the couch. Isley stood up and came from behind the desk.

"Get down on your knees," she ordered, and Sienna did as she was told.

"It was you, wasn't it?" Sienna questioned as Isley pointed her weapon at her head. "It was you who killed Kojo, Drew, Franklin, and Jackson, right?"

"I didn't kill Kordell."

Isley stepped up and put the barrel of her gun to Sienna's head. "I know it was you who ordered Brendon to kill me. Kordell would have wanted to talk."

"That was just business. You were a cop."

"I'm still a cop." And she hated it.

"Since you're not here to arrest me, I'll give you half a million dollars tonight if you don't kill me. I will leave New York, and you'll never see or hear from me again."

"I know I won't ever see or hear from you again. Goodbye, Sienna," Isley said and shot her in the head.

She went back behind Sienna's desk and sat down. Isley picked up the phone and dialed a number.

"Hello, Sienna."

"No, this is not Sienna. Do I have the honor of speaking with Joey Toscano?"

"You do. Who is this?"

"My name is Veronica Isley, Mr. Toscano. I'm the woman you knew as Shanice Hardaway."

"I thought you were dead."

"Obviously, I'm not dead. But Sienna, *she's* dead."

"What can I do for you?" Joey asked calmly, but he was thinking that it was ballsy for her to be calling, so he was intrigued.

"You and I need to have a conversation."

In addition to her medal for Meritorious Police Duty, Veronica Isley's reward for her participation in the successful undercover operation was to be assigned to a radio car with an old racist cop that she couldn't stand. Isley had been a drug dealer a lot longer than she'd been a cop, and she hated being a cop. She was Shanice Hardaway, and she was damn good at being a drug dealer.

Chapter 46

"Burbank Tower, this is Citation 8121K. Entering left downwind Runway 33."

"Citation 8121K cleared to land Runway 33," the Tower responded.

"Citation 8121K cleared to land Runway 33," Rain confirmed and began landing procedures.

Once Rain landed the Cessna Citation at Hollywood Burbank Bob Hope Airport, she thanked Jake for letting her fly the jet and exited the aircraft. Rain didn't have a driver's license, much less a pilot's license, so she always appreciated that he let her fly. Erykah had arranged to have a limousine waiting for her when she exited the aircraft.

As the limo drove down Santa Monica Blvd. on the way to the hotel, it occurred to her that since she became a member of The Family, she had rarely taken a day off, much less a vacation. The last time was a weekend trip to St. Martin with Von Preston. Well, this wasn't a vacation; it was a business trip. In that day and back to New York the following day. But she had never been to Los Angeles before and had no idea if she'd ever be back, so Rain planned to enjoy and pamper herself until it was time to take care of the business she had flown all that way for.

When the driver arrived at the Four Seasons Hotel Los Angeles in Beverly Hills, Rain checked into one of the property's deluxe balcony suites. Once she tipped the bellman handsomely, she went out on the balcony and took in the view. Standing there, she thought about her plan for the day and the work she needed to put in. That wouldn't occur until sometime after one in the morning, so she had plenty of time.

She was no tourist, and although she was thinking about watching the famous L.A. sunset, Rain Robinson had never been much of a beach girl, so she had no intention of doing either of those things. What she did have planned, or more correctly, what *Erykah* planned for her afternoon, was a visit to the hotel spa for a massage and a facial. But first things first. She was hungry after the long flight from New York.

She went back into the suite and headed for the mini-bar. After grabbing a bottle of tequila, Rain looked to see what they had to eat.

"Kit Kat Bar, premium chocolate, chips, popcorn, and nutrition bars."

She shook her head and picked up the room service menu. She had Panino Con Pollo on the balcony, and then it was off to the spa.

"Loraine Robinson, I have an appointment."

"Yes, Ms. Robinson. Please come this way."

When Rain left the spa, her entire body felt refreshed, and her skin felt amazing. She'd gotten the Swe-Thai massage, which was said to restore energy, increase flexibility, and enhance circulation. In the mood to pamper herself, which didn't happen often, Rain also got the Knesko Rose Quartz Gem-clinical facial, which uses precious gemstones, minerals, and clinical ingredients to treat the skin holistically.

"I may actually do that again," she said and thought about making getting massages and facials a regular thing.

When she returned to her suite, Rain had time to kill before her dinner reservation. Even though she wasn't planning on going to the beach, she did buy an Alaïa Trikini one-piece swimsuit and a Camilla silk floral maxi coverup for the occasion, so she went downstairs and posted up at the pool for a couple of hours, sipping cocktails and people watching.

Her dinner reservation was at Spago of Beverly Hills, one of L.A.'s more iconic fine-dining restaurants. Since it was just an overnight trip, she only brought two outfits by Versace to wear for the evening. She tried on the black leather zip-front minidress and Versace strappy leather sandals but thought that it would be more appropriate for what she had to do that evening. So, instead, Rain chose the dark orchid Versace satin cutout minidress that was draped elegantly in silk, with a slashed cutout at the bodice and Versace strappy satin sandals.

That night at Spago's, Rain dined on Black Pearl Kaluga Caviar because she'd never had any before and the True Wagyu New York Striploin, grilled over hardwood. Dinner was excellent, *but caviar is overrated,* Rain thought as she returned to the hotel to change for the evening. That night, Big Night recording artist Cristal was appearing at The Wiltern, a concert hall in the Wilshire Center. Since being boss of The Family came with perks, Rain had orchestra seats and backstage passes.

"Rain!" Cristal shouted when she came into the green room. "I am so glad that you could make it."

She hugged Rain and introduced her to the assembled celebrities, most notably, her good friend, movie star Mason Grant, as well as the other musicians, guests, and hangers-on that usually surrounded Cristal wherever she went.

"You know it's a shame that I came all the way to L.A. to see your show, and I can't get you to play Purple Rock."

"It is, girl, a damn shame. I will have to speak with Gladys about getting me in there," Cristal promised.

Rain leaned closer to Cristal. "You tell Gladys that you talked to me about it personally, and I said that I would consider it a personal favor if she'd let you play Purple Rock."

Cristal leaned back and looked at Rain for a second or two without speaking before she smiled and whispered, "Did you just threaten Gladys?"

Knowing that Gladys was scared to death of her, Rain smiled. "No, girl, that was just a friendly request. Now, if she chooses to take it as a threat, that's on her."

The after-party was being held at a place called Crocker Club. When Rain entered the club, she looked around for her prey for the evening but didn't see him anywhere. She had been assured by usually reliable sources that he would be there after one in the morning and wouldn't be hard to find. Rain glanced at her watch.

"Twelve forty-five," she said aloud. "Patience." She went to the bar. "Patrón, neat."

"Coming up," the bartender said with a flourish and dropped a napkin on the bar in front of her.

Forty minutes later, Rain was on her third Patrón when she saw her prey for the evening seated at the bar with another man. She finished her drink, tossed a twenty on the bar for a tip, and stood up. After she took a peek in the Versace Large La Medusa leather tote she was carrying, Rain approached her prey.

"Excuse me, gentlemen."

They stopped talking and looked at Rain from head to toe. "Damn," one said.

"Mind if I join you?"

"Not at all," the other said excitedly, and Rain opened her bag.

"You Chet French?" She stepped closer to him and touched his chest. "The nigga they call 'Big Frenchie'?" she asked very sexily.

That put a big smile on his face. "That's me." He leaned closer to Rain. "And what's your name, sexy?"

"Me?" Rain put her hand on her gun. "My name is Rain Robinson."

"Oh, shit," he said and pushed the man that was with him into Rain and ran.

Rain came out with her gun and opened fire as Big Frenchie ran. Then he dove for the ground. The man that was with him pulled out his gun and fired at Rain. She returned his fire, and as she sought better cover, she became mad that Big Frenchie had gotten away. While the people in Crocker's scattered at the sound of the shots, Rain hit the man in the right shoulder with her next shot.

He turned over a table, sprang up quickly, and fired a few rounds at Rain. She fired back and caught him with one to the chest. He kept firing until Rain put one in his head. Rain watched as his body hit the floor hard.

Rain looked around for Frenchie. "Shit!" she shouted when she didn't see him. She put her gun back in the leather tote, dropped her head, and headed quickly toward the exit.

Wondering how the fuck she found him, Big Frenchie had slipped into the men's room to hide out. He came out when the shooting had stopped. When he saw her heading for the door, Frenchie took out his gun and fired several shots in her direction.

As the crowd scattered again, he took cover behind some tables and continued firing at Rain. She took out both of her 9-mm weapons and began firing at him on the run, seeking better cover. It was then that Big

Frenchie came out from behind the table and made a run for the exit, busting shots all the way. Rain fired and hit him with a shot to the back that sent him flying to the ground. Then she walked up to him, shot him twice more, and got the fuck out of Dodge.

Epilogue

As men approached from all directions, Kirk pulled up to the gate and showed his badge to Ronald.

"State your business."

"Detective Kirkland, to see Mr. Black."

He lowered his weapon and nodded to his men. They went back to their posts, and he opened the gate. That evening, Mr. and Mrs. Black were in the media room, talking over drinks, when Chuck knocked on the door.

Shy had just pointed out to him that he should have waited until the doctor removed Wanda from her medically induced coma before he did anything. But that's not what he did. Somebody had hurt Wanda, and somebody needed to pay a price for that. It reminded him that, at his core, he was still "Vicious Black," and sometimes, his judgment needed to be called into question.

"What is it, Chuck?" Shy asked.

"Kirk is here to see you, Boss," he said, and Shy frowned. "Send him in."

Less than a minute later, Chuck opened the door, and Kirk entered. "Good evening, Mrs. Black."

"Hello, Detective Kirkland."

"I hope that I'm not intruding"—Kirk looked toward Black—"but I have a question I need to ask you."

"Then I will leave you gentlemen to talk." Shy kissed her husband and stood up. "Good to see you, Detective," she lied and left the room.

Kirk pointed at the door when it closed. "She doesn't like me, does she?"

"No, she doesn't."

"Didn't think so."

"Cassandra doesn't like cops."

"I'll try not to take it personally then."

"Can I get you something to drink?"

Kirk thought for a second. "Sure, why not? I'm off duty."

Black smiled and stood up. "What are you drinking?"

"Whatever you're having is fine."

"I'm drinking Rémy Martin, Louis XIII," he said and went to the bar to pour.

"That's fine."

Kirk sat down while Black poured a glass for him and refilled his. He handed the detective his drink and sat down.

"You know, as long as we've known each other, this is the first time we've drunk together," Black said and raised his glass before he took a sip.

"That's because I'm particular about who I drink with."

"So am I."

Kirk took a sip. "That's smooth."

"What'd you need to ask me?"

Kirk drained the glass and put it down. "I wanted to ask you about Lisa Austin."

"What about her?"

"Our forensic accountant got an anonymous email that connected her with Thomas Gates and provided details of the chronology of transactions that she used to pay him." Kirk paused. "I assumed that came from you. From your hacker, what's her name—Carla."

Black nodded in acknowledgment and recognition that Kirk knew about her. *He is a detective and a good one,* he thought and realized that he should expect no less.

"That I knew."

Although Carla's chronology wouldn't be admissible in court, it was more than enough to obtain a warrant to get the information legally.

"What I wanna know is why? Why hand Lisa Austin to me? Not that I don't appreciate it, but why?"

Black drained his glass. "You want another?"

"Thank you."

"Because we agreed. You tell me what you know, and I tell you what I know. Remember?" Black went to the bar, returned with the bottle, and refilled their glasses. "I just kept my word."

"You did." Kirk picked up his glass. "But what I'm curious about is why. Why not deal with her yourself? We haven't found Gates and Bracy, and I know we're not going to." Kirk paused to see if Black would acknowledge the killing of those men. His facial expression did not change. "So why not deal with her yourself and disappear Lisa Austin?"

"I don't kill women."

"No." Kirk nodded. "You get Rain to do it for you."

The End of *When It's Over*

Mike Black will return in *This Time, Baby*.